MAYBE MAGIC

ASH FITZSIMMONS

MAYBE MAGIC

THE LOST HALLS, BOOK ONE

MAYBE MAGIC. Copyright © 2025 by Ash Fitzsimmons.

Print Edition ISBN: 978-1-949861-69-3

Cover design by MiblArt.

www.ashfitzsimmons.com

CHAPTER 1

By my fourth day in the woods, I'd decided that running away from home wasn't all it was cracked up to be.

Oh, I knew how to camp—I'd been on hunting trips as a kid, and I could make a shelter and start a fire with flint and tinder—but those had been trips of short duration, and always with other people. This time, I was alone, I wasn't entirely sure where I'd landed, and I hadn't yet dared to start a fire for fear of detection. My mom and dad were good folks, and I loved them to bits, but they'd have dragged me back in an instant if they'd found me.

Home wasn't a *bad* place. I wasn't beaten or starved, and I grew up surrounded by family—my grandparents, my aunt and two uncles, and a mess of cousins. Home was a safe haven, I'd always thought, as if the split rail fence around the perimeter of the compound could keep the outside world at bay. East Branch had long been our family's shelter, and it would continue to protect us if we stuck together and maintained its borders—if we depended on each other.

Like every child born at East Branch, I knew my role from a young age: help farm the plots and tend the livestock, learn to hunt and fish, and once I was grown, marry and try to make babies. So many of the couples on the compound struggled to get pregnant or carry a baby to term, and no one had more than three children, though not for lack of effort. But that was how it had always been, so we knew to expect difficulty. And in general, we did our best, as continuing our community was of paramount importance. We fed ourselves with our crops and our few kills, and since it took an awful lot of hands to feed everyone, deviating from the normal life plan at East Branch was almost unthinkable—as unthinkable as leaving, really. Might as well take food out of your family's mouths.

Yet here I was, all the same, halfway up a mountain and not looking back.

I don't know when my dissatisfaction with East Branch began to fester. Perhaps I spent too long listening to my parents' radio, trying to make sense of the world beyond the fence. Maybe I stared too much during my one and only trip to town to fill up the generators. Or it could have been that I was eighteen, a few years away from marriable by most estimations, and the best option available to me was David Amos.

David.

My cousin was a month older than me, he was easy on the eyes, and while we were undoubtedly kin, we weren't as close as our shared surname might suggest. Heck, there were lots of us Amoses in East Branch. But David always felt more like a brother to me than a potential husband, and when I tried to picture him that way, my skin crawled. Plus, I was pretty sure he was interested in Hannah Church, so that left me with paltry options: Marshall, David's little brother, or Sebastian Amos, who was only thirteen. I'd *babysat* the Amos twins, Sebastian and Stephanie—I couldn't imagine marrying one of them.

Frankly, I wanted more than that. The world outside East Branch was huge and unknown and terrifying, but I had to see what it could offer.

Unfortunately, my initial impressions of freedom hadn't been great. I'd sneaked out in the dark hours of Thursday morning, and the rest of that day had been fine, but it had rained steadily throughout Friday and Saturday, and everything about me was still damp on Sunday. The sun was beginning to decline that afternoon, and though I had hours of daylight left to figure myself out for the evening, I suspected that I'd be going to bed wet and hungry once more. I'd brought only two days' rations with me, I hadn't tried to trap so much as a squirrel yet, and the few berries and mushrooms I'd found around my campsite did little to supplement my stores. My only saving grace was that I wouldn't freeze in the mid-June warmth, but without a fire, I'd still be unpleasantly chilled come nightfall.

Discomfort and prudence warred within me as I considered the little fire ring I'd built. The wood was wet, but I had a flint, and I thought I could get *something* going with enough effort. Some folks with the touch in East Branch could light fires with a flick of their fingers, but my touch was pretty weak by comparison, and I'd always needed mechanical help. But assuming I could start a fire, did I dare to risk it? I didn't recognize these hills, but could there be a search party trailing me? If they saw smoke, they'd surely investigate. Better, perhaps, to forgo the fire and shiver for another night in my shelter of branches...

The sound of approaching footfalls snapping twigs and crunching decaying leaves yanked me from my deliberations, and I strained to listen. Deer? Bear? One of my cousins? I couldn't say, and I didn't have time to run. Hoping for the best, I quietly detached my bow from my pack, nocked an arrow, and knelt partly behind an oak, waiting.

It wasn't a bear, fortunately, nor my parents come to claim me. Instead, to my surprise, I saw a blonde woman approaching. She was perhaps a little taller than me, and definitely a few years older, with a mild tan. Her hair was pulled back in a loose tail, exposing her ears—which, I noticed, were pocked with multiple sets of stud earrings that glinted in the sunlight. She wore jeans and a blue T-shirt, and the strap of a bulging canvas sack ran diagonally across her chest. She hadn't seen me, as her attention was focused on the stand of purple-flowered woundwort at her feet. Reaching into her bag, she extracted a small pair of shears and began cutting back the stalks, harvesting the young growth.

If I stayed very still, I thought, she might not notice me. A patch of mushrooms or wild blackberries could catch her interest...

And then my nose began to twitch.

Though I scrunched my face and tried to hold back the sneeze, my body betrayed me, and the stranger quickly straightened and searched for me. "Hello?" she said, putting her shears away. "Who's there?"

Briefly, I thought of sprinting off down the mountain, but I didn't want to abandon my pack...and besides, I told myself, it wasn't like the woman was *armed*. I was the one with a bow and quiver.

At least I'd had sense enough to keep my headband on.

Rising from my hiding place, I put the bow aside and showed her my empty hands, a gesture of good faith. "Hi," I croaked, my voice rusty from several days' silence and little water.

She smiled back at me. "Hey, there. Sorry, I didn't mean to startle you. Out for a hike?"

"Uh...yeah, I guess," I fibbed. "You?"

"Foraging." Giving her sack a pat, she said, "Making some bath soak for my friend, and I wanted a couple clippings to dry. Did you see that massive stand of mint back there?" she asked, thumbing one hand over her shoulder. "I know it's an aggressive plant, but it smells so *nice*. So, where are you heading...uh..."

Following her line of sight, I glanced back and saw my shelter on full display. "Oh...you know..."

The woman's tone changed in an instant. "Are you camping out here?" she asked, concerned. "Like...primitive camping?"

I'd never heard it called such, but then folks outside East Branch did go about matters somewhat differently, or so I'd been told. "Uh, yeah. I was going to make a fire."

Her brow furrowed. "Not with wood that wet, you're not, unless you're hiding kerosene in your bag." She stepped closer. "Are you okay? Do you need help?"

Before I could answer her, my stomach growled, and I made a face. "No, no, I'm fine—"

"Has someone hurt you? Are you hungry?"

Well, there was no point in lying about the last question. "I haven't been able to trap anything yet..."

"Here, sit down," she said, and took a spot on a fallen log at the edge of my makeshift camp. "I didn't bring much..." Reaching into a pocket on her sack, she extracted something about as long as my hand and wrapped in printed foil. "Granola bar?"

I'd never had a granola bar, but hunger won out. Thanking her, I ripped into the wrapper, then bit off a chunk of the foodstuff within, a chewy, compressed loaf of oats and dried fruit. It was sweeter than I'd expected, but I barely tasted it in my haste to swallow it down, and then I licked the sticky residue from my fingertips.

Once I'd come up for air, the woman asked, "You want to tell me what you're really doing out here, hon?"

I couldn't trust her—she was an outsider, and I didn't know the first thing about her other than her apparent love of flowers—but she'd fed me, and the lengthening shadows and my damp clothes shoved caution to the back of my mind. "I ran away from home," I mumbled, balling up the wrapper.

She held out her hand. "Here, I'll take that." Once she'd tucked the garbage into her bag, she asked, "How old are you? Be honest with me."

"Eighteen."

She squinted at my face, then seemed to decide that what I was telling her was plausible. "If you're eighteen, it's not running away. You're a grown-ass woman, and you can go anywhere you want. So...where are you heading?"

I shrugged. "Don't know. Just not back there."

"I see," she said lightly. "Keeping your options open, eh?"

"Guess so."

After a moment's hesitation and further study of my

campsite, she held my gaze and murmured, "This seems like a pretty miserable night to be camping, especially without a tent. Ground's still wet. Why don't you come home with me for the night?"

I said nothing, watching her as if I could suss out her true motives from the faint shifts in her expression.

"No charge, no strings, and I won't make you go back to wherever you came from," she continued. "I've got a spare bedroom, and I don't know about you, but I could go for some dinner. Look, I'm sure you're capable of handling yourself," she said, nodding toward my shelter, "but I'd hate to leave you out here alone for the bears to find. Do you have a pistol, at least?"

"Got this," I replied, lifting my bow.

"That's, uh...something," she allowed. "Maybe not great against a hungry bear, though. So, how about it? Hot meal, dry bed?"

My childhood lessons warned me against accepting her offer in the strongest of terms. Outsiders were *not* to be trusted, not with anything, and we couldn't afford to let them get too close...

But that was the voice of East Branch, wasn't it? If I wanted to make a fresh start beyond the community, then I would need to trust *someone*...and this someone was dangling the promise of food and a roof in front of me.

I would think better with dinner in my stomach, I mused, trying to reason with my old anxieties. Plan better. Perhaps the stranger would have an idea about how I could proceed, or at least more granola to share.

Be brave, I told myself. *Be brave or scurry home.*

"You're sure you wouldn't mind?" I asked.

"Of course not." Smiling, she rose and brushed off her jeans. "Come on, grab your stuff. Let's get back to my truck, and we'll see what we can do." As I collected my few possessions and lashed my bow into place, she added, "I'm Jane Fortune, by the way. Nice to meet you, uh..."

By the inflection in her voice, I could tell she was fish-ing for a name, but I wasn't that comfortable yet. "Nice to meet you, too."

She nodded, letting it go, and pointed to a barely marked trail. "This way. We've got about a half-hour hike ahead, but hey, we'll build an appetite."

As we walked, the woman—Jane—didn't ask me many questions, which I appreciated. Instead, she offered tidbits about herself, and I suspected she was trying to put me at ease, seeing as I'd agreed to go with a total stranger.

"I live in Ragged Gap," she said, looking over her shoulder to smile at me. "*Technically*, I come from South Carolina, but I haven't lived there since I was a few weeks old, so that doesn't really count, right?"

I mumbled something in the affirmative. As an East Branch native, I knew the nearest town was Whitford, but I'd only visited once. I had no familiarity with Ragged Gap or South Carolina, but I didn't want to betray my ignorance.

"Grew up here, just me and my dad," she continued. "I got a job out of town a few months back, but I come home on the weekends to check in. And see my boyfriend," she added, chuckling. "Don't worry, he doesn't live with me—he's got a place in Whitford. Tonight will just be us girls, yeah?"

"Sounds nice."

"Great! Here's what I'm thinking: let's go home and get you settled, maybe a hot shower, some dry clothes, and then we'll worry about dinner. Will that work? I mean, if you're starving right now, I'll drive through McDonald's on the way."

Since Jane was the one offering the food and accommodations, I didn't want to come across as greedy. "Uh…sure. That's fine."

My stomach growled again, and she laughed. "No harm in a pre-dinner snack, though, is there? I haven't been grocery shopping, but I should have some chips and cookies in the pantry."

She kept up the light conversation until the trail ended in a set of rough-hewn stone steps down to a gravel patch by a paved road, empty but for a scuffed blue truck. "Here we go," said Jane, leading me toward the vehicle. "Let me just get the keys…"

Riding in the enclosed portion of cars was a definite novelty for me. I'd hopped into the bed of one of the community's old trucks as a child when we went out to the fields to weed or bring in the harvest, and I'd likewise ridden back there, gripping the sides for dear life, when my parents took me with them to Whitford that once. The inside of Jane's truck offered cloth-covered seats and carpeting, and it smelled of something bright and sharp that I couldn't quite name, though I suspected the little pack of orange liquid clipped to the console had much to do with the scent.

"Buckle up," she said, trading the strap of her sack for a shoulder belt that pinned her to the seat, and I copied her. I didn't know how I would remove the belt again once the metal tab locked into its holster, but if I were observant, perhaps Jane would show me the trick without forcing me to ask.

She slipped the key into its slot, and the truck rumbled to life with an unexpected blast of cold air and voices from a radio—a commercial I recognized with a fast-talking man who offered low, low prices on quality used cars. She snapped off the radio before I had quite gotten past my surprise that the truck came equipped with one, but she didn't start driving right away. "Listen," she said gently, "you're safe with me. Whatever's going on, we'll figure out your next step. I can call out of work tomorrow, no worries. And if this is something bigger than the two of us can handle, I've got some friends from college down in Atlanta who help women in crisis. There's a shelter, food, clothes, job training. If you need something like that, I'd be happy to call."

"Thanks. Is Atlanta near Ragged Gap?" I asked, feeling

out the unfamiliar town names.

Jane's eyebrows rose. "Uh...well, Ragged Gap is about ten miles away, so not exactly." I must have seemed confused, as she clarified, "It's next door to Whitford, you know? Whitford's in the northeastern valley, and Ragged Gap's in the southwestern."

"And...Atlanta?"

"Atlanta," she said, drawing out the word, "is about two hours south of here." She regarded me strangely. "Have you never been?"

I shook my head.

"*Never*? I thought most of the schools around here would at least have a field trip to the Capitol..."

"Homeschooled," I mumbled.

"Ah. Me, too, but my dad used to take me down to visit." She moved a lever and turned the wheel, and eased the truck onto the road. "He wanted me to tour the Capitol and all—thought I should know something about state government—but we went to see the Braves play, visit the zoo, the Coke museum...he sat through *The Nutcracker* four Christmases in a row when I was little," she added, smiling to herself. "Terrible traffic, but Atlanta's worth a visit."

She drove us along the winding two-lane road that cut through the wooded hills, giving me a moment of silence in which to breathe, and I made up my mind. "Maebe."

"Maybe what?" she asked. "Visit Atlanta?"

"No, uh...that's my name. Maebe. Maebe Amos."

"Huh. That's...not one I've heard before."

"It's for my great-aunts," I explained. "Mae Belle and Belinda. They died before I was born. My parents didn't like either of those names, but they wanted to name me for both, so..." I shrugged. "Maebe it is. M-A-E, not M-A-Y."

"Gotcha. Well," she added, grinning, "at least you have an interesting one. I ended up with *Jane*. How boring is that?"

"I don't know any Janes," I offered.

"Because it hasn't been really popular since, like, the 1920s. I had a great-aunt named Jaena, apparently, but I guess my folks wanted something more normal." She paused, then asked, "Any siblings? I'm an only child."

"Same." She had, I recalled, mentioned living with her father, and I decided not to pry as to her mother's whereabouts.

"And you're from around here?"

"Uh…yeah." Wasn't I? Surely I hadn't walked *that* far.

Though I was, admittedly, being evasive, Jane didn't press me for details, but I caught her sneaking glances at me as we drove along.

The woods gave way to settlement—Whitford, I thought—and then we slipped between two hills and emerged into what seemed to be a much larger town. "Ragged Gap," said Jane as she stopped at an intersection. "As the crow flies, it's not that far from home to where I was foraging, but there's no straight, easy drive. You're not getting carsick, are you?"

I assumed she meant queasy and shook my head.

"That's good. We're just up there," she said, and pointed to a narrow road snaking along a hillside.

Once we'd gained a bit of altitude, I looked out through the trees and got a better sense of the *sprawl* of the place. Ragged Gap was, I supposed, the collection of buildings in the middle of the valley, but the ringing hills were pocked with houses—or what I could see of them, at least, given the leafy summer. The road dipped again as it wound around the mountain, and as the houses grew sparse, Jane turned onto a street that would barely be wide enough for two cars to travel abreast, then slowed in front of a stand of trees that gave way to a cabin.

"Here we are," she said, and pulled off the road onto a patch of gravel—the parking area, presumably. In East Branch, we kept our two trucks in a barn, but I supposed it made sense that Jane should leave hers at her house.

The cabin was tidy, a single-floor wooden structure

quite a bit smaller than some of the houses we'd passed on the way up. The windows at the front were closed, and I worried about the heat situation within the building—didn't she understand the use of cross-drafts? But Jane seemed unbothered as she cut the engine and released her belt, and I fiddled with the buckle until mine came free, too. I climbed out of the truck and grabbed my pack, then followed Jane up the porch steps. She didn't enter the house right away, but rather reached for a black panel on the door that suddenly glowed with blue numbers. After she tapped four in sequence, I heard a whirring sound, and a light on the panel turned green.

"Keyless lock," said Jane, turning the handle. "Since I'm gone pretty regularly, this is easier if I need someone to look in on the place."

That she needed to lock the house at all was a foreign concept—so much at East Branch was produced and shared by all, and I'd never seen a building with a lock on the door. But outsiders were different, I reminded myself, then followed her inside.

A wave of icy air washed over me as I crossed the threshold, and I gasped and stepped back. Jane spun around, concerned, then seemed to realize what was troubling me. "Sorry, is it too cold? I can raise the temperature."

"How…what…" I stammered, looking around for an open window or a fan.

"Central air conditioning. It keeps the place cool, and then there's a heater for the winter months. Come on in, it won't hurt you."

I tried to get my bearings as she closed and latched the door behind me. To my left was a sitting area with a plush couch and a pair of chairs arcing around a stone hearth and the flat black rectangle hanging on the wall above it. A door opened at the back of the room, but what lay beyond it was darkness. Straight ahead, through a side opening, was a wooden table for four set with blue placemats—the kitchen, presumably—and behind that was what seemed to be a window that stretched from the floor nearly to the ceiling.

Jane casually flipped a switch on the wall, and lights blazed to life above us. I couldn't hear a generator—did outsiders use quieter models? Surely something had to be powering the mysterious air conditioning, which seemed like such an extravagant waste of fuel.

"I bought this place in a foreclosure auction a few years ago," said Jane. "It wasn't in great shape, and I've been kind of slow in renovation, but the roof's solid. Let me show you the guest room."

She led me into the kitchen, then turned to the right, where a short hallway offered three open doors. "That one's my room," she said, pointing to the right. "You'll be over here, and the bathroom's in the middle."

Following her to the spare bedroom at the back of the house, I squinted against the sudden brightness when she turned on the overhead lamp, which hung from the base of a mounted fan, its blades designed to mimic thin woven wicker. The light spilled upon sandstone-colored walls and a polished wooden floor, upon which rested a large bed with a beautifully carved headboard and footboard, the tops of which curled away from each other. The bed was equipped with the thickest mattress I'd ever seen, which she'd covered with a dusky green coverlet and set with blue and brown pillows. The rest of the furniture matched the bed—a nightstand with an electric lamp and clock, a dresser and mirror set with another lamp and a pair of un-burned purple candles in low glass holders—and a blue rug by the bedside completed the room.

"Here you go," said Jane, pulling a folded contraption from the empty closet, and leaned it against the wall. "Luggage rack. Just put your stuff here and get situated, and I'll be picking up in the bathroom when you're ready."

She left me alone to contemplate the lovely furniture and the shaded window and the cold air blowing from a vent in the ceiling. As she bustled about next door, I carefully put my bag on the rack and untied it. Nothing I had with me seemed clean enough to touch Jane's linens, so I spread my clothes on the floor, trying to decide which of my things was the least damp and dirty. It was, unfortunately, a tossup.

I suppose I took longer than I'd anticipated, as Jane returned and found me studying my few clothes. "Everything okay?" she asked, looking over my work. "Oh—hey, want me to run your stuff through the wash while you're showering?"

As I'd done my share of washing among my chores, I was aghast at the notion of asking my host to launder my clothes. "Thank you kindly, but I couldn't ask that of you—"

"It's no trouble," Jane interrupted. "I'll pop them in the machine, and they'll be done in an hour or so."

I frowned, then asked dubiously, "Washed and dried?"

"Yep. There's a trick to mine," she said with a wink, and gestured toward the clothes on the floor. "Let me get those started."

Not wanting to offend her, I bundled them up and handed them over, and she coaxed me into the bathroom.

"Good *heavens*," I whispered as I stared around the cavernous space. The bathroom was massive, far larger than the bedroom, and I wondered how it all fit into the house. At home, our bathroom could be crossed in two long strides, a windowless room large enough for a wooden tub lined with a tarp and a shelf for the pitcher and bucket. The outhouse was, of course, a separate building in the back. *This* room, however, was bright and white. Beneath a window fitted with distorting glass sat a deep porcelain tub large enough for two. Beside it was a glass-walled cubicle almost larger than my parents' entire bathroom, though I wasn't entirely certain of its function. On the other side was a door cracked open to reveal what had to be a flush toilet. I'd heard of such, but I'd never seen one at East

Branch. Flanking the door were a pair of long counters in what I would come to recognize as smooth white marble, one of which was littered with bottles and glass cannisters.

"Here," said Jane, patting the other counter, "you can put your toiletries anywhere you like on this side. Do you need anything? Toothbrush, floss, comb? I've got extra."

Ordinarily, I cleaned my teeth with a baking powder paste, but I'd left even that behind. "Um…I have a comb, but that's all," I mumbled.

"Don't worry." She smiled and dug under her counter, then produced a clear bag stuffed full of interesting objects. "Can't beat dentist samples," she said, and laid several items by my sink, all of which I would need to examine once she'd gone. "I've hung a towel and washcloth right there for you," she continued, pointing to the bar on the wall beside the glass cubicle. "Want help getting the shower started?"

"Please."

To my surprise, she ignored the deep tub and stepped into the cubicle just far enough to turn a gray metal knob in the wall. Water immediately began to fall from a square apparatus near the ceiling, and she twisted the knob until the water steamed. "Left for hotter, right for cooler," she instructed as I gawked. "Shampoo, conditioner, and body wash are in those bottles, and…here, how about a little ambiance?" She tapped a panel on the wall outside the shower, and the dark gray surface lit with colors and words. With a few more taps, the lighting within the shower dimmed and began cycling through blues and greens, while soft, unfamiliar music trilled over the noise of the falling water. "Best I can do for a spa mix," she said almost apologetically, "but if you want to try aromatherapy next time, I'll fix you up. Want me to take those clothes, too?"

I stepped into the toilet room and disrobed—everything but my headband—then wrapped myself in the impossibly soft towel she'd offered me and passed her my things. "Just yell if you need me," said Jane, heading for

the door. "And don't worry about the music and lights—
they'll stop a few minutes after the water shuts off."

Finally alone, I removed my headband and took a ten-
tative step into the cubicle, and my muscles melted at the
caress of the hot water. Jane had turned off the main lights
as she left, leaving me feeling almost like I'd jumped into
the pond on a summer day and was staring up at the distant sun...though far warmer and accompanied by what
sounded like musical pipes. Accustomed to washing everything with soap, I read the bottles Jane had left for my use
and applied their contents in order, and when I finished
and emerged from the cubicle, I was pink all over and
smelled of flowers.

Hesitantly, I flipped the little white toggle by the door,
and the lights came on again.

Remarkable.

The bathroom was designed with a pair of real mir-
rors—like the ones in our trucks, but far larger—and the
one nearer the shower had steamed over. I wrapped myself
in my towel and took stock of myself in the far mirror as I
dripped on the rug. My brown hair had darkened almost to
black from the water, and it hung limply over my shoulders and halfway down my back. My eyes, also brown,
were somewhat bloodshot, which I attributed to the poor
sleep I'd had over the last nights. The rest of my face was
unremarkable, flushed from the warm shower and far
cleaner than it had been in a few days, though I'd managed
to scratch my forehead near my right eyebrow on an errant
branch—an annoyance but not an emergency.

I flipped my head over and squeezed the water from
my hair, then borrowed the brush Jane had left to detangle
it, carefully working around my ears. I'd accidentally
brushed *them* enough times to be cautious. While I had no
ribbon on me, I noticed a small blue box and found that it
contained a spool of waxy white string. Deciding that
would do in a pinch, I tied back my damp hair and considered the result.

Not bad. Not great, but not bad.

"Everything all right in there?" Jane asked through the door. "I've left a bathrobe on your bed while your clothes are in the dryer."

"Just fine, thanks!" I called back. "I'll be out soon—"

"No rush. I'm sorting my plants in the kitchen."

The other items from the—what had she called it, the dentist?—could wait. In my haste to leave the bathroom, I almost forgot my headband, then spotted it on the counter and quickly backtracked.

The band was just a strip of blue cloth about three inches wide, but my parents had stressed to me its necessity since I was a small child. If I ever left East Branch, or if strangers came onto the compound land, I needed to cover up. Blend.

So, I tied the headband over the top half of my ears once more, then reached beneath it to unfold them flat against my head.

There. Nothing to see.

CHAPTER 2

"Your soaps smell much nicer than the soap at home," I said, peeking into the kitchen. I'd never owned a bathrobe, but I'd gotten the hang of Jane's loaner and managed to preserve my modesty.

She looked up from the counter, where she was bundling her plants, and beamed. "Thanks! I used to make and sell them. Did you ever see Fortune's Fancies products around town?"

I shook my head. "Afraid not."

"Eh, that's all right. I sold at the Mercantile for a while, then at The Robin's Nest and Ragged Gap Apothecary, but I've just been selling off my current stock for the last few months. New job doesn't leave much time to pour candles and make soap. That said," she continued, grinning as she tied together a bunch of lavender for drying, "a girl needs her hobbies, and even if I'm not selling, I've got time to make batches for personal use. Friends and family, see?" A pair of small nails hammered into the cabinets on either side of the sink gave her a place to run a piece of string, to which she'd been hanging bundles with clothespins. "Let me check your laundry—it should be about ready. Do you want to borrow a hairdryer?"

Having no idea how to use such a thing, I declined. "It'll dry by bedtime," I assured her, and glanced out the tall window beside the kitchen table. It was, I realized, a door, a pane of glass marred with a wooden handle. Beyond the door, the land sloped down to a shallow creek before rising again. I saw a small garden out back, but the only thing within it appeared to be wildflowers. "Are there chores I could be doing?" I asked Jane.

"Nah. You're my guest, and it's all in hand. Be right back."

She disappeared into a small room at the far side of the kitchen, then quickly returned with her arms full of my things. "Here you go, fresh from the dryer."

My clothes were warm and supple, not nearly as stiff as they usually were after a wash day, and they smelled faintly of lavender. "Oh, wow…"

"Why don't you go fold those before they wrinkle?" she suggested. "Or you're welcome to hang them in the closet. Get dressed, and I'll meet you out here."

Jane had, I noted, already changed clothes. "You're not going to bathe?"

"Took a birdbath in the sink to get the sweat off. I'll be fine," she said, and shooed me on my way.

I made short work of my laundry, folding everything neatly and tucking it into the topmost of the dresser drawers, then slipped into a remarkably clean blouse and summer-weight trousers. By the time I returned to the kitchen, Jane had finished with her plants and was hunched over…*something* on the counter, a slim black rectangle attached to a similar base. It wasn't a type of book, that I could tell, but…

"What's that?" I asked, pointing to the object.

Jane's brows rose. "This? Just a laptop." She turned it around, revealing a glowing panel like the one in the bathroom wall. "You, uh…you've never seen a laptop?"

"No. What *is* it?"

"It's a computer." She sounded surprised by the question. "Here, come check it out. It won't bite."

I drew nearer, and Jane slid to one side to show me the panel. "You've got your screen here, your keyboard down below, and here's your mouse."

"*Mouse?*"

"The old ones looked kind of like mice. This moves the

cursor around the screen," she explained, and dragged her finger to show me. "I was just checking restaurant hours. I don't feel like cooking tonight, but it being Sunday, some of my go-tos close early. This one should work: Jay-Jay's Bar and Grill." She tapped her finger, and the view changed to a picture of small blocks of text. "They're new and a little out of the way, so the tourist traffic is minimal, and the food's not bad. See something there you can eat?"

I must have seemed perplexed, as Jane said, "Let's try this again. Jay-Jay's is a restaurant. Ever been to one?"

"No," I confessed.

"Huh. Well, we go there, you tell them what you want to eat from that menu of choices, they make it, and I pay them. Simple."

"I don't have any money—"

"Which is why I'm paying," she said, and squeezed my shoulder. "We'll check it out, and I'll answer any questions you have once we get there."

We loaded the truck again, and Jane drove us off through the deepening evening shadows. Leaving the mountain for the valley, she joined a number of vehicles on the wider roads, but our traveling companions fell away as we passed a lit-up cluster of buildings. "Downtown Ragged Gap," said Jane. "It's cute, but it's also a pain to try to eat downtown when there are tourists around."

"Tourists?"

"People from elsewhere who rent cabins in the area for a few days. They hike or fish or buy handicrafts or get drunk, and in the fall, they swarm the area to see the leaves change. Tourism keeps this place alive, but that doesn't mean we like to fight them for tables. Hence Jay-Jay's."

Jane stopped a ways past town at a long building broken up by colorful signs. At the far end, the name of the restaurant glowed in big red letters, and Jane parked near the front door. A wide space between the building and the road was covered with smooth stone hatched with white lines, and tall light-topped posts planted at regular intervals cast their glow on the few vehicles nearby.

"This is called a strip mall," said Jane. "Not aesthetical-ly glorious, but it's practical. You've got a drugstore at the end, a secondhand shop, a *surprisingly* good wine store"—she pointed to each as she named them—"that place sells candles, they do shoe repair, and that empty one used to be a meat and three. Another restaurant," she explained.

"What happened to it?"

She grimaced. "Way too many health inspection scores in the sixties. This way."

Like Jane's house, Jay-Jay's was chilled to an absurdly low temperature, but none of the few people in the build-ing seemed to mind. Past a wooden stand sat a dozen ta-bles in different configurations—some set for four, others for six or eight—all covered with black cloths and ringed with identical wooden chairs. More tables had been built into three of the walls, but instead of chairs, thick green couches with seats facing either direction were slotted into the gaps. The fourth wall was mostly covered with glass shelves full of bottles, separated from the rest of the room by a long counter lined with wooden stools. A glowing panel—perhaps something akin to Jane's laptop—was mounted near the ceiling by the bottles, and the three men sitting at the counter kept their eyes trained on the chang-ing picture.

A fourth man, who wore all black and stood drying a glass behind the counter, nodded to us and said, "Sit any-where you like. We'll be right with you."

Jane led me to one of the wall-mounted tables and asked, "Booth okay?"

"Uh...sure."

She slid in on one side, and I did likewise, facing her over the tidy black cloth. The table was equipped with salt and pepper, plus a bud vase holding a single rose. I reached out to touch its pink petals, then jerked my hand back in confusion.

Jane chuckled. "It's fake, hon. They probably don't

have the budget for fresh flowers."

A moment later, a blonde woman in a black outfit like the glass-drying man's approached with a pair of folded booklets in her arms. "Hey, y'all, sorry about that," she said, all smiles. "I'm Tracy, and I'll be taking care of you tonight. What can I get y'all to drink?"

Jane didn't give her name in response, which I found odd, but I supposed she knew best. "Hey, there. Sweet tea for me, please, and Maebe..."

I shrugged helplessly.

"How about water?" she told the woman.

"Sounds good." She scribbled on a small pad of paper. "Get y'all started with some appetizers? Spinach dip? Stuffed mushrooms?"

"Yeah, let's get a spinach dip, and do you have any fried green tomatoes left tonight?"

"Sure do. One order?"

"Yes, ma'am, thank you."

"Great. I'll put these in and get those drinks, and I'll give y'all a minute to decide on the rest."

Once she'd bustled off, Jane leaned toward me and lowered her voice. "That's our waitress. We tell her what we want, and she brings it over. So, what would you like for dinner?"

I unfolded the booklet Tracy had left in front of me, a big piece of paper encased in a smooth, clear coating, and saw the text I'd glimpsed on Jane's laptop written across both of the inside pages. "I, um...I don't know. There's a lot..."

"The chicken fettuccini alfredo is pretty good. Ever had that?"

"No..."

"Okay. The breaded pork chop is decent..." Her eyes scanned the booklet, and she grunted. "Tell you what, let's do something easy. Do you like cheeseburgers?"

"Sorry, what's a cheeseburger?"

She looked up at me bemusedly but quickly composed

her expression. "Ground beef, slice of cheese, lettuce, to-mato, onion, pickles, ketchup, mustard, and mayonnaise in a bun. Personally, I'd add bacon and leave off the onion, but whatever makes you happy. Comes with fried pota-toes."

That didn't sound bad at all, and I let Jane order when Tracy returned with our drinks. "You're welcome to try my alfredo," she added when we were alone again, "but I won't be offended either way." Folding her hands on the tabletop, she blew out a long breath, then said, "I don't mean to pry where it's not my business, and I am *not* trying to offend you, Maebe, but it's kind of obvious that you've been, uh…sheltered."

"Yeah," I replied, laughing weakly.

"I don't want to hurt your feelings—"

"You're not," I insisted. "That's one of the reasons I ran away from home. My family's taught me plenty of use-ful things, but I hear about so much on the radio that I don't know, and I…I suppose I wanted to see what else was out here."

"Did you not want to go to public school?"

"We don't do that. Kids are taught by the community. That's how it was for my parents, and their parents, all the way back. Just…how things have always been, I guess."

"Where are you from?"

Though prudence shouted that I couldn't trust Jane, practicality reminded me that she was feeding and shelter-ing me, and the question was reasonable. "East Branch," I said. "Do you know where that is?"

To my surprise, her face lit up. "Oh, sure! I mean, I've never been out there, but yeah, I know where East Branch is. You hiked a pretty good ways."

"We don't really have visitors," I mumbled, which wasn't untrue, though a more accurate statement would be that the community didn't *want* visitors and took pains to keep them at bay.

"Sure—everyone around here knows that," she said,

then leaned close again. "My boyfriend is actually from East Branch, and I've been trying to convince him to let me meet his family, but he's not ready yet."

I stared at her, shocked, but before I could say anything, Tracy appeared with a tray of small plates, serving dishes, and utensils rolled in cloth napkins. Warning us that the dip was hot, she returned to the kitchen, and Jane took up the serving spoon. "It's mostly spinach, artichoke, and cheese, and it's addictive. Want some?"

As she put a scoop on my plate, I managed to blurt, "*Connor?*"

"Yeah, Connor Willow. Are y'all two, uh…related?"

I laughed at the question. "*Everyone* at East Branch is family. Connor's not my close cousin—I only have one, Eugene, and he's just six. Connor and me…" I paused, trying to map our families in my memory. "We're third cousins, I think, but not *just* third cousins. Like, if you go back far enough, you find the same people in your families."

"I see. Try the dip before it cools."

Following her lead, I scooped it onto a small piece of toasted bread and took a bite. The flavors were different but delicious, and my empty stomach demanded more.

Jane smiled as I inhaled my portion, then handed me the spoon for seconds. "Con mentioned that some of the families out there are, uh…pretty close."

A jolt of fear hit me in the gut, and I stiffened and forced myself to swallow. "What has he said about us?"

"Nothing bad," she replied, grabbing a tomato slice from the plate and taking a bite. "But I know he's protective of East Branch, so I'm not pushing him to give me the tour. I'd love to see it, meet his family, but on his terms."

That put me slightly more at ease, and I went for a third helping of the dip, which really was fantastic. As my stomach's cry for food began to quiet, I said, "You know Connor's parents died, right?"

"Yeah, he told me. I'm sorry I never met them."

"They were pretty nice," I replied. "Tom and Debbie. I was, like, nine when they died, so I didn't know them all that well, but it was a big deal when they visited. They brought food and sweets and parts for the generators. Kerosene. Showed up with a butchered deer one time, and *that* was a good dinner." Dragging my toast through the dip as I chased a piece of artichoke, I said, "It was a huge scandal when they moved out, or so I've heard. *No one* ever leaves East Branch. They may have been the very first."

"And now you," said Jane.

"Yeah," I mumbled. "And now me."

"You're not sure about this?"

Not at all—I was a roiling ball of conflicting feelings—but I tried to make sense of them for Jane. "I want to see what's outside of East Branch, but if I go, it hurts everyone else in the community. We don't have as many people there now as there were in the past, and it takes a lot of hands to grow food and fix barns and…and wash *so* many clothes. There are no fancy machines that do it for you. We have generators, see, but they're for necessities or emergencies, not for something frivolous like that. Or that's what my parents would call a laundry machine," I added, hoping I hadn't insulted Jane. "*I* think it's wonderful. Does Connor have one?"

To my relief, she smiled. "He's got a perfectly serviceable washing machine, though his dryer is on its last legs. But listen, hon, you're allowed to explore," she said. "Just because you were born in a place doesn't mean you have to stay there. And like I said, if you're eighteen, no one has any right to force you to go home. You're of age."

I frowned. "Really?"

"Yeah. You can't buy booze yet, but you can move out of your parents' house. So, here's to figuring yourself out," she said, lifting her glass. "And if you need a place to crash for a while, maybe I can help you."

As I was scraping the last of the spinach dip from the serving bowl, Tracy returned with the next dishes, and I found myself staring down a stack of meat, vegetables, and bread so thick that I could barely hold it. "They don't mess around with burgers here," Jane told me, picking up her fork. "Go for it."

Despite the sheer quantity of spinach dip I'd consumed, I found my appetite renewed by the smells of charred beef and fried potatoes, and I tucked in with a speed that would have left my mother appalled.

Glancing up at the counter as I ate, I noticed that most of the men who'd been sitting there had left. The man in black, having cleaned the glasses, hunched behind the counter and stared at something oblong in his hand, while the lone diner—or drinker, perhaps—swirled his beverage and shot the last of it back in a quick gulp. With that accomplished, he slid off his stool, then reached beneath his shirt and extracted a handgun, which he aimed at the man in black. "Empty the register," he demanded. "I won't hurt you if you don't try nothing, but give me the money, *now*."

I froze, burger still in hand, but Jane's look turned steely as she put down her fork and slid off her bench. "What are you doing?" I whispered.

"*Stay put*," she ordered, then stood and cracked her knuckles.

The man behind the counter looked her way, and the robber turned around. "Sit your ass back down, bitch," he snapped, waving the gun at Jane. "I'll deal with you in a minute—"

Jane whispered so softly that I could barely hear it, and the air in front of her distorted as if it had suddenly become water. She held her left hand out, palm facing the robber and fingers splayed, and the distortion rapidly grew until it was taller and broader than she was.

"Put down the gun and get out of here," she said, her voice low and sharp.

"The *fuck*—"

"Last warning."

The man in black wisely dropped behind the back of

the counter.

An instant later, the robber fired his weapon twice at Jane. Before I could scream, both bullets ricocheted off the barrier she'd erected and fell to the thin carpet.

A shield, I realized. She'd created a *shield*. Some folks with the touch could make a small one, maybe the size of their hand, but Jane's was *massive* and strong enough to stop bullets…

The robber's eyes went wide, and he took a step back. "What the hell—"

With another whisper from Jane and a quick flick of her free hand, the robber was lifted off his feet and tossed—not toward the laden glass shelves behind the counter, for which I suspected the man in black was relieved, but rather toward the swinging kitchen door. He bounced off the floor and groaned, dropping his gun in the process, but Jane gave no quarter. She picked him up again, then sent him sailing headfirst into the door and jogged after him.

I dropped my dinner on the table and followed. As I pushed open the door, I saw the robber moaning in pain, sprawled on the tile and holding his head. The employees stood around, gawking, but Jane, having dropped her shield, took charge. "This asshole just tried to hold up Zach at the bar," she announced. "Got a closet handy?"

"Hell, we've got a whole fucking fridge," a bald man in a soiled white apron replied. Dropping a long knife on the steel counter, he stormed over to the robber, hoisted the injured man's torso off the floor in his muscular arms, and dragged him to the back of the kitchen. Tracy opened a wide metal door in the wall, and the aproned man shoved the robber inside.

"He might be concussed. Probably don't want to leave him there long," said Jane. "Could someone call 911?"

She turned, spotted me standing behind her, and shepherded me back into the dining room. "You okay, Zach?" she asked the man in black.

He nodded, though he looked shaken. "Yeah. Shit. *Thanks.*"

"I hate to ask, but could we get to-go boxes?"

Zach hurried out from behind the counter with white containers and made quick work of packing our meals and tying them into a sack. "This is on the house," he said, pressing the bag into Jane's hands.

"No, I can't—"

"Seriously. Just go before the questions start. No cameras in here, so, uh…you should be good."

"Still…" She reached into her purse and pulled out a ten-dollar bill. "That's all the cash I've got on me, but if you could give that to Tracy—"

"Absolutely," he said, taking the money from her. "Y'all go."

We'd almost reached the door when Jane looked back and said, "I hope we're square now."

Zach laughed incredulously. "Oh, yeah. We're good. Be careful, Jane," he added as we walked out into the night.

I'd barely fastened my restraint belt when Jane sped away from Jay-Jay's. "Sorry," she said as I yelped and clutched at the door. "I'd just rather not be here when the police show up."

"Isn't Connor police?"

"In Whitford. This is Ragged Gap," she replied, and blew out a long breath as she turned onto a side street, apparently taking a different route home.

Though I had a million questions, the first one that popped free was, "Why did you ask that man if you were square?"

"Square. Even." She slowed at an empty intersection, then rolled on through. "A few months ago, my dad got in some trouble, and these guys broke into his house and wouldn't leave. I wanted to get them out, but I needed the Ragged Gap cops to be distracted in case anyone called in a disturbance, so, uh…" She paused. "I'm not sure 'frenemy' is the right word, but anyway, the owner of Mystic

Mountains downtown agreed to throw a massive party that night. Zach attended, and I know he got arrested for public intox and public nudity, so while I suspect he had a *great* time, I do feel bad that he's got a record now. The good news," she continued, barely slowing at the next intersection, "is that while I'm still not on the best of terms with the Mystic Mountains crowd, I can trust them to keep their mouths shut."

She glanced my way as she drove, and I must have looked spooked, as she said, "I'm not going to hurt you, Maebe. Promise. That's not who I am. I, um...I've got some *talents*, as I guess you saw tonight, but you're safe with me. That said, if you're uncomfortable, I won't be upset. We can go back to my place, and I'll find a shelter—"

"You have the *touch*!" I cried.

"Uh...yeah. Something like that."

"I didn't know that anyone outside East Branch had it! Except Connor, I mean, but he's one of us..." Struggling to find the words for my racing thoughts, I asked, "Does Connor know?"

"Heh. Very much so. I've been trying to help him improve his focus, actually. Do you...have it?"

"A little. It's not impressive—not like *that*," I said. "I've never done anything like you just managed. That shield! And how did you throw him so far? He had to have been heavy..."

"Natural strength and practice. I train these days." Turning toward the mountain, she said, "So...how about we go home and finish dinner, and if you'd like, maybe I could show you a trick or two after that."

I grinned. "Really?"

"If you're okay staying with me. I mean, if you'd prefer, I could drop you at Connor's..."

"Could I stay? Please?"

"Sure, hon," she replied, and I caught her little smile as we drove on.

CHAPTER 3

Back at Jane's house, we sat at the table in the bright glow of the electric lights and ate our reheated food. She explained to me the concept of a microwave oven and demonstrated its efficacy, though I was somewhat lost as to the mechanics that night. Honestly, I was too frazzled to care. The combination of exhaustion and my stomach's satiation lulled me toward sleep, but the shock of witnessing Jane casually throw a grown man across the restaurant, *twice*, pushed thoughts of bed from my mind.

Once we'd finished, Jane topped up our tea glasses—I'd tasted hers and decided I liked the sweetened brew—and then she sat back and raised an eyebrow in challenge. "Want to show me what you can do?"

I bit my lip. "My touch isn't as strong as yours..."

"That's okay. Neither is Connor's. But let's see what you're working with."

Most of my family members had the touch to one degree or another. Connor's parents had been the big exception; neither showed evidence of the touch or any physical abnormalities, and from what I'd gathered, they'd been able to blend outside the commune. But Connor had the touch, and so they'd brought him back as a boy to learn the basics. I'd received the same sort of lessons: how to block blows with energetic fields, and how to move small items with your will. Neither regularly worked for me, but the latter was the more challenging, as objects simply seemed to ignore my requests. But I'd stumbled upon a workaround in that I could coax the air to lift things for me…from time to time.

If the stars aligned and I had my mind *just* right.

Jane had left a few items on the cleared table—our glasses, salt and pepper shakers, a stack of paper napkins—and I opted for the easiest of the lot. I exhaled and waited until I felt the fluttering of the tiny power stir within me. With a whispered prayer for cooperation and a slow ripple of my fingers, I willed the air around us to lift the topmost napkin, which floated upward and spun in place before I relaxed and let it float down.

"Not bad," Jane declared, putting the napkin back on the stack.

"Not good, either," I muttered. "Stuff won't move for me unless I make a breeze."

"Hmm." She took a sip of tea as she considered the problem. "You know, when I was a kid and my dad was teaching me, he used to nag me about focus. I would get so annoyed whenever he got on to me about it, but in retrospect, he was absolutely right."

"What do you mean?"

"Well…ever played with a magnifying glass in the sun?" When I shook my head, she explained, "Sunlight falls all day, and the world generally doesn't combust, right? You might get a sunburn, but you don't catch fire."

"Sure…"

"But if you *focus* that sunlight, take it and compress it to a much smaller point, you have a strong, bright beam that can do damage. Set leaves on fire, toast ants—"

"*Yikes.*"

"Yeah, that's pretty cruel, but kids are awful. Anyway, same principle applies with magic."

"Magic," I echoed.

"The touch. My talent. It's the ability to work magic," said Jane. "That's what you're doing. When you're young and untrained, you don't tend to focus your will sufficiently, so even if you get the result you were after, it's sloppy or a waste of energy. I've been tutoring Connor to tighten his focus, but for you…" She pushed back from the table. "Wait right there."

A few minutes later, she emerged from her room carrying a thin wooden rod about a foot long. It was unornamented but clearly had been worked, as its surface was smooth and oiled. "What's that?" I asked.

"This," said Jane, giving it a flick, "was my wand when I was a kid. Basically, you focus your will on the wand, and it acts like a magnifying glass to narrow that focus into what you want it to do. Eventually, you grow out of it, but for now, why not give it a try?"

I took the wand from her and clutched it in my fist, then considered the napkins again.

"Sorcerers mostly use words to focus our will," Jane murmured. "Speak what you want to happen."

"Sorcerers?"

"People like me…and probably people like you and Connor. I suspect there's a sorcerer or two deep in your family," she replied. "Not something we can solve tonight, but for now, try out the wand."

I closed my eyes for a moment, clearing my thoughts, then felt for my touch, aimed the tip of the stick at the and napkins, and whispered, "Fly."

The napkins shot from the table as if they'd been hit by a storm gust and slowly drifted to the floor.

Jane chuckled at my embarrassment. "Solid effort," she said, and summoned the napkins back to the table. "We need to work on your control, but I'd say that's a fine start." Catching me stifling a yawn, she said, "How about we pick this up tomorrow, eh? You could use a good night's sleep."

While she sent me to the bathroom to brush my teeth, she bustled around the house, then joined me. "I put a glass of water on the nightstand in case you get thirsty, but you're welcome to whatever's in the kitchen," she said. "And I misted some lavender spray on your sheets—it helps me sleep."

"Thanks. Uh…" I held up a small box of toothpaste, the back of which I'd been reading for instructions, and made a face.

Jane gave me a brief demonstration at her sink, and aside from the strong mint flavor, I didn't find the experience unduly weird. In truth, my teeth felt oddly smooth, which Jane assured me was normal.

She bade me goodnight at my bedroom door. "Come get me if you need anything," she insisted. "Or yell. I won't mind."

But she needn't have worried. Maybe it was the lavender spray, or perhaps my miserable nights in the woods caught up with me, but as soon as I stripped off my dinner clothes and collapsed into that miraculously soft bed, I knew nothing further.

The next morning, I came around to the combined scents of lavender and bacon, an unusual duo that whispered to my half-sleeping mind that something wasn't quite right. Gradually, I became aware of the unfamiliar mattress beneath me and more conscious of the smells of another person's house, and I bolted upright in bed with a gasp as I tried to remember where I was.

Big bed. Water untouched on the nightstand. Electric lamps everywhere. Fan still turning overhead despite the cold air blowing from the ceiling vent…

Jane's house, I recalled, and exhaled as my heart slowed. This was Jane's, and I was safe. Jane, who had the strongest touch I'd ever seen.

I glanced at the dresser, where I'd left her wand, and grinned in the twilight of the shaded room. The window in the guest room faced west, and I appreciated not waking to the sun in my eyes for a change. But the smell of cooking bacon told me Jane was already awake, and manners dictated that I offer to help her with breakfast.

Groggily, I slipped on her borrowed bathrobe, tightened the belt, and came around the corner to find that my hostess wasn't alone.

"Connor!" I cried, clutching the robe closed at the neck. "When did you...uh..."

My cousin, who'd been working at the counter behind Jane, was oddly dressed in a navy collared shirt, tie, and pleated trousers. An unfamiliar patch was affixed on his sleeve just below the shoulder, and when he turned, I saw a piece of gold-colored metal pinned on one side of his chest. He wore a black holster at his belt, in which I spotted the handle of a gun. I wasn't entirely sure what he was doing—the steel contraption on the counter was yet another of the peculiar gadgets in Jane's house—but as the plate beside it held a short stack of browned bread, I assumed it was some sort of toasting implement.

He looked up from his work, grinning, but his smile quickly faded as his eyes widened. *"Mitta—"*

"Hey, sleepyhead!" said Jane, turning from the spitting skillet with tongs in hand. "Just about to make some eggs. Is scrambled okay..."

In that moment, as they stared at me—Jane with surprise, Connor with horror—I realized I'd forgotten my headband, which had landed in my pile of clothes the night before.

I hastily pulled my hair forward, trying to cover the problem, but the damage was done.

Jane cleared her throat. "Sorry, brain fart," she said, resuming her work with the bacon. "So...scrambled?"

"Sure, thanks. Excuse me," I mumbled, and darted back into my room to fix the problem.

As I wrapped my headband and straightened out my ears, I tried to tell myself that this wasn't a colossal disaster. Jane was dating Connor, yes? Perhaps he'd mentioned this. And since she had the touch, maybe she knew other people with the same...feature. But then again, recalling how Connor had looked at me, I suspected that this might be new to her.

I went ahead and dressed properly while I was in there, then slipped back into the kitchen to see Jane still at the stove, now working on a skillet of eggs while the bacon cooled, and Connor standing close behind her, speaking so quietly that the cooking noises almost covered him. "It's harmless," I heard him say. "Out at East Branch, it's called 'the flop.'"

Okay, this was definitely a matter he hadn't broached with her yet.

"Usually goes hand in hand with the touch," Connor continued as she stirred the eggs. "It's just a weird birth defect in the community, you know? Like that blood disorder with the Blue Fugates or dwarfism and polydactyly in the Old Order Amish. What's it called..." He snapped his fingers. "The founder effect. Need caffeine."

Jane muttered, and the kettle rose from the stove, swerved around Connor's head, and flew toward the sink, where it filled of its own accord.

"I could have started that..." he protested.

"I don't trust you with sharp objects or fire when you're coming off an overnight shift," she retorted, then spotted me and smiled again, though the gesture seemed tenser that time. "Hey, hon. Ever had hot tea? Or do you like coffee?"

"Neither's really known at East Branch," Connor mumbled.

"Then perhaps we should start with orange juice. Con, would you..."

"On it." He opened the big metal box sitting against the wall to light and a rush of cold air—a refrigerator, I assumed, as the tea Jane had pulled out for us the night before had been chilled. There was only one at East Branch, an old green box that was used purely to hold produce during the canning process. Convincing it to function was often a two-day project.

Connor extracted a carton and poured pale orange liquid into three glasses, then carried them to the table while

I stood awkwardly by. "Have a seat," he told me. "And hey, mitta," he murmured, patting me on the shoulder. "Glad to see you're all right."

My anxiety spiked. "Did Mom and Dad tell you—"

"Not yet, but we should probably let them know you're not dead, hmm?"

Now *that* was a thought nearly concerning enough to put me off my breakfast, but then Jane and Connor brought the eggs, bacon, and toast to the table, and I decided I could eat a little.

They settled in, and I thought for a fleeting moment that the issue with my wardrobing error might be forgotten. After a few bites, however, Jane looked between Connor and me and said, "I don't mean to be rude, but *what* is the flop?"

"It doesn't hurt," I said.

Connor, who'd been shoveling eggs onto a piece of bread, put down his fork and glanced at me briefly before turning to Jane. "It's weak cartilage in the top of the ear. Doesn't affect hearing or anything, but it does look a little different. And if you come out of East Branch and you've got the touch, odds are better than decent that you'll have the flop as well."

"But not you," Jane pointed out.

He rubbed the back of his neck and winced. "Well...actually, I did."

"*Did?*"

"Yeah. My parents didn't have it, so they thought I might come out normal, but then I got the touch *and* the flop, so...yay." He shrugged and sipped his steaming tea. "They didn't have money to throw around, and I have no idea whether their insurance would have covered something like that, but my pediatrician was a saint and arranged reconstructive surgery when I was a few months old." Leaning toward Jane, he cupped one hand around his ear and angled the round top toward her. "If you look in the back, you can barely see the scars. They weren't noticeable by the time I started kindergarten, and thank God for *that*. I can't imagine what sort of hell school would have been like had I not had surgery," he added, chuckling.

Jane inspected the back of his ear, her brow puckered. Apparently, Connor's explanation had raised more questions than it had answered. "Maebe, I hate to ask, but could I see your ears again, please?"

I cut my eyes to Connor, who shrugged.

"Sure," I said, and loosened the knot of my headband. "Hold on, let me unwrap this..."

When I pulled the headband off, Jane didn't flinch or shy away, but her eyes narrowed as I tucked my hair back. "Kind of like a puppy, right?" I said, trying to make light of the situation, and briskly turned my head to make the floppy bits bounce. "Really, they don't hurt unless I try to comb them."

She hesitated, then started to reach for me. "May I?"

I obliged, leaning closer, and felt her unfold and raise my ear. "You can give it a squeeze," I offered. "It's weird, I guess."

But she wasn't interested in the defective cartilage. "Your ears are pointed," she murmured.

"I told you East Branch is insular," said Connor. "It's been there a long time, the gene pool is...*limited*—"

"No, this...I'm not so sure this is a weird mutation," she replied, and gently released me. Sitting back in her chair, Jane looked from me to Connor, biting her lip as she thought. "Yours were like Maebe's?"

"More or less," he admitted. "Mom tucked my baby pictures away in the china hutch if you're dying for proof, but yeah. Same issue."

"Con, they're *pointed*."

He grimaced. "Honestly, if that's the worst birth defect to come out of East Branch—"

"No, no," she said, and clasped his hand. "Honey, I'm not talking about inbreeding. Look...when you first showed me that you had talent, I told you there might have been some sorcerers at East Branch along the way, right?"

"Yeah..." he said, nodding.

"But in light of *that*," she continued, cocking her head toward me, "I'm not so sure. What if it wasn't sorcerers?"

"What else could it be?"

"*Elves*," she murmured.

He laughed aloud. "You're kidding, right?"

"Not at all."

"Elves," he said with evident disbelief. "In Appalachian Georgia. Does that make *any* sense?"

"I don't know. I mean, there's Liliol ti'Cren in Virginia—"

"She's a transplant, right? Like your dad."

"Yeah, but it *could* happen."

Connor seemed unpersuaded by this line of reasoning. "East Branch has been here since before the revolution. It's *old*. What are the odds of having elves in that mix? And besides, if there *were* elves, aren't they immortal? We've got a burying ground on the property if you want to see how many people die out there."

"Con—"

"My dad died of colon cancer. You ever heard of an elf with freaking *cancer*?"

Jane took a deep breath. "No," she said softly, "I haven't. Not yet, anyway. It's not like I'm an expert. But I *do* work with elves, and I'm telling you that Maebe's ears look like a shortened version of what I see on just about a daily basis."

Finally, I got a word in edgewise: "What are...elves?"

"I'll explain," she said to me, then turned her attention back to Connor. "And that's evidence of another problem. Sweetie, I know you want to protect East Branch," she said, "but do you realize that Maebe doesn't know what a computer is?"

"They're...sort of luddites, I suppose," he reluctantly replied.

"She doesn't know where Atlanta is. What to do with toothpaste. How a restaurant works. Can you sit there in good conscience and let your cousins *live* like that?"

"It's all they know—"

"And Maebe, at least, wants more."

Connor looked my way, and I nodded.

"I don't blame you," he said to me. "Really. I'm the lucky one. If you want out, I'll help you find your feet. But I can't just sweep into the compound and drag them into this century," he continued, turning to Jane. "I can't *expose* them like that. They don't know how the outside world works, and once you factor in the touch and that pesky little birth defect...I mean, even if we could arrange plastic surgery for everyone who needs it, you're talking about parents and grandparents who've never left this *county*. They'd be a freakshow or worse if the extent of the situation in there came to light."

"I hear you," she said, holding his gaze. "And I'm not suggesting we call CPS. Not right now, anyway. But...will you try something for me?"

"What'd you have in mind?"

Releasing him, she cocked her thumb over her shoulder toward the working part of the kitchen. "Get something out of the fridge. Don't make a sound, not a *peep*. See if you can do it with gestures alone."

"Do you want Jane's wand?" I offered. "She let me use it last night, and it's helpful—"

He shook his head. "I've got it, mitta, Thanks." Staring at the refrigerator, Connor inhaled deeply and blew out a long breath, then uncurled his fingers toward the door and cocked two back. The door opened with ease, almost slamming into the stove until another gesture caught it. He squinted at his target, the juice container, and with a twitch of his hand, it floated off its shelf and onto the table between him and Jane. With a satisfied smirk, he waved the door closed again, then looked at his girlfriend and folded his arms. "See? I've been practicing."

To my surprise, she closed her eyes, sighed, and rested her forehead on her fingertips.

"What?" Connor asked. "I *have* been practicing!"

"I believe you," Jane mumbled. "The problem is I've been teaching you wrong."

"Huh?"

"All these months, I've been working on verbal spells with you. Focusing mantras, all that jazz."

"Right…"

She raised her head. "You have *never* accomplished anything with a spoken spell as easily as you just did that. No fucking wonder. I'm an *idiot*."

"You're not an idiot, Janie. I've always done both together," he protested. "That's how I was taught."

"And it was overkill because all you need are gestures."

He paused, perhaps considering the ramifications of that declaration. "Is that a bad thing?"

"No," she replied, and weakly laughed as she poured herself more juice. "Sorcerers tend to rely on spoken casting. Elves primarily gesture."

She was halfway through her juice when Connor, who'd been staring at his plate with a troubled expression, spoke again. "You really think I'm part *elf*?"

"Could be. I don't know what to tell you, but…I *do* know someone who might have an idea about how to proceed."

They shared a long, silent look.

"You want to call your boss," Connor muttered.

"I absolutely do."

He sighed, shook his head, and resumed his attack on his cooling breakfast. "All right, fine," he said with resignation. "Just…no field trips to East Branch without me."

"Of course not." She rose, kissed his temple, and plucked a black object off the counter. "I already put in my vacation notice for today. Wonder if he's aware."

I watched her tap at the device and hold it to her ear, and Connor whispered, "It's a phone. Newer than the one at home."

"*Oh*," I whispered back, then fell quiet as Jane started speaking.

"Morning. Sorry to bother you," she said, and paused. "Yes, sir, I'm in Ragged Gap. Something's come up...*no*, no, he's okay. Or he was when we last spoke, I mean. Dad's finishing the weekend brew today, and I'm not disturbing him. But I've got a bit of a situation, and long story short, I need to bring someone in for genetic testing..."

Her eyes drifted toward Connor as she listened. "Actually, no, not him, and in any case, he needs to sleep after his shift. His cousin. Er...third cousin, I think. She wasn't sure. Anyway, don't hold me to it, but I *think* she may be somewhat elven," she said slowly.

The pause that time was longer.

"I've got reasons for my suspicions," she said, "but I'd rather not muddy the waters until someone can give me a straight answer about species. So, is there any way you could get me a visitor's pass? Call over to Laws and explain why I'm coming to see Canna?"

Jane smiled as the person on the other end replied.

"Great. I'm going to finish breakfast and get cleaned up, and we'll come through Central. Hope this is reason enough for the impromptu personal day..." She grunted indignantly. "Have I *ever* come to work hungover?"

"Might want to eat," Connor told me. "Sounds like you've got a drive ahead of you."

CHAPTER 4

By the time Jane finished her call, I was concerned and thoroughly lost. "Sorry," I said as she put the phone down, "but *what* is going on? Where are we heading?"

Jane looked at Connor. "Do you want to tackle that, or shall I?"

"Let me." As Jane returned to her seat, he pushed aside his plate and folded his hands on the table. "It's all right, mitta. You're safe. You can trust Jane." I must have seemed skeptical at that, as he insisted, "Really, you can. She's got weirder things going on in her life than anything East Branch can throw at her."

"Probably true," Jane murmured, and sipped her tea.

"And she knows how to keep a secret. Jane's not going to let anything happen to you, okay?"

"Okay," I replied, though I wasn't entirely confident in the situation.

"So, uh…" He squinted at the ceiling as if hoping to find assistance in the plaster. "There's a place Jane wants to take you. The entrance is…what, about an hour's drive?" he asked Jane.

She nodded. "If traffic cooperates. It's near Central, over the border in South Carolina."

That meant little to me, but I nodded along and tried to keep up.

"And this place," Connor continued, "it's…well, I've never been, but there's tons of folks in there with the touch. Like, they've got *strong* touches. Stronger than anyone at home."

"That's where I work," Jane added. "My job out of town? It's over there."

"You want to talk about strong touches," said Connor, nodding to her, "this lady right here can run circles around you, me, and maybe all of East Branch together."

"Oh, certainly," I concurred. "You should have seen her last night."

Jane grimaced. "We don't need to—"

"What happened last night?" Connor asked me.

"Jane took me to eat at this place…um, Jay-Jay's? I think? And there was a man with a gun who threatened a friend of hers, so she made a shield and distracted him, and his bullets *bounced off*."

Connor's dark eyes widened. "Come again?"

"I mean it! And then she threw him across the room, and while he was down, she thew him into the *next* room, and he hit his head, and they put him in a refrigerator, and then we left with takeout."

He turned to Jane with an annoyed scowl. "Firebug, *why* am I just now hearing that you stopped an armed robbery? And who witnessed this?"

"Zach from the woo-woo brigade," she replied. "He got arrested at Stephanie's mystical rager, so he's not going to say a peep. And I didn't say anything because it's not your jurisdiction, hon," she added, leaning over to peck him on the cheek.

That appeared to do little to pacify my cousin. "Maybe it's just me, but personally, I'd like to know if someone's shooting at my girlfriend."

"What're you going to do, drive over to the Ragged Gap PD and rough up the perp? I'm fine."

"*I'm* not! I'd prefer to keep you free of bullet holes, if it's all the same to you!"

She patted his hand. "We got free dinner out of the deal."

"That is *not* compensation for getting shot at."

"It was a *huge* shield," I said, trying to help. "Biggest

one I've ever seen."

"I bet," Connor muttered. "New rule, mitta: you'll be fine with Jane, but if anyone starts shooting, let her handle it."

"No one's going to shoot us in Beukal," said Jane. "And what's this 'mitta' I keep hearing? Is that your nickname?" she asked me.

I shook my head, bemused by the question. "No, I don't have a nickname. I'm just Maebe..."

"It's a term I've only heard at East Branch," Connor explained. "Means 'little sister.' We use it for all our younger female cousins."

"Huh. Where's it from?"

"Beats me. I mean, I'm not shocked that the community has its own slang, but don't ask me where it originated."

Silently, I made a note of this development. It made sense that we would use words the outsiders did not—after all, they certainly had a vocabulary I struggled to understand.

"Anyway," said Jane, turning to me, "I'd like to take you to this place and let my cousin check you out. She's a doctor, more or less—oh, no, she's medically trained," she hastily clarified as my brow knit, "but they work with magic in tandem with more mundane treatments. There's a blood test she can do that will hopefully tell us why you have the touch."

"What good would that do?"

"Possibly quite a bit. If it turns out that your ancestry isn't fully human, these folks might be willing to help you. Give you an education, perhaps, or at least teach you to use your talent. I don't know for sure, and depending on what the test turns up, there could be some political wrangling involved, but this might be a chance for a better life for you outside of East Branch."

An education. A *real* education. And if they could help me with my touch...

"Does it hurt?" I asked. "The test, I mean."

"Ever had blood drawn?"

I shook my head, and Connor muttered, "They don't go to the doctor unless a limb's hanging off."

"*Noted*," said Jane. "No, Maebe, it doesn't really hurt. She'll probably take blood from a vein in the bend of your arm. It's not *comfortable*, but it's pretty quick. I've had it done," she added, "and Canna's great. She'll answer your questions."

Again, I looked to Connor for reassurance, and he nodded. "I've met her a few times. She actually stitched me up last month after a home repair gone sideways…"

"Takes more than a little blood to dull her appetite for brunch," Jane teased. "That woman loves an omelet." Seeing my confusion, Jane said, "Nothing too serious—Connor sliced his hand on a knife. And since Canna has four kids, her purse is practically a medical kit."

"With potions," Connor added.

"*Good* ones. But here's the deal," Jane told me, sobering. "Let me take you to see her. If you get uncomfortable or want to go home at any point, just say so, and I'll drive you back here. Promise."

Frankly, I was nervous. Ragged Gap was the farthest I'd been from home, and now I was to go even farther? Meet more strangers?

"Does she have the touch, too?" I murmured.

Jane nodded. "She's a sorcerer like me. Better trained, actually. But if you make things move around her, she's not going to scream and run."

If Connor thought it was safe, and Jane was going to be there…well, that was good enough. "Okay," I said, hoping I didn't reveal my anxiety, and picked up my neglected bacon. "When do we leave?"

As soon as breakfast was finished, Jane sent me to finish dressing while she and Connor cleaned up the kitchen. He knocked and poked his head into the bathroom a few minutes later as I was brushing my hair. "Going home to get some sleep," he said. "If your parents contact me, what do you want me to say?"

Briefly, I mulled over my options, then turned to the mirror and began wrapping my headband. "Tell them I'm all right and need some time, yeah?"

"Can do. I'm going to rearrange my schedule, so I'll probably see you back here tonight." He paused, then added, "This place Jane's taking you...you should keep your headband on unless Jane says it's okay to take it off."

That wasn't a thrilling prospect—with the summer heat, the cloth left my head sweaty and my ears itchy—but I said, "Understood."

Stepping into the bathroom, Connor lowered his voice. "It's not forever, mitta. Jane can change her appearance with her touch, and she knows how to make jewelry that lets other people do the same. There was a kid here a few months back who had a pair of *horse* legs and a tail, and Jane could make her look absolutely ordinary."

I perked as I saw where he was going. "She could do the same for me?"

"I'd bet on it. Probably not today, since you're going to be out, but I think she could work something up for you. *If* you want," he stressed. "I'm not saying you need to change anything, Maebe."

"Says the one of us who got his fixed."

Connor rolled his eyes, then patted my shoulder. "Tell me everything tonight, eh?" he said, and left me to my work.

Shortly after he departed, Jane and I climbed into her truck, Jane equipped with a tall metal cup she'd filled with hot tea. "Buckle up," she reminded me, snapping on her belt, and backed onto the road.

"So...where are we going, exactly?" I asked, clutching the plastic cup of iced tea she'd poured for me on our way out the door.

Jane chuckled. "You'd think that would be an easy

question, wouldn't you?"

"Is it far?"

"Again, you would think that'd be an easy—*shit*." She pulled hard to the right, muttering profanities, as a car came barreling up the road,. "Sorry, hon. Okay, uh…let's start with the easy part. Ragged Gap is in Georgia, yes?"

"All right," I replied, having no reason to doubt her.

"We're up in the northeast corner of the state. In a little bit, we're going to pick up Highway 76 and take it southeast over the state border into South Carolina. Now, we don't go far into South Carolina, only about an hour, but we'll end up close to a town called Central. There's an undeveloped lakeside area west of Central, and hidden in there is a portal."

"What's a portal?"

"Well, this one is a doorway between worlds. Where do I start with this?" she muttered, scowling at the road as we descended the hill. "The beginning, I guess. Right. So, a long time ago—way before East Branch existed—there were people living in our world here who weren't human."

I frowned at Jane, considering that. "What do you mean?"

"Some had the touch, you'd call it. Others were every bit as smart and creative and what have you as humans, but they looked different." She paused, gathering her thoughts. "I told you I'm a sorcerer, yeah?"

"Uh-huh."

"We look human, but we're not. There's the whole 'magical powers' thing, but we also live about three centuries, and we age pretty slowly."

My eyes widened. "So, you're, like…"

"Oh, no, I'm just twenty-eight," she quickly reassured me. "But I won't look my age much longer—I'm at that point where aging sort of levels off. Anyway, because we look so much like humans, there's this hypothesis that sorcerers started as a freak human mutation—like blue eyes, say, but on a radically weird scale. I think it's plausible, but some folks take it *really* personally, so best not to speculate in public."

I put that aside for later. Insulting someone who could throw me across the room seemed like a terrible life plan.

"Now, you asked earlier what elves are," she continued, skirting the main part of Ragged Gap. "Considering the spectrum of intelligent non-human species, they're close to the 'passably human if you squint' end, but they're something else entirely. Magically gifted, for one thing. Immortal, for another."

"Huh?"

"They don't die of natural causes," she explained. "You have to, like, stab them or shoot them or set them on fire. Otherwise, they just keep going. And they age *super* slowly—my boss looks a few years older than I am, but he's, like, almost seven hundred years old."

My jaw dropped, and I quickly sipped my tea to cover.

If Jane noticed, she had the grace not to mention my reaction. "Like I said, if you squint, you might not notice an elf at a distance, but a few characteristics set them apart from your average human in a crowd. They tend to be thin in their build, so no linebackers...uh..." She glanced at me. "Ever seen a football game?"

"No..."

"Well, then, your average elf is probably slimmer than Connor," she amended. "Very high cheekbones, and they've got more pointed teeth than you might expect. A bunch of them are vegetarians these days, but I'd hate to get bitten by one." Again, she paused. "And then there's the ears."

My own had begun to grow warm under my headband, but I resisted the urge to reach up and scratch them. "Are they like mine?"

"Kind of. They're pointed like yours, but they don't flop over, and if I'm not mistaken, they're a little longer. But...I mean, I'm no genetic expert, but if you combined human and elven genes enough times, you might end up with someone who looks like you."

I nodded, mulling that over. "And...there are elves where we're going?"

"Elves, sorcerers, trolls, nymphs, gnomes, and more," said Jane. "All sorts of folks. You've got centaurs—they look pretty much human to the waist and like horses below that, four legs and all. Fauns are a similar idea, but they're kind of goatish. Big, curly horns and those weird goat pupils but only two legs. Nagas...same principle, but the bottom half's a giant snake, and they can unhinge their jaws like no one's business. *Freaky*."

I winced, as I wasn't exactly fond of snakes of normal size.

"There are others, but I think I'm overwhelming you as it is," she said, softly laughing. "There won't be a test, I promise."

"I'm holding you to that," I replied, cocking my cup in her direction.

"No worries. So...there are *billions* of humans out there, and that population has grown just about every year. Individual humans might be cool with magic—I mean, I've got a friend in Ragged Gap who's as human as they come, and she just rolls with the weirdness by now," said Jane—"but in general, humans get freaked out if they experience real magic, and when they're scared, they attack. I imagine that's why the folks who founded East Branch made a community for themselves." She paused at an intersection and sipped her tea. "Long ago, there were non-human communities here—villages of sorcerers, troll clans, the elven Halls, and so on. Humans spread out and got too close, some of them saw magic as inherently evil, and they started eradicating non-human populations. By the fifteen hundreds, something had to give. A group of sorcerers holed up at...well, at my boss's old fortress and created a pocket world."

"What's a—"

"Pocket world? An artificial world separated from this

one—the main one—but anchored to it at certain points. It's magically created. Let me see…all right, have you ever seen a piece of lace put over, say, a tablecloth? A doily, a placemat, something like that?"

I nodded. "Sure. My mom makes beautiful lace, and so does her mom. They put it out on the table for special meals, but they use different tablecloths beneath it."

"Great. So, imagine that the main world here is the tablecloth, and the pocket world is the lace. Not as big, not as solid, and it sort of sits on top. Does that make any sense?"

"I…think so?"

"It's really okay if it doesn't," Jane replied with a little smile. "I'm throwing a lot at you, all at once."

"I'm following," I insisted.

"Stop me if that changes…and hold that thought," she said, pulling up to the edge of a much wider road and looking back at the oncoming cars. Once the path was clear, she accelerated into a right-hand turn and picked up speed. "This is Highway 76. Just about straight on to Central," she said. "Where was I?"

"Lace."

"Gotcha. Okay, the pocket universe—the lace, if you like—is called the Pactlands. Or rather, that's the English translation. Once it was built, all of the non-human peoples signed this governing agreement called the Pact, and then they moved in and started over. The sorcerers who built it wanted to stick it somewhere out of the way, just in case the magic failed, and since a bunch of them were Europeans and this was the fifteen hundreds, they anchored their capital in what's now Virginia, just a little west of Richmond…two states up from South Carolina," she added. "It's a long drive. That's where we're heading."

"But I thought you said we'd be there in about an hour," I pointed out.

Jane grinned. "We will be, and you can thank the portals for that. Portals are doorways, like I said. Within the

Pactlands, there are portals in the major towns, and you can use them to get between places. The external portals, however, all go to the same spot in the capital. Central is the one nearest to Ragged Gap…and East Branch," she allowed. "The only portal in Georgia is around Surrency, and that's, like, a five-hour drive."

I hesitated, then asked, "Do they hurt?"

"Not at all," she said gently, and reached over to pat my knee. "Feels about like this, so if you can put up with my driving, the portal will be a breeze."

Thus reassured, I sat back and drank my tea, watching the morning lighten around us. The highway wasn't busy, just a strip of asphalt with yellow lines down the center, hemmed in by trees in full summer leaf and the logs and wires my dad had once told me were power poles. Soon enough, we crossed a bridge, and Jane announced, "Welcome to South Carolina!"

I didn't think it looked all that different from home—not at first. After a time, I noticed that the mountains seemed smaller in the distance, and overall, we seemed to be descending. Jane must have noticed my bemusement, as she asked, "What's on your mind, Maebe?"

"What happened to the mountains here?"

"What do you mean?"

"Where did they go?"

"*Ah.*" She smiled as she drove. "You've lived all your life in the far southern end of the Blue Ridge Mountains. That's part of the Appalachian chain. *Very* old mountains—the Rockies out west put them to shame in terms of size, but that's only because the Appalachians have been around so much longer that time has worn them down. We're now at the far eastern edge of the Blue Ridge, heading into the Piedmont—that's a big plateau running along the chain," she explained. "Past the Piedmont, the land flattens out. You might see the occasional hill, but the mountains don't rise like you're used to."

A world without tree-covered mountains hemming me

in like fingers around a cupped palm seemed utterly alien, and even the land around us felt almost too open without those protective guardians.

"The Pactlands is pretty flat," Jane continued, skirting a dead squirrel. "Less aesthetically interesting, but there's more room for settlement and farming—and since that world was built, I understand why they prioritized livable land over scenery. There *is* a mountain range, the Edolis, but it's not quite like home. No trees to speak of."

"Did they not plant any?" I asked, perplexed by the obvious oversight.

"Oh, they planted some—it's not for lack of trying. The problem is that nothing but grasses naturally grow well in the Pactlands. Something to do with the artificial nature of the world. I can't give you the full explanation," she said apologetically, "because that goes into the sort of theory I've only begun studying. Suffice it to say that most of the Pactlands is a prairie, and when they want to grow actual food, they've got to shore up the connection to the outside world with magic, and that's not easy. There's a nice sort of wilderness park where they've managed to make trees grow," she continued after a sip of her drink. "Decently close to the capital, all things considered. When I came over for the first time, my cousin's husband took me out there to show it off. I mean, I appreciate the work that went into making and sustaining it, but for folks like you and me, it's nothing extraordinary."

Honestly, I had enough to muddle through that day without trying to contemplate what a flat, treeless world might look like, and so I pushed that to the side to deal with later. "So," I said after Jane sped around a slower car, "you think Connor and I are, uh…elves?"

"My guess is partly elven, but I can't say for sure," she replied. "All we know is that *someone* up y'all's family trees wasn't human. How far back, how many people that might have been, exactly what sort of non-human progenitors we're dealing with—that's something I can't tell you. But my cousin Canna can run the blood test and tell you what you are, which would be a start."

I nodded, letting that sink in. "And if you're right, you think someone would send me to a real school?"

"I...think that would be logical, and if I have any input, I'll push for it. But there might be political problems to work through first."

"Like what?"

She groaned and propped her elbow on the door. "Each group in the Pactlands retains some vestiges of its prior governance, hierarchy, traditions, whatever you like, some *much* more than others. Elves are some of the worst in that regard—they've kept up with their own aristocracy. Back in the day, the rich and powerful families operated under the Hall system—fairly feudal, if you know what I mean."

I didn't, but I smiled and said nothing.

"The Halls were actual strongholds—buildings—back then. These days, there are mansions all across the Pact-lands for the lords and ladies of their Halls, and the old families try to one-up each other. All but my boss, I think."

I frowned. "Does he not care?"

"He doesn't have to. Before the Pactlands, he was king, and no one seems to have forgotten that." She glanced my way, then laughed at my surprise. "He heads the Division of Intelligence now. That's where I work—I'm a trainee agent. If it turns out that you've actually got an elf or two in the family, maybe the director will know how they got there. He's the one who authorized this trip."

"Connor doesn't like him," I murmured, recalling his reaction at breakfast.

Jane shook her head. "Con's not quite sure what to do with him, and they didn't have the smoothest of starts. But Con can deal with himself for now. Assuming you're partly elven, what happens next may come down to whether one of the Halls will claim you—and for that, we might need a little pressure from on high, you know?"

The notion of politicking was unfamiliar to me. Disputes over matters of importance were few and far between at East Branch, and the elders in the community collectively made the decisions that affected us all. But I didn't want to tax Jane more than I already had, so I sat back and drank my tea, watching the trees rush past and letting the truck's radio cover my anxious silence.

CHAPTER 5

Jane told me not to be alarmed when we turned off the main road and onto a dirt lane, but she needn't have worried. After an hour of driving past houses and shops and other vehicles, I didn't mind the break. Barely rutted, the road wound through the unfamiliar woods for a bit, and then I saw its terminus up ahead, where it disappeared into a stand of pines.

Suddenly, a dilapidated house came into view at the end of the road. "What..." I whispered.

Jane laughed to herself. "That's the portal entrance. It's hidden unless you know what you're looking for, and intent will trigger the spell to reveal it. Neat, huh?"

It was more than neat—this was *magic* on a scale I'd never imagined, far beyond anything my weak touch could accomplish. To Jane, however, this seemed like nothing more than an ordinary Monday.

"The portal is around the back," she continued. "Technically, it's inside the building, but the entrance is at the rear. Hang on..."

She slowed and bumped her truck over the weeds around the side of the house, which seemed poised to collapse at any moment, like the rotten old barn at East Branch that all the adults forbade the children from approaching. When she reached the rear, I was shocked to see that most of the outer wall was missing, as if it had been peeled away. Time had not been kind to the interior, littering it with junk and sowing weeds, but I had only a moment to worry about snakes hiding within when Jane stopped the truck, reached up to her sun visor, and pressed a button on a little black box.

Not three seconds later, a male voice came through the speakers of the truck. I couldn't understand a word he said, but Jane answered him in the same strange tongue. After a brief pause, the male voice spoke once more, and Jane leaned back in her seat.

"Portal attendant," she explained, and drank the dregs of her tea. "For the external portals, they only allow one vehicle in at a time. Apparently, DPP is sending a convoy back through right now, so we've got to wait a few minutes."

"DPP?" I asked.

"Division of Plants and Potions. They regulate production and distribution—my dad's a grower and brewer back in Ragged Gap, and they send quarterly inspectors. With that many in the field, they've probably just busted someone's illegal operation."

"Police?"

"Sort of, with specialized jurisdiction. What you might think of as the regular police are at the Division of Laws. That's where we're headed," she said, then quickly added, "You're not in trouble, Maebe—my cousin works there. I wouldn't take you somewhere I thought was unsafe, okay?"

Thus set somewhat more at ease, I studied the back of the house while we waited. "So, the portal's in there? Behind a door or something?"

"Not quite," said Jane. "You'll see."

Before I had time to grow too bored, I spotted flashes of light in all colors deep within the house. The lights grew in number and intensity, and then a bright white spot appeared at the center. "What—"

"Portal's opening," Jane replied, and shifted her truck into drive. "Almost there…"

The white spot rapidly swelled, covering my view of the house with a glimpse of the inside of a large and not at all crumbling building—perhaps something like a barn, I mused, but far larger than any barn I'd ever seen. A little barrier blocked our path just within the portal, and to its left was a glass-walled cubicle smaller than Jane's shower.

"Don't be afraid," she murmured, driving forward. "Just a portal booth. I've got this."

She eased through the portal, and I looked back as it quickly closed behind her. When I faced the front again, Jane had stopped the truck and opened her door, and the strangest creature I'd ever seen stepped up to the vehicle. Male, I thought—he had a neat beard, anyway—though quite short for a man, but that wasn't what caught my eye. Rising from his forehead were thick horns like a ram's, which wrapped back around his slightly pointed ears. He wore a dark green shirt but nothing below the waist, and his legs, covered in curly brown hair, ended in hooves.

I did my best to school my expression while he conversed with Jane, smiling and patting the open door. She handed him a piece of folded black leather, which opened to show metal within, an eight-pointed star shape with a green ring in the middle, surrounding what I supposed to be letters. The goatish man nodded at this display, then stepped back into the booth, climbed onto a stool, and began to type at an apparent computer. He called to Jane, who replied and closed her door, and a moment later, the barrier before us rose to give us passage.

"We're in," Jane said cheerily as she drove across the building. "Let's get out of here…"

"Um…uh…that…" I floundered briefly, too stunned by what I'd witnessed to speak coherently. "That…what…"

"He's a portal attendant," she said. "They check credentials. My badge was fine, but he had to look you up. Your temporary permission has come through, so we're all nice and legal."

"But…but he…"

"Faun. I mentioned them, yes?"

She had, but actually seeing one was a rather different matter. "And...there's more of them here?"

"Oh, sure. I know it's a lot to ask," she said, heading for the exit, "but please try not to gawk at folks. I'm happy to answer any questions, just...you know, don't stare."

And with that, she pulled out into the sunlight. I looked back to take note of the building we'd left—not a barn, as I'd imagined, but rather a circular structure with a domed brown roof. The pathway out turned onto a ringing road, and Jane sped away.

"Hey, Maebe?" she said as I watched the building recede behind us. "Turn around."

I did, then caught my breath. "Oh, *wow*."

The world was indeed flat and treeless, and I could see far enough into the distance to spot the massive cluster of buildings up ahead, structures taller than any I'd ever seen. Some flashed in the light, and I gawked in spite of myself.

"That's Beukal," Jane told me. "The capital city. It's not huge, as cities go—Atlanta's bigger—but it's the largest settlement in the Pactlands."

"We're going *there*?"

"Nothing to worry about, hon."

I stared out the windows as we passed huge swaths of grassy fields, green with the season. With no vehicles behind us, Jane slowed as we neared a strange, twisted bush about hip-high and asked, "Want to guess what that is?"

I peered at it as we passed. "I don't know. The leaves look kind of like an oak..."

"Bingo. That's what a mature oak tree looks like around here. See why the whole place isn't forested?"

She sped up again, and I glanced back, feeling sorry for the weird little tree that had managed to sprout in such terrible soil.

Jane described our surroundings as the buildings began to rise around us. "Outskirts of town," she said. "We're going into the city center, into District 2. That's where Laws keeps its tower. See?" she asked, pointing through the windshield. "It's the tallest one in town. Canna's office is about two-thirds of the way up, so she's got a great view from the patient rooms on that floor…*when* she stops. They keep her busy in there."

I didn't say anything, but I rubbed my legs and tried not to calculate how many stairs I would need to climb. Only the barns had staircases—our homes were single-floor dwellings—and while I knew that some buildings had multiple stories, I'd never been faced with one so tall. My legs, still a little sore from my hike over the last days, were just another problem for my anxiety, which rose with every intersection we crossed and every strange creature we passed. By the time Jane parked beside the massive glass spire, I would have given serious consideration to ducking behind the bushes and being sick had there been any bushes on offer, but the neat lawn provided no privacy.

Jane waited while I slid out of the truck, then locked up and escorted me through a set of double doors into the tower. Past the glass wall, the entrance hall was covered in polished white marble, and our footsteps echoed. The ceiling rose at least twenty feet, and as I took it all in, I calculated that my family home could easily fit within the space. A few benches lined the walls, some occupied, and I tried to be stealthy as I sneaked glimpses of the other people around us: an ordinary-looking brunette in a floor-skimming green robe, a man with a neatly braided white beard who stood only as tall as a young child, a massive being with purple skin, tusks, and a dark tuft of hair, who held an undersized paperback in one clawed hand as it waited.

Jane led me past them all to a wooden desk midway along the hall, where a long-haired blond in a black shirt was frowning at a panel—another computer, I supposed. He looked up at our approaching footsteps, noticed Jane, and nodded in apparent recognition, then spoke to her. She answered him, smiling, and signed an open book on the desk. He turned to me and said something, but Jane swooped in before I could start flailing, and the two wrapped up their brief conversation as he lifted the handset of what I took to be a phone.

His ears, I noticed, were pointed, but unlike mine, they stuck straight up from the sides of his head. The tips poked a good inch through his hair.

I caught Jane's eyes and mouthed, *Elf?*

She nodded, then claimed a free bench on which to wait. Once I was seated beside her, she leaned close and whispered, "He's the lobby attendant—you can't just walk around this building by yourself if you don't work here. Canna's on her way down."

A few minutes later, one of the sets of metal doors at the back of the lobby opened with a chime, and a woman came striding out. She was tall—I could tell that even at a distance—and her open purple coat, which fell to mid-calf, swished as she walked. Her brown hair was pinned back but for a few stray wisps that had escaped their bindings. Jane rose and waved, and the woman smiled as she hurried toward us. They hugged briefly, and then the woman took a closer look at me, her green eyes narrowing as she studied my face. She spoke unintelligibly to Jane, who murmured, "Haven't had a chance to think about a language potion. We just met yesterday."

"Oh!" she replied, but didn't miss a beat. "Hello, there," she said to me, her words oddly accented, and stuck out her hand. "Canna Nerin."

I shook it. "Maebe Amos."

Her head cocked. "Just maybe?"

"Maebe is her name," Jane explained. "It's spelled differently."

"I see. Sorry," Canna told me, grinning abashedly. "I'm not too familiar with human names—"

"My parents made it up," I said, shrugging. "It's fine."

"Noted, then." Looking back at Jane, she said, "Your message was a little sparse on detail. Want to tell me what's going on?"

"Sure, but not in the lobby. Can we go to your office?"

"Of course." She started off toward the metal doors, and Jane and I trailed after her.

Beyond the doors was a tiny room the size of a closet. I'd barely stepped inside when the doors slid shut behind me, and I spun around as Canna flashed a badge like Jane's and pushed a small circle marked with a strange symbol on the front wall. The circle was one of several dozen, which ran up the wall in a pair of neat lines, each bearing a symbol or two. Before I had a chance to ask about them, the room shuddered and began to move, and I screamed.

"*Whoa*, it's okay!" said Jane, grabbing my shoulders. "You're fine, Maebe, it's just an elevator."

"A *what?*"

"An elevator," she repeated. "Unless you want to walk up all those stairs…"

"Done that. Not recommended," Canna muttered.

I tried to catch my breath and noticed a panel above the doors, on which different symbols rapidly flashed. "This is…magic?"

"No, sweetie, this is good old-fashioned mechanics. I'll show you how it works later, all right?"

I nodded.

"Deep breath?"

Following her suggestion, I pulled myself together, though Canna regarded me curiously for the rest of the ride.

When the elevator chimed again, the doors opened, but the room beyond us had changed. Instead of the marble lobby with its soaring ceiling, this hallway was much more practical, still about ten feet high but with tile floors and cream-painted walls. A man in a purple coat like Canna's walked past, escorting a faun in a black shirt with one arm in a sling. We'd barely stepped out when a door down the hall opened, and a creature like the purple one in the lobby, albeit gray, stuck its head out and looked around until it noticed Canna. It called to her in what sounded like a low-pitched female voice, but when she answered, the creature grunted, left the room, and marched off down the corridor.

"Tricky patient?" Jane murmured.

Canna made a face. "Swift Rapids has a centaur in there. He's a detective, and he's normally a sweetheart, but he's got some issues out the back end, if you follow, and he's *sensitive*. Even when you get them numbed, protocol says to use the buddy system when approaching a centaur from behind. Those hooves have minds of their own."

"You're welcome," she replied with a smirk.

"I'll withhold judgment on that until you tell me what brings you here, but...yeah, I've taken my share of hooves. Occupational hazard."

As I trailed Canna through the door-pocked hall, I whispered to Jane, "What *was* that?"

"Troll," she whispered back. "She's a healer, too. Not going to hurt you."

Though I wasn't convinced of *that*, I stayed quiet until Canna showed us through one of the identical doors and into a small room. It had no window, but electric lights in the ceiling cast a warm glow around the space, which was dominated by a metal desk and a cluttered counter. Two old metal chairs sat on the visitors' side of the desk— utilitarian if not exactly welcoming—and I couldn't have begun to guess at the contents of the many bottles and boxes stashed around the room. The only feature that gave it personality was the photographs, which depicted a large, dark-haired man and four small children. We had a camera at East Branch, one used only for special occasions, and my mother said that the film it required was almost impossible to find. Canna easily had twenty photos taped to her cabinets, a staggering excess. Around the pictures were exemplars of children's artwork—finger paintings, abstract drawings whose subjects were known only to the artist, a halfway decent rendering of a sunset in crayon— presumably the work of the children in the photos.

Canna shut and locked her door, then said, "Close your eyes, dear."

I did as she said, but the bright flash that followed shone red through my eyelids, and I opened my eyes in alarm. "What—"

"Privacy spell," said Jane. "Now we can speak freely."

"And I can't wait to hear *this* one," Canna replied, leaning against the counter. "Have a seat," she added, gesturing toward the chairs. "No need to stand for me. So, what brings you here?"

I sank into one of the chairs, but Jane stood beside me and rested her hand on my shoulder. "Maebe is one of Connor's relatives from East Branch."

Canna's brow furrowed. "The compound?"

"Exactly. She's got talent, just like he does. But there's something else you need to see."

I looked up at Jane in query, and she nodded. "Could you take off your headband, hon? It's all right."

Hesitantly, I unwrapped the cloth strip and pulled it away, then ran my hands through my hair to fluff it. "It looks a little weird," I told Canna, "but it doesn't hurt or anything…"

The woman was a professional, and to her credit, her reaction was raised eyebrows instead of a gasp or worse. "That's different," she murmured, and straightened. "May I…"

"Sure." I tucked my hair back behind the ear closer to her and tilted my head, and she carefully lifted the top part to examine it. "This is pretty common at home. We call it 'the flop.'"

"Connor had it, too," Jane told Canna, "but he had reconstructive surgery as a baby."

"*Seriously?*"

"He told me this morning, I had no idea. But talent, plus ears like that…"

"Suggests elven extraction, doesn't it?" said Canna. "Easy to find out. Let's get her tested."

Releasing me, Canna returned to the counter and began digging through drawers. "The analysis will take only a few minutes. I can look for genetic markers, certainly, and check her against the database. Do we want a health panel…" Her voice faded when she turned and looked at me.

Though I was trying my best to be stoic about the situation, my heart hammered behind my ribs, and my palms had begun to sweat. I suppose my face betrayed me, as Canna's eyes softened, and she put the items she'd collected on the counter. "It's all right, dear," she said, and perched on the edge of her desk in front of me. "I'm sorry, are you afraid of needles?"

"I don't think she's ever been to a doctor," Jane offered, and I nodded.

"*Oh*. Okay, don't worry," said Canna with a smile. "Everyone has a first time. Let's take this slowly, yeah? Would that work?"

I swallowed my fear. "Uh…okay."

"Good," she said in a tone that sounded eerily like my mother's. "I'm a healer. That means my job is to make you feel better and fix whatever's bothering your body. In this case, I can do a diagnostic test—or rather, our machine can do the difficult part," she said, pointing to a black box squatting on the counter. "That'll tell us *what* you are, most basically, but I can ask it to run additional tests on your blood sample, which will give us some insight into how you're functioning. Blood sugar, cholesterol, iron, and so on. Now, you look pretty healthy to me just sitting there, but looks can be deceiving. How old are you, dear?"

"Eighteen last March."

"Mm. And you've *never* had a checkup?"

"No…" I said, slumping in my chair.

"Oh, sweetie, I'm not upset. You haven't done anything wrong," she reassured me, and patted my knee. "But you *are* growing up, and if you stick around here, I would strongly recommend some follow-up visits. Happy to make the arrangements—just not today. One healer's probably sufficient for now, right?"

She grinned, and I smiled back at her, relieved.

"Do you have any questions?" Canna pressed.

Plenty, but I didn't want to annoy her. "Um...how does that thing figure out what I am?" I asked, nodding toward the black box.

"It looks for the presence of particular genetic markers, and then their frequency..." She paused as my face scrunched. "I'm not being clear, am I?"

"I...I didn't go to school," I mumbled. "Home-schooled. But there's lots I don't know, I guess, and—"

"Sweetheart." She held out her hands, and I placed mine atop her waiting palms. "It's all right to not know something. There are plenty of things I don't know, and the same goes for Jane. We're all getting by as well as we can. You don't need to feel bad or apologize."

"It's just kind of overwhelming," I whispered.

"And that's okay. Here's the thing, Maebe: you are in charge of your body. Unless you're unconscious and in desperate need of emergency care, I'm not going to do anything to you without your permission. I *want* you to ask questions and be comfortable, and in here, there are no stupid questions. Promise."

"Thanks."

She gave my hands a squeeze before releasing me. "Let's go to basics. Every cell of your body contains genetic information—the instructions that make you *you*. Your genes are unique, but the same sequences of information occur in the same places across a species. For instance, Jane and I don't have identical noses," she said, glancing at her cousin, "but we have noses in the same spot on our faces, and the basic design is the same."

I nodded. "Okay..."

"Now, what we've found is that there are particular sequences that only happen in certain species. Jane might pass for human on sight, but if you run her blood—which I have—you see sorcerer markers in the usual places and none of the human-only markers. And some species have different numbers of chromosomes, too, which makes this easier...uh, the molecules in which genetic material is kept," she clarified. "Sorcerers, elves, and humans have forty-six, for instance, but trolls have forty-eight, and nymphs have fifty-four. So, if you get a sample with fifty-four chromosomes, you know you're dealing with a nymph, see?"

"I think so."

"But that's just the genetic side of what the analysis will do," she continued. "It'll also give us some readings about how much of different things we see being transported in your blood. That, in turn, will give us an idea of how your body is functioning. Unfortunately, this works better when you haven't eaten because food can mess with your numbers, but if something's wildly off right now, it'd be good to know. So, with all that in mind, may I run your sample?"

"It's not going to hurt?" I asked.

Canna wiggled one hand. "Just a little prick while I get the needle in your arm, and then some mild discomfort for a moment. Nothing so bad that you should need a painkiller."

Deciding to trust her, I thrust out my arm and braced myself.

She wrapped a tight band around my upper arm and pressed on the bend in my elbow, then grunted to herself and released the band. With that accomplished, she sprayed something cold on my skin and told me to sit still while she prepped the needle and a clear tube. I watched as she eased the needle in, and the tube immediately began to fill with blood. "You've got good veins," she told me. "Thanks for making this easy. One more vial of blood, if you please..."

As I held an absorbent pad to the wound to stop the bleeding, Canna fiddled at the machine. "Just running a cleaning cycle," she explained, and by the time that had finished and Jane was taping a bandage on my arm, Canna had prepared my sample for analysis. She popped it in and started the process, then typed and swiped at a computer beside the machine until the picture changed to what she needed.

The initial results weren't long in coming. "Right," Canna murmured, watching the computer. "Assuming you're not secretly a troll"—she glanced back at me and winked—"your numbers are good. Everything's in normal range…okay, and no traces of known potions in the sample. That's expected, yes?" she asked Jane.

"I haven't given Maebe anything."

"Perfect. No active infection…and she needs her shots," Canna said. "I can put her on a course similar to the one used for Sage, if that's how we want to proceed."

"Shots?" I asked.

"They help teach your body how to fight off certain illnesses…though if you're elven enough, they might not be so crucial. Let's see…"

A moment later, Canna muttered, "*Huh*. Interesting."

"And?" asked Jane.

She turned around, an inscrutable expression on her face. "Elven and human markers. Majority elven."

CHAPTER 6

I wasn't sure how to feel about that, but Jane, at least, seemed shocked. "Like...half?"

"Approximately seventy-three percent," said Canna. "And Maebe's from *East Branch*?"

"I...I thought they might have had a sorcerer or two somewhere back along the line—"

"This is more than one or two, I'd think. If East Branch is a fairly closed community, then a *significant* chunk of the foundational stock was probably elves." Shaking her head, she asked, "What the heck is going on in those mountains of yours, anyway?"

I sat there in silence, trying to absorb what Canna was saying, and watched as she put a blood sample into a gray machine further down the counter and attached her computer. She cleaned up the black machine, and as she was disposing of the trash, the gray machine beeped. Bending over to read the computer, Canna reported, "No match. That's not unexpected."

"What does that mean?" I asked.

"This machine compares your genetic profile to the ones we have in a protected database—government officials, parents with missing children, and such. I'm not surprised that you don't match, but I wanted to be sure." She studied me for a moment, then asked, "Maebe, would you mind if I called in a colleague? Another healer," she added. "I've never seen an ear condition like yours, and he might have some insight."

I shrugged. "Sure, if you want..."

"Thanks," she said, and slipped out of the room.

Alone with Jane, I looked at the black box, my guts knotting. "What does all of this mean?"

She sighed. "Well, it explains where your talent comes from. More than that…I'm not sure yet, but we'll get to the bottom of it," she said, and gave me a tight smile.

I'd barely had time to begin properly fretting when Canna returned with a tall, thin man in a purple coat. He wore his dark blond hair back in a bun, leaving his pointed ears on clear display—and when he opened his mouth, I understood what Jane had meant about elven teeth. While the top two in the front looked flat and normal enough, the rest were far sharper. He spoke as they walked into the room, then caught sight of me in my chair and stopped in his tracks, his jaw dropping as his unfamiliar words were cut short.

Canna closed the door and quietly said, "Hirral, this is Maebe. She doesn't speak Pactish yet, so…"

He gawked at me for a moment longer, then pulled himself together and cleared his throat. "Uh…hello, youngling. I'm sorry, you…you took me by surprise."

"Sorry," I mumbled.

"You've done nothing wrong. Though I will go ahead and apologize for my accent," he added with a half-smile. "It's been quite some time since I had cause to go out-side."

"Want to see her report?" Canna asked.

"Absolutely." He waited while she tapped at her computer, and then a piece of paper was spat from another machine tucked into the back of the room. When she passed it to him, his eyes widened as he read. "Seventy-three percent? Her parents are…what, an elf and half-elven?"

"Nope," I told him, "they look like me. Most folks in our community do."

He frowned at me over the report. "Community?"

"It's a settlement outside in Georgia," Jane offered.

"Do you know—"

"I've heard of it, never been. You've got elves there? Growers?"

"No," she said, "it's an old community, highly insular, and they have no idea that they're anything but human. Apparently, most of them have at least minor talents, and then there's the flop."

I lifted one of my ears between finger and thumb and let it fall. "It's pretty common back home. If you've got the touch, you probably have the flop, too."

Hirral looked to Jane again, who explained, "'The touch' is what they call magical ability. Maebe can cast— she did it last night. It's not strong, but she's also untrained."

"Remarkable," he said, "and *very* curious."

"I've never seen anything like her condition," Canna told him, "so I was wondering if you knew of any other cases."

He shook his head. "Not personally, but I know what *that* is. Cifyent."

"Sorry," said Jane, "I don't think my language potions covered that one…"

"They wouldn't, not unless you needed High Elvish for…I don't know, cultural studies," Hirral replied with a shrug. "*I'm* certainly not fluent. But cifyent has been documented for centuries, so the old name stuck. It's a birth defect, harmless but odd looking."

My cheeks began to heat.

Unaware of my embarrassment, he continued, "The last recorded cases were before the Pact, so it hasn't been well studied, but the thought is that it's the result of a recessive mutation. The cartilage in the upper ear is structurally deformed, so the top falls over."

"And…what, the mutation has died out?" Canna asked.

"Before today, I might have said yes." Staring at me, Hirral said, "It was incredibly rare in the northern Halls, but it was occasionally seen in some of the southern ones.

Of course, since *they* were wiped out, I would have thought cifyent went with them. And you say this is *common* in your community?" he asked me, his eyes narrowing.

"Almost everyone has it," I replied, fighting the urge to fidget under his gaze. "It's…just us, I guess."

He mulled that over, then looked at Canna and said something I couldn't understand. She replied in kind, and he focused on me again. I'd seen that sort of intense stare before, but usually from a kid in possession of a dead animal and a good poking stick. Finding myself on the receiving end was thoroughly uncomfortable.

At least Canna picked up on my condition. "Thank you, Hirral. I don't think I need to stress that this is to be kept quiet for now."

He snorted. "Uh, *no*, you do not. What's the plan?"

She folded her arms as she turned to Jane. "Medically, I'm not sure, but this seems like the sort of matter your boss would want to know about."

"Her boss?" Hirral asked bemusedly.

"I'm over at DOI," Jane replied.

"*Oh.*" He retreated a pace, lifting his hands in surrender. "Understood. And he's old enough—he might have seen this condition before the Pact."

"He's aware of the situation," said Jane, pulling her phone from her purse, "but yeah, I'll share the update."

With that, Canna shooed Hirral out and followed him, giving Jane and me a moment's privacy. She tapped at the phone, then put it on Canna's desk and pivoted toward me. "You okay, hon?"

"I think so…"

"I'm not impressed with his bedside manner, to be frank."

Though my flushed face surely revealed my true feelings, I tried to downplay them. "I'm sure he didn't mean anything—"

"He asked Canna how inbred you were."

I stiffened in my seat. "Does *he* know about East

Branch?"

"No. Deduction," she explained. "If you have a small community with lots of people showing the same rare trait, there's a good chance that they've been marrying each other for a long while. But you heard Canna—you seem pretty healthy. And if your family's a little too connected, that's not *your* fault."

While I didn't understand everything Canna had said to me that day, I knew enough about the community's problem. My grandpa—my dad's father—cared for the few horses we had on the property, the ones used to help with plowing. He had one stallion, two mares, and a handful of geldings, but when he bred the mares, he always sold or traded the foals to outsiders. I'd cried one fall when he sold off a little filly I'd come to love and wanted to learn to ride, but Grandpa was firm. Horses born in East Branch couldn't stay, no matter how pretty they were. As I grew older, I saw the problem: the foals had only their parents and siblings on the property, and when the mares went into heat, that was setting up a disaster. Breeding half siblings to each other wasn't good for the horses, Grandpa had explained, and so, whenever he needed a new mare, he traded for unrelated stock.

But no one was trading *people* with East Branch. We certainly didn't marry our siblings, and first cousin marriages were rare, but most of us surely shared ancestors. *Inbred* wasn't a word used around home—we preferred *close*—but I knew what it meant, and I was old enough to have heard that closeness blamed for the number of failed pregnancies.

"We're going to figure this out," Jane continued, giving my shoulder a pat. "Okay? At least we've got the process started..." Her phone beeped, and she plucked it up to take a look. "Great, he's waiting. Let's go."

"I don't want to be a bother—" I began.

"You're not. Want to put your headband back on before we walk out of here?"

Working quickly, I retied it and fixed my ears, and Jane opened the door just as Canna returned. "Thanks so much," Jane told her, printed report in hand. "We're off to DOI."

"Any time." The two exchanged brief hugs, and Canna smiled at me. "Let me know what I can do for you. I'm happy to make some calls to other healers to get you fully checked out."

I thanked her, but in truth, I wasn't thrilled with the offer. Canna had been gentle, but if Hirral was more the norm, I had no desire to be prodded and stared at.

Jane led me into the elevator and back to the lobby, and then we hopped into her truck again. "The biggest of the agencies are all headquartered in District 2," she said, pulling into traffic. "Laws and DPP have the flashiest of the buildings—DPP built its glass tower first, and then Laws came along and built a bigger one—but DOI went for something more subdued. It's only about half a mile, so don't get too comfortable."

Subdued was a relative term. Soon, we pulled up at a windowless stone building that, while not as shiny as the tower we'd just left, still rose ten stories above us. Jane drove up to a little hut like the booth back at the portal and flashed her badge, and the woman inside nodded. The air in front of us, which shimmered like a heat mirage, suddenly stilled, and Jane eased forward. "Barrier spell," she told me, heading down a ramp into the darkness below the building. "And should you break through that, there are more spells on the elevators and the stairwell. Good luck getting out of the parking garage."

To my surprise, the underground space was well lit once we cleared the ramp and neatly marked for cars. Most of the spaces were painted with symbols, and Jane parked in one about halfway across the garage. "Reserved parking is nice," she said, cutting the engine, "but you've got to have status before you get a spot close to the door. Come on, let's walk."

I didn't mind—the garage was cool for summer, much like the world above. On the far side, Jane led me into another elevator, then showed her badge to a domed white circle set beside the buttons, which flashed red. "We're in," she told me with mock gravity. "And going all the way up. Just stick with me."

The elevator doors opened onto the nicest hallway I'd ever seen: twelve-foot ceilings, thick carpeting in dark blue and gold, and brass lamps set along the stone walls between the wide wooden doors. Noticing my hesitation, Jane wrapped her arm around my shoulders and escorted me down the hall, then poked her head into an open doorway and said something I couldn't understand. The person inside—a sorcerer, I thought—spoke back to her, and Jane walked on to the door beside it, which had to open into a corner space. "Secretary," she whispered. "I didn't know if we'd been added to the official schedule."

She rapped twice on the door, which clicked open and swung inward. "Come in, Jane," a male voice called, his accent unplaceable to me.

I followed her into an office just as nice as the hallway and at least as large as Jane's den. A dark, heavy, polished wooden desk with brass details faced the door, atop which were situated a pair of what had to be computer screens. To our right was a matching rectangular table set with eight ornate chairs and a pair of glass bowls holding mints. On the left was an oversized couch in navy leather, flanked by a pair of armchairs positioned around a wooden coffee table. Behind the couch, an enormous and very full bookshelf covered the wall from corner to corner. To my surprise, the wall behind the desk featured a floor-to-ceiling window, beyond which I could make out rooftops and a green patch. Since the building *had* no windows, I assumed the impossibility before my eyes was the result of magic.

A redheaded man sat at the desk in a large leather chair, which rocked back as he stood. He gestured lazily at the door, which shut and latched, then said, "No need to stand there. Come in, have a seat."

Jane perched on the couch, and I joined her, trying not to be obvious as I studied the man. He seemed young, maybe Connor's age—there didn't appear to be even a hint of gray at his temples—and his loose hair fell over his shoulders and down the front of his sleeveless robe. The garment was strange, charcoal gray and embroidered with silver thread at the collar, unlike anything I'd ever seen sported in East Branch or elsewhere. He wore a cuffed black button-up shirt and trousers beneath it, nothing flashy, but his dark shoes were polished. And even from across the room, I could see the tips of his ears poking through his hair—another elf, no question about it.

As he drew near, he held my gaze and grinned. "*There* you are," he said. "I was beginning to wonder when we'd meet."

I looked back at him blankly, but Jane jumped in. "This is Maebe. You know about her?"

"*Know* is a rather strong word, but I have been seeing flashes." He took the nearer chair and regarded me with evident curiosity. "Maebe, you said?"

"Maebe Amos," I mumbled. "Hi."

He smiled again and sat back, crossing his legs. "I'm Diriem. All right, Jane, I'm listening. Why did you bring another Georgian here?"

"You tell me," she replied, and handed him my report.

Watching him, I knew the instant he reached the part she'd wanted him to see. "Seventy-three percent?" he asked incredulously. "Where on earth did—"

"East Branch. I mentioned she's Connor's kin, yeah?"

He stared at her for a moment, and a strange expression crossed his face, a look of comprehension that rapidly shifted toward a wince. "Close kin?"

"Third cousins," said Jane. "But this is East Branch, so—"

"It's probably more than that," he finished. "You said she's talented?"

"Not well trained, but she's got something."

"My touch isn't strong," I told him. "Connor can, like, open the refrigerator and get things, but I'm not, um...I mean, I try..."

"It's all right," Diriem murmured. "I suspect we could find a good tutor for you."

"And that's not all," Jane interjected. "Maebe, hon, I hate to ask again, but would you..."

"Sure." I untied my headband but glanced back at Diriem before I removed it. "Uh...this might look weird, so, you know, brace yourself."

His mouth twitched. "Consider me braced. Go for it."

Apparently, he wasn't as braced as he'd imagined, as he leaned toward me with saucer eyes when I freed my ears. "Heavens..."

"Canna called in another healer," Jane told him. "He said it was—"

"Cifyent. That's a *cifyent* case."

She smirked. "For having seen flashes, you seem surprised."

"I've seen nothing with the wrapping off," he protested, then sat back and shook his head. "An incredibly rare birth defect, but harmless," he said to me. "Honestly, I haven't seen that in centuries."

"Guess it's not as rare as you think, since most of us have it," I replied.

Diriem's eyebrows shot toward his hairline. "Excuse me?"

"At East Branch.," I said, trying to sink into the cushions. "If you've got the touch, you probably have the flop, too."

"Connor had it at birth, come to find out," Jane added. "So, yeah, looks like there's a whole quasi-elven community in my backyard."

He rubbed his face and scrunched his eyes shut. "Any idea as to *how*?"

"No clue yet. Question."

"Shoot."

"Is there a term in Elvish that sounds anything like 'mitta' for a younger sister? Maybe a younger female relative?"

Diriem's eyes opened, and he made no effort to hide his surprise. "Not in Low Elvish, but in *High* Elvish, that would be 'mitha.' A younger sister, cousin, close friend...but it's a fairly informal term, and I can't imagine that it's found its way into anything ceremonial. Why do you ask?"

"Because Connor called her 'mitta' all through breakfast."

"Could be an East Branch thing," I suggested. "'Mitta' for younger girls, 'catta' for younger boys—"

"Mitha, catha," said Diriem. "That's too close to be coincidental."

"So, why do our elves in the holler use loan words from High Elvish?" Jane asked.

He sat quietly for a moment, staring into space, and I was growing concerned when he slowly said, "I don't know, and the only conclusion I can draw seems impossible."

Jane frowned. "How so?"

"The languages were already dividing when I was a boy. What we think of now as Low Elvish was a northern development—if you look closely enough, you'll see traces of Germanic borrowing in there. Not German, but the older forms of the Nordic tongues. There was a pronunciation shift as well, plus local dialects, and eventually, a clear divide began to manifest. That didn't happen in the south. They were *much* more particular about preserving the language—and with so many human settlements and competing tongues around the Mediterranean, I understand the impulse. But for a community to be using High Elvish now, plus the incidents of cifyent..."

He looked at Jane, but if he was expecting her to finish that thought, he was disappointed. "Sorry," she said, "I'm not following."

"Southern Halls."

She sucked her teeth. "Not to be difficult, but I don't have an encyclopedic knowledge of Hall politics."

"*Right.*" Leaning back in his chair, Diriem closed his eyes again and started to rub his temples. "At the time of the Pact, the northern Halls and a few of the southern—ti'Cren, ti'Grell, ti'Vir—joined up when I told them it was the only way, but my counterpart in the south refused to relinquish his crown. We sent scouts in the first years following the Pact to check on them, see if they'd reconsider, but within five years, the scouts could find no trace of them. Their fortifications and settlements had been razed, and farsight showed nothing."

"Farsight?" I echoed.

He paused, seemingly surprised by the interruption. "It's what we call a wild talent. I see flashes of the future...or potential futures, really. Useful on occasion. Anyway, I tried for *months* after the last scouting expedition, and I couldn't see a single person I'd known. We could only conclude that they'd been annihilated...just as my farsight had predicted."

His hands dropped, and when his gray eyes opened once more, they fixed on mine. "But now there's Maebe here, who's high-percentage elven, uses words in a language long dead, and exhibits cifyent, a known trait in the *southern* Halls. It sounds impossible...but there's the matter of her name as well."

I sighed. "*That's* just my parents being too creative for their own good. I had great-aunts named Belinda and—"

"No, not your personal name. Your family name."

I squinted back at him. "What, Amos? It's not that weird..."

"Not on its own, no, but in combination with everything else I know of you..." He chuckled mirthlessly and shook his head. "The last king in the south, the one who refused to sign the Pact and save his people—he was Ivari *ti'Ammaas.*"

As I sat there, trying to slot this information into my already racing thoughts, Diriem propped his elbows on the arms of his chair and steepled his fingers. "I believe it's time I took a closer look at East Branch. Maebe, why don't you tell me about your people?"

I don't know why I did it—prudence counseled me to say nothing and run home. But as Diriem waited, I licked my lips, then said, "We've got records. You might start there."

CHAPTER 7

"I'm sorry about this," Jane called from the kitchen that afternoon over the sizzle of her skillet. "I'm normally in Beukal during the week, so the dinner options here are pretty minimal. But I've got some frozen sausage patties, if that would help."

"Sure," I said.

"Really, if you hate pancakes, just tell me, and I'll ask Connor to pick something up on the way."

"Pancakes are fine, thanks."

Frankly, she could have served last summer's potatoes and a hunk of questionable cheese, for all I cared. Jane had plopped me down in front of the television upon our return to Ragged Gap, and having never been exposed to such, I was exploring Netflix and having the time of my life. The remote control—which felt like magic, even though Jane swore it wasn't—made sense after a few minutes of practice, and overwhelmed by the choices available to me, I passed the time scrolling through the menus and reading about my options.

She abandoned the stove for a moment and stepped into the den. "Doing okay in here? Are you thirsty or anything?"

"I'm fine," I said, and smiled up at her. "Need help?"

"Nah. Sorry this isn't more entertaining…"

"Jane," I said, putting the remote aside, "I'm sitting inside, there's cold air blowing on me, the outhouse is *in* the house, and, like…" I gestured to the TV. "This is pretty nice."

"All right," she said, though she sounded skeptical, and returned to the kitchen. "Oh, *shit*, don't burn on me..."

Jane was, by her own admission, not the world's finest cook, and the smell of overdone pancakes wafted between the rooms. I didn't mind. By the time Connor walked in, a man with a funny accent was narrating as some lions chased a baby wildebeest, and I might have forgotten to blink for a bit, so intent was I on watching the scene play out.

"Hey, mitta," he said, dropping a bag by the door. "How was the trip?"

The wildebeest went down, and I paused the program before the lions could disembowel it. "Kind of crazy." Quickly, I took him in: he'd switched to jeans and a green collared shirt from the morning's dark blue outfit. "You changed clothes."

"And cars," he said, then smiled at Jane as she walked in. "Hey, Firebug. Breakfast for dinner?"

"Struggle meal." She kissed him and nodded to his bag. "Thanks for coming."

Chuckling, he replied, "When my girlfriend asks me to spend the night, I'm not going to say *no*. So, tell me all about it. What's the verdict on Maebe?"

She tugged his arm. "Come with me so I can get the rest of these pancakes made. Maebe, want to join us?"

Reluctantly, I abandoned the television for the kitchen table and a glass of tea while Jane flipped the current pair of pancakes before they could char. "Canna did her bloodwork," she said as Connor leaned against the counter with a beer. "Numbers are good...and she's about three-quarters elf."

He froze, can halfway to his mouth. "Come again?"

"Technically, seventy-three percent. And there's a massive wrinkle."

Connor sighed and put his beer down. "How bad?"

"Not so much bad as perplexing, but it caught Diriem off guard."

"You told him?"

"I took Maebe by after her report came in." She slid the pancakes onto the growing stack, covered them with foil, and ladled out a fresh batch. "He's been getting flashes of her, he said, but apparently not one with her headband off. I've never seen him so surprised."

"And how did Oz the Great and Powerful take that?"

Jane shot him a glare over her shoulder. "In short, he thinks East Branch may have been settled by elves everyone in the Pactlands thought were dead. The ear flop ran in some of those Halls, and you've retained bits of High Elvish."

"Huh?"

"He thinks 'mitta' and 'catta' are corruptions of 'mitha' and 'catha,' which have about the same meaning. Oh, and the last king in the south came from Hall ti'Ammaas, which sounds too much like Amos to be pure chance, or so Diriem thinks. Long story short, Maebe could very well be descended from royalty."

Connor snorted. "Hell, if that's the case, we probably all are." He retrieved his beer but paused before drinking to give me a long, searching look. "*Seventy-three* percent? Really?"

"According to Canna. And I suspect you're somewhere up there, too." She checked the pancakes, then put her spatula aside and folded her arms. "If you want, I'll take you to Canna to check. Or bring her here with her mobile unit—I'm sure she wouldn't mind."

He shook his head. "Thanks, but not now," he muttered, and drank. "That's, uh...that's not a question I'm ready to deal with yet. Whether I'm not even majority human."

"Either way, it's not a bad thing," Jane murmured, and slid closer to kiss his cheek before returning to the stove. "But it's up to you, babe. If you want to talk about it, I'm here."

Connor set the table and drank quietly while I told Jane

all about the program I'd found, hoping the change in topic would lighten the mood. But despite my best attempt at impersonating the narrator, Connor remained pensive, and he didn't let the matter drop even after Jane brought the pancakes and sausage to the table. "What do we do?" he asked as she put a leaf-shaped glass bottle on the table. "Are they going to get Maebe in school, or..." Catching me examining the bottle, he said, "Maple syrup. Sweet and sticky. Pour it on."

Jane nudged it my way and spread a pat of butter on her serving. "Well...Diriem wants to visit East Branch."

He laughed aloud. "That sounds like a *terrible* idea."

"I told him about the records," I said, pouring out a small puddle of syrup to taste it.

"*Maebe*—"

"He thinks he can read them!" I protested. "Nobody else can, so what's the harm in giving him a shot?"

My cousin groaned to himself. "Mitta, you're smarter than that."

"He was nice."

"Doesn't matter. What are the elders going to do if we show up with outsiders, eh? You see that going well?"

"If we explain..."

"And this could be important," Jane cut in, holding Connor's stare. "Maebe said you've got a record of births and deaths, but no one can read the first few pages?"

He nodded. "Births, deaths, marriages, the usual. The book's probably as old as East Branch. And yeah, the entries at the beginning are unreadable—they're not in English. I didn't even recognize the letters," he said, sawing into his stack. "The first bit...I think it's more than just names and dates, but it can't be translated."

"Isn't there a chance that those pages could tell you how East Branch came to be? Who your people are?"

"Possibly," he muttered.

"Then what's the harm in giving Diriem a peek? He might be able to offer you some answers."

Connor's mouth tightened. "Look, if he wants to see the records, that's one thing. It's getting him out to East Branch that's the problem, and I can't bring the book to him. It doesn't leave the community."

"Couldn't we *try*?" I asked. "And Jane says she's never been out there—what if they both came?"

"That's...not much better."

"Seriously, if you say she's your girlfriend, no one's going to shoot her."

"So you assume," Connor grumbled, but he seemed thoughtful as he chewed. "Maebe's got a point. If she and I get out of the car first and clear the air, then we might avoid violence."

"You're that worried?" Jane asked.

"I don't like taking chances where you're concerned."

"And I appreciate that, but I do want to meet your family."

He grunted and attacked his pancakes again. "My parents are gone, and so are my grandparents. The closest family I have left is Uncle Alan, my mom's big brother. He and Aunt Helen have a couple of kids older than us, Candice and Mason, and they're each married with kids of their own."

Candice had married Gregory Amos, Mason had married Iris Smith, and both were rare families with three living children...including David Amos, my best but unwanted prospect in East Branch.

"I still want to meet them," said Jane. "If they're important to you, then that's all the convincing I need."

Connor's face worked as he ate in silence for a moment, and then he put down his utensils and took a long swig of beer. "No offense to you, Maebe, but East Branch is a shithole."

Taken aback, I stopped eating, even though the syrup was delicious enough to lick off my plate. "Is *not*."

"It is. My folks were the first to get out," he said to Jane. "Maybe ever. With my Associate's degree, next to the rest of the community, I might as well have gone to Harvard. It's…" He struggled for the words. "It's a shithole, but I've got to protect it. If the true situation out there came to light, if CPS got involved, if satellite trucks parked outside the fence…I don't know how they'd function, Janie. Forget magic—they're dirt farmers living without basic utilities, and everyone's cousins to everyone else half a dozen ways."

"It's okay," Jane murmured.

"No, it isn't. Look at Maebe," he continued, glancing across the table at me. "She's got no ID, no documentation, not even a birth certificate. She's technologically illiterate, and I'd be shocked if she could get a job in Whitford. Most of them make you apply online, anyway, and I know damn well she can't type."

I slumped in my chair, my cheeks heating.

"At East Branch, folks are taught to farm, to hunt, to manage the touch if they've got it, and to try to make babies. That's it. And it's fucking embarrassing."

Jane looked between the two of us, seemingly torn as to who needed reassurance more, and settled on Connor. "Hey," she said, gripping his arm, "you remember how my grandfather murdered almost all of his children? Whatever can be said for East Branch, there are worse families out there. And at least you had two parents, right?"

"Sorry," I interrupted, "your grandfather did *what?*"

"He's a monster, and now he's doing life in prison," she replied, then turned back to Connor. "If you don't judge me for Gerem, then I'm sure as hell not judging you for a bunch of farmers at East Branch."

He met her gaze.

"I love you," she whispered.

A slow smile crossed his face, but the troubled look never left his eyes. "You really want to foist your boss on East Branch?"

"He might be able to help, that's all I'm saying. But if you think this is too risky…"

Jane allowed that to hang, and Connor released a long breath. "All right," he mumbled. "Tell him I'll do it. But I'm chaperoning, and if he puts one toe out of line—"

"He'll behave," she assured him, then caught my eye and winked. "Maebe, how are the pancakes?"

"Great," I fibbed, and forced a few more bites down to sell the lie. The pancakes weren't terrible, but Connor's words had stolen my appetite.

Jane and Connor retired around nine, leaving me with the remote and the refrigerator all to myself. Too troubled to sleep, I watched more of the nature program and drank tea, hoping that would calm me enough to let me crash on the couch, but I found myself unable to concentrate and slipped out the glass kitchen door to the warm June night.

Summer evenings aren't quiet, filled as they are with the sounds of frogs and owls and crickets, but at least it wasn't a bad cicada year. I brushed off a wooden chair on Jane's small patio and took a seat, watching the lightning bugs flash all through the woods around us and occasionally sneaking peeks at the sky. The moon, nearly full, was on the rise, and though I couldn't see it from the rear of the house, the long shadows of the trees showed me its ascent.

Alone with the night and my thoughts, I finally stopped to attempt to process everything I'd seen and heard that day. A new state. A new *world*. A city of glass spires and magical windows and half-goat roadway attendants and elevators and so very many words I couldn't read or understand. A strange, sobering thought that I wasn't entirely human and never had been, that there was a *reason* for the quirks that made my community keep the rest of the world at bay.

My community.

Despite my long-simmering dissatisfaction with East Branch and my desire to see the possibilities outside, it had always been *home*. Generations of my people had lived and died on that property, had scraped the land and raised their families and persevered, and that was my inheritance. But to hear Connor speak of it as he had...

It's a shithole.

Alone among all of us, Connor knew what the outside was like. If he thought East Branch was so bad—if he thought I was too ignorant to even find work—then what was to become of me? Of *us*? If I left to get an education and didn't return, the community would be all the poorer...but if I were to be educated elsewhere, would I even want to return? This was only my second night under Jane's roof, and already, I dreaded the thought of returning to a home with no electricity and the misery of a summer-baked outhouse. And none of Jane's comforts were magical—well, except the bathroom, she'd admitted that afternoon, which she'd redone with magic because doing it the hard way would have been a drawn-out disaster. Heck, I couldn't blame her. But oversized bathroom aside, did ordinary people beyond East Branch live like *this*? Air conditioning and fans, electric lights and laundry machines, a stove that heated at the turn of a dial, water that ran hot and cold from taps all over the house? A TV with thousands of programs at the click of a remote? And computers—which, admittedly, I still didn't understand, but they seemed like useful things.

Would my cousins delight in these facets of the larger world as much as I had, or would they shy away? If I managed to drag part of East Branch out to see what awaited, would the outside come and peer in? And if it did, how would it react? Curiosity? Disgust? Pity?

I shouldn't risk that. It was selfish to take actions that could have ramifications for the whole community without discussing the matter.

But I'd seen so much already in less than two days. And if I could get a real education, learn to use my touch...make something of myself...

If I were responsible, I'd call the whole thing off. I'd

pack my things, thank Jane for her hospitality, and ask Connor to drive me home. I'd tell my family that I got lost in the woods and say nothing about where I'd actually been. Wouldn't that be for the best? I'd seen how upset Connor had been. And the way Hirral and Diriem had stared at me—I didn't want that for my family, did I?

No, of course not. No one wants to be studied like a two-headed calf.

But.

Maybe someone in the Pactlands could help us. If we learned to really use our touches, then perhaps we could improve East Branch. If we all had a little more education, if we could get our ears fixed, then we could integrate into Whitford, step into the light without fear of being noticed. We could live in houses with water and power and mattresses that weren't stuffed with corn husks.

Maybe—just maybe—I could find my way back to the city of towers and magic. Maybe someone there could finally lead me toward a path I wanted to follow.

Or it could all turn into a disaster the like of which East Branch had never known.

The door slid open behind me, and I turned as Connor let himself out, barefoot and wearing only a pair of sweatpants. "Hey, mitta," he murmured, closing it behind him against the bugs. "You're going to get eaten alive by the skeeters if you sit out here all night."

"Just thinking," I said.

"Not tired?"

"Not yet. The TV's interesting."

"And I saw your tea glass on the table. Caffeine's not helping the situation." I frowned up at him, and he explained, "It's a stimulant, and you're not used to it. You might be awake for a while yet."

"Oh," I muttered, feeling stupid once again. One more thing I didn't know. "Why are *you* awake?"

Connor sighed. "Because Jane is asleep, and as usual, she's stolen all the covers. I went to grab that blanket off the couch and found you out here."

"Mm." A lightning bug flew close, and I caught it in my cupped hand. "You two aren't married yet, right?"

"No, we're just dating. We've been testing each other out, I guess you could say. I met her last November, and that was that. Head over heels." He paused to pull up another chair and joined me as I let the lightning bug fly on. "Things aren't so rushed outside East Branch, but...between you and me?"

"All right."

"I'm pretty sure I'd like to marry her."

I smiled in the darkness. "*Might* have noticed that."

"Did you, now?"

"You weren't making a secret of it," I said, and swatted at a mosquito on my bare arm. "Is Jane part elf, too?"

Connor leaned back in his chair and stretched his feet in front of him. "Heh. No. She's all sorcerer. Most of them are in the Pactlands, but there are a few sprinkled here and there. Jane, her dad, folks with permission to hide in plain sight."

"She's got a really strong touch."

"*Yeah.* Ever seen her play with fire?"

"I don't think so..."

"Don't worry, she will. She's got a natural affinity for it. Pyromancer, they call her."

My brow scrunched. "*What?*"

"Or that's what Jane and Yacovi call it in English, at least. 'Pyro' comes from the Greek for 'fire.' In the Pactlands, they've apparently got more pyromancers like Jane, hydromancers—they're unusually good with water— floramancers like Jane's dad, who can grow plants really well..."

"And farseers?"

"They can see the future or the past. Jane works with a bunch of them."

I hesitated, then asked, "Why don't you like her boss? He seemed okay."

Tucking his hands behind his head, Connor huffed a sigh. "Back in February, Jane was in trouble, and we went on the run. Decided to try to find her mom—she walked out when Jane was a baby—and we followed this tracker thingy all the way to California. Other side of the country," he added. "Took us days to make the drive, especially with the Rocky Mountains in the way. So, we finally get to this little town, and the tracker leads us right to her mom's *tombstone*."

"Oh, gosh…"

"Yeah. Janie…it was a bad day. Her dad was stuck in the Pactlands, this asshole Forum representative who turned out to be her dear old granddad was trying to kill her, and then throw her mom on top of it all. Anyway, we went to get some food that night, and suddenly, there were two guys coming up to us in the restaurant who damn sure weren't speaking English, and I thought we were going to have to fight a couple sorcerers right then and there. Turns out it was Diriem and one of his minions. They'd been remotely stalking us."

"So…did they help Jane?" I asked.

"Yep. Got the mess cleaned up, exposed her granddad, got her dad his freedom again…and then Diriem offered her a job. She says he's been great."

"But?"

Again, my cousin sighed. "Nothing's *wrong* with him, I guess," he grudgingly allowed. "It's just…I'm relatively competent, yeah? Not with my touch, sure, but as a grown-ass man, I've got most of my shit together. I mean, if you call 911 in an emergency and you're in Whitford, there's a decent chance I'll be the one responding, and folks are okay with that. But then he swooped in, and…you know how little kids will say crazy stuff, and you just go along with it to humor them because they're kids and don't know any better? That's kind of the feeling I got from Diriem. Like he thinks I'm this dumb kid."

"Jane said he's pretty old," I offered.

"*Oh*, yeah. Dirt. Still…" His chair creaked as he shifted his weight. "We didn't meet under the best of circumstances, so that may have a lot to do with it. I don't think he's planning to hurt you, if you were worried about that. And I don't think he'd hurt East Branch *intentionally*, but I don't need someone marching in without letting me make the introductions. Last thing I want is shots fired out there."

I nodded to myself, then tried to shift the conversation to a happier track. "So, when are you going to marry Jane?"

Connor chuckled. "Direct, aren't you?"

"Curious," I replied, and slapped at another bug.

He didn't answer immediately, and when he did, his voice was softer. "I love her. And for some unfathomable reason, she loves me, too. But practically speaking, I don't know how we'd work out."

"Because she works in Beukal?"

"Nah. If she told me tomorrow that I needed to follow her there, I'd do it. Now, don't go giving her any ideas, mitta," he teased, "but that's the truth. The problem is my lifespan."

I frowned at him, barely visible as he was in the faint glow of the TV that spilled into the kitchen. "You're healthy, right?"

"Far as I know. My physicals are good. But if I live to, say, ninety, I'll be lucky. Jane might see three hundred. Sorcerers live *much* longer than humans do, and they age slowly, so by the time we're in our eighties, I'll be an old man, and she won't even be middle aged."

Hoping I wasn't about to upset him, I said, "Except…we're not quite human, right?"

"We still die like we are. And I love Janie to death, but I dread the day that she wakes up and decides she can do better than a small-town cop with too few relatives and an expiration date two hundred years ahead of hers."

The crickets buzzed around us as we sat there without

speaking for a time, and I watched the lightning bugs, hoping my eyes would start to droop.

"I'm sorry about what I said at dinner," Connor finally murmured.

"About what?"

"Home. And you. It was unnecessarily harsh."

"But you weren't wrong," I replied. "Connor...what we should we do? Take Diriem home or stop this now?"

He thought for a moment. "I don't know what the right answer is," he began, "but I'll tell you true, mitta: East Branch is dying. Maybe not in our lifetime, or in the next generation's, but it can't go on forever."

While I knew in my heart that he was right, that did nothing to untie the knot in my stomach. "Things could change..."

"Our numbers have dropped. The community's had problems having children for ages, and now we know for sure that the flop is a birth defect...a *recessive* birth defect," he muttered. "Do you know how screwed up a gene pool has to be for something like that to become common? If things go on like they always have...I mean, I don't want to imagine what East Branch will look like in a hundred years' time, *if* the state doesn't step in first."

"What do you mean?"

"I mean folks out here know that place ain't right. I play off the rumors as much as I can, but people in power in this county know the situation out there is weird, to put it mildly." He blew out a long breath. "East Branch needs help, whether the community can see that or not. And right now, much as I don't like it, our best bet may be intervention from the Pactlands."

With that, he stood and grunted as he unkinked his back. "Come on, Maebe. Let's try to sleep, eh? Tomorrow could be a *strange* day."

Connor turned off the TV, grabbed a blanket, and returned to Jane's room. As the house stilled again, I lay on my borrowed bed, staring up at the ceiling fan and waiting for sleep to take me.

My attempt at running away seemed so petty now, so small. This wasn't just my future on the line anymore.

Whatever I did next, it had to be for East Branch.

CHAPTER 8

While we were finishing breakfast Tuesday morning—egg sandwiches from a place called McDonald's, which Connor had slipped out early to purchase—a car slowed and pulled into Jane's driveway. She perked at the sound of the tires on gravel, then rose to investigate, with Connor right behind her. When she opened the front door, she laughed, then called, "Oh, slumming it, are we?"

"Good morning to you, too," said a voice I recognized as Diriem's. Swallowing the last of my sandwich and licking my fingers clean, I hurried to join them.

"A Mercedes," she teased. "How very plebian."

Connor, who'd stepped onto the porch, craned his neck to see the back of the sleek gray sedan that had parked behind his vehicle—an SUV, Jane had said. "Ooh...would we call an S-Class *plebian*?"

The man walking around the car was redheaded like Diriem, but his face seemed much more human than I remembered. Combined with his white button-down and dark trousers, he looked fairly ordinary, even if he wore his hair too long. "This is a perfectly serviceable vehicle," he protested. "Nothing eye-catching. You can't tell me you never see a Benz up here."

Jane folded her arms and cocked a brow.

"Look, I cannot pull off a farm truck. The illusion only works to a point."

"*Sure*, boss. Come in. There's tea."

"Thank you. Connor," he said, nodding to my cousin, and followed Jane into the house.

We reconvened in the kitchen, where the man with Diriem's voice and someone else's face was considering the boxes of tea bags Jane had left on the counter. "Um…excuse me," I ventured.

He glanced up, noticed me, and smiled—a perfectly normal, not at all worryingly sharp smile. "Ah, Maebe. You lurk well."

"You, uh…you look different…"

"A temporary situation," he replied, and made a quick gesture in front of his face. Instantly, the features I recognized returned, and he grinned at my surprise before switching them back. "It's called masking, and it's a necessary skill out here. We can do it without significant difficulty, as can sorcerers," he explained, nodding to Jane. "Everyone else uses jewelry to blend in. You know, you can put that headband on, but I've got *slightly* more work to do to escape notice."

"Yes," Jane deadpanned, "like not showing up in a rare sportscar."

Diriem rolled his eyes. "You're never going to drop that, are you?"

"It's a very nice Lotus, but it just ain't subtle. The last time he visited me here," she added, looking my way, "he came in a car that cost more than what I paid for this house."

Connor coughed to interrupt. "The good news today is that it doesn't matter what you drove over—we're taking my ride."

"I don't mind driving," Diriem began, but Connor emphatically shook his head.

"Absolutely not. Here's the deal," he said, staring Diriem down from the other side of the counter. "This is not a dick-measuring contest. You don't know East Branch. *I* do. And we're playing this my way so no one gets shot this morning. Got it?"

Diriem held up his hands in surrender. "Your show, Chief."

"*That* has nothing to do with it. Law enforcement won't go out to East Branch unless they're invited in, and that hasn't happened in the last thirty years. Folks are twitchy around outsiders, and when strangers pull up, the guns come out. Add Maebe to the mix after she's been gone for a few days, and I can only imagine that emotions are going to be running high. Now, I know damn well you can shield, but I'd really prefer to avoid a shootout with my kinfolk, so here's how this is going to work. I drive. Maebe sits up front with me. You two stay in the vehicle until I say it's clear," he instructed, glancing at Jane. "Is that understood?"

"No argument," she murmured.

Diriem nodded. "I'm not here to antagonize anyone."

"I get that," said Connor, "but it's going to take a little convincing to get everyone on the same page." Pointing to the empty mug beside the tea boxes, he asked, "Want to take that to go?"

A few minutes later, the four of us loaded up, Diriem with a loaner metal travel cup from Jane. I climbed into the front seat of Connor's vehicle, which was much nicer than Jane's old truck, and buckled in. Connor slid behind the wheel and looked down at my feet. "You're not bringing your stuff?"

"I'm not ready to go home yet," I told him.

"Fair." He cast a glance back at the rest of the passengers, then drove over Jane's scrubby grass to get to the road.

I couldn't have guessed how to get home from Jane's place, but Connor apparently knew the way well. He said almost nothing during the drive past Ragged Gap, and when I sneaked looks at him, I noticed the tightness in his jaw.

The fact that Connor was worried did nothing to make me feel better. I'd been gone since early Thursday morning, and I hadn't left so much as a note for fear that my parents would track me down. After five days, they might fear the worst, and guilt roiled my guts. I didn't want to hurt my family, just see something of life beyond East Branch, but I suspected I'd gone about it all wrong.

Connor didn't slow when we hit the Whitford town line, but he skirted the little commercial district and kept heading northwest toward the woods. All too soon, I spotted the familiar split rail fence demarcating the border of East Branch, and Connor pulled onto the dirt turn-off beside the paved road. As usual, the wooden gate was latched. "Stay put," he told us, unbuckling. "I'll get the gate open."

Once we'd passed through and he'd latched the gate back, he proceeded at a crawl down the rutted dirt path toward the heart of the settlement, past the thick woods that shielded East Branch from the road, then the cornfields and the apple orchard, and then the pasture where our few cows grazed. Houses began to pop into view, the old log homes our ancestors had built and their descendants had maintained against rot and termites and time. I looked away as we drove by my family's home, afraid of what I might do if I spotted my parents at the door, but I needn't have worried. As we approached the end of the road and the meeting house, I found a crowd gathering to confront us—including my parents—many of them carrying guns and anyone with the flop sporting a hood, a headband, or one of the thin cloth hats common around the community during the summer, which covered the back of the neck and tied under the chin.

Connor stopped and turned off the engine, his jaw set. "Mitta, let me go first. Janie, Diriem, y'all stay put until I say otherwise."

He opened the door and slid down from his seat, bare hands visible. "It's me!" he called to the assembled. "It's all right!"

"Connor!" cried an older male voice, and I spotted Alan Black pushing through the crowd, hat tied on and shotgun pointed at the ground. "Hey, boy!" he said, smiling tensely. "What brings you out here?"

"Well, for starters—"

"*Maebe!*" my mother screamed, catching sight of me as I exited the vehicle. "Oh, good heavens, Maebe! Where have you been?"

She and Dad grabbed me before I could take more than a few steps away from the SUV, both hugging me so hard I could barely breathe. I could feel my mother crying as she clung to me, and as I twisted to gasp for air, I saw Connor at the center of a knot of happy people slapping his back and thanking him for bringing me home.

"We've been worried sick," Mom said, dragging my attention back to my parents, who still gripped my arms as if they feared I'd bolt. "What happened, baby? Where did you go?"

Before I could answer that, Connor raised his voice above the hubbub. "Folks, I've brought guests."

That chilled the mood in a hurry, and Mom yanked me further away from the SUV.

Alan, backed by his wife, Helen, my grandpa, and John Amos, demanded, "What do you mean, *guests*?"

"It's all right," Connor said again with remarkable calm, considering the number of guns ringing us. "One of them is my girlfriend, Jane—"

"*Girlfriend?*" Alan echoed. "You're seeing an outsider, boy?"

"She's got the touch," Connor replied, focusing on the elders. "Stronger than anyone's here. Actually, she's been helping me strengthen mine of late." When that didn't trigger an outcry, he continued, "Jane's from Ragged Gap, in the valley south of ours. She knows a little about East Branch, and she can *absolutely* keep a secret. I'd stake my life on it. And she's been wanting to meet my family."

Alan still didn't look thrilled, but he softened. "Well, now, that might be fine…"

"And we've brought along a…a friend of hers," said Connor. He's got the touch, *big* time. Could be stronger than Janie's."

"I told him about the records," I cut in, and fought the urge to shrink back when the elders turned to me. "The ones no one can read. He says he might be able to."

"Maebe Amos, what were you thinking?" my mother whispered, tightening her grip on my arm, but I focused on the elders, who were conversing among themselves. After a moment, Alan looked back at Connor. "You trust this...*friend?*"

To my surprise, Connor didn't hesitate. "Yes, sir. He did right by Jane when she was in trouble, and he can keep his mouth shut. He just wants to help."

Again, the elders deliberated, but then Alan gave Connor a curt nod, and he beckoned the others out.

"Where have you been, girl?" Dad asked, drawing my attention to them once again.

I didn't see a point in lying, but the full truth could perhaps wait. "Out there. I've been telling you for years that I want to see what's beyond East Branch, so I left."

"We've barely slept in days," he said, taking a tone I knew well from my childhood shenanigans. "Your poor mother has been *ill* with worry, and you—"

"I'm sorry," I said, looking them both in the eye. "I...shouldn't have left like that without telling you. But I'm okay. Jane found me in the woods and took me home with her, and she's been really nice—she's got water flowing in the house and everything. Oh! And we went to a place called a restaurant for dinner, and this man tried to rob it, and Jane threw him across the room with her touch. Didn't even sweat. She's *so* strong."

Jane's appearance outside the SUV stopped my parental chastisement for the moment. "Hey, y'all," she said, smiling even in the face of the community's arsenal. "I'm Jane Fortune. It's so nice to finally meet Connor's family."

Alan kept his gun pointed down, but he stepped out of the pack to confront her. "You've got the touch, do you?"

"Yes, sir."

"Show me."

She flicked her hand and whispered, and a thick coil of flame ignited around her wrist like a bracelet. As the crowd murmured, Jane twisted her hand until the fire thinned into a rope, which she began to twirl like a lasso.

Alan's eyes widened as he gawked at the demonstration—a fair response, as no one in East Branch could manage anything close. "How...how do you..."

Jane extinguished the flame with a twitch of her fingers and showed him her empty, unburned hand. "It's magic. That's what the touch is, magic. My dad and I both have the talent for it, and I promise you, I understand that this isn't something you go blabbing about all over town." When he still looked troubled, Jane said, "If it helps, my dad's a moonshiner, too, so I know the importance of being...*selective* in your conversation."

He frowned and looked to Connor. "Moonshiner?"

"Someone who distills liquor without a license," Connor explained. "I keep telling you that what goes on here is illegal."

His uncle shrugged. "There's no harm in it, boy."

"Until someone goes blind, but whatever," Connor muttered.

Jane grinned as she sidled closer to him. "No wonder you aren't horrified by Dad's operation—you've got your own 'shine hookup."

"Believe me, his product is *far* better."

Before they could get into the details of East Branch's stills, Diriem joined Connor and Jane and nodded to Alan, the apparent spokesman for the elders that day. "Good morning," he said, keeping his empty hands low and visible. "Are you Connor's...uncle?"

"That I am," Alan replied tersely. "And you are?"

"Diriem."

"Huh. What's your business here? You from Whitford?"

"No..." He looked to the side and spotted me watching with my anxious parents, then turned back to Alan. "Have you ever wondered why you and your neighbors alone, of all people in this region, have talent? The touch, yes?"

"We're not the only ones," he said, pointing to Jane.

Diriem shook his head. "Her family came from else-where. My understanding—and please correct me if I'm mistaken—is that yours is an isolated community several hundred years old, and many of you have the touch...and a rare birth defect. Maebe called it the flop."

Alan stiffened. "There's nothing wrong with us. It's just a quirk—"

"I mean no offense," Diriem quickly soothed. "You're right, it's harmless. But the last time I knew of a communi-ty with that *quirk* was the sixteenth century, and my people believed they were wiped out."

He frowned. "Your people?"

With a gesture, Diriem unmasked.

The folks closest to him gasped and backed off, and my parents tried to pull me away as I struggled against them. But though I could see Alan's unease, he held his ground and kept his grip on his gun.

"The reason you have the touch and the flop is because you're not fully human," Diriem continued. "Maebe was tested yesterday—what was it, twenty-seven percent hu-man?" he asked me.

I nodded and finally shook off my parents. "Yeah."

"Thought so. Anyone here with the touch is likely to show similar results."

"What the hell *are* you?" Alan asked, his voice low and wavering.

"Not a danger to you," Diriem replied. "Tell me, do you know the term 'elvaniri'?"

He seemed momentarily taken aback. "Uh...yeah. It's what the *old* old-timers used to call people with the touch, but...gosh, I haven't heard that since I was a child. Why?"

"*I* am elvaniri. Full blooded. And that term comes from

a dead language barely ever spoken these days. I learned it as a boy, but that was close to seven hundred years ago."

Alan eyed him skeptically. "Come again?"

"We age slowly," said Diriem, shrugging. "But anyway, the last group I knew of who used that language for more than ceremony also occasionally produced a child with flopped-over ears. Unflopped, they looked like this," he added, tucking his hair back. "We thought those people had been killed, but now, finding you here—obviously not fully elvaniri, but with talent, a few surviving words of a very old language, and that *quirk* of yours—it suggests something remarkable."

Again, Diriem looked my way for a moment before turning back to Alan and the other elders, some of whom had regained their courage sufficiently to come closer. "I understand that you've been here for a considerable time, and you've resisted integrating into the neighboring towns...not that I blame you. I live in a place that's safer. Somewhere you wouldn't need to worry about your appearance or your gift—because that's what your touch is, a gift. Perhaps there's something we could do to help you. Maebe wants an education, but even those uninterested in further schooling should learn how to use their talents. Might make your lives easier," he said, glancing around the crowd. "But for today, at the very least, I can probably tell you what's in your old records if you'll allow me to see them."

Alan considered that briefly, then untied his hat with his free hand and pulled it off, revealing his own flop. "We...we'll need to think about things, talk about them..."

"Of course. Nothing need be decided today."

"But if you think you can read the records, then I don't have a problem with it. What say you?" he asked, looking at the other elders. Helen and my grandpa nodded, and though John seemed less sure, he didn't protest. "All right, good enough. This way," he said, and started toward the meeting house, gun down.

Connor and Jane started after him, and I slipped closer, trying to avoid my parents' iron hands and litany of questions. "Community meeting house," I heard Connor tell the newcomers. "It's where they gather to make decisions. Anything important is kept in there—the deed to this land, bills of sale, the phone."

The meeting house was always dark—the windows were too small to properly light it, especially with the trees around—and Alan lit one of the oil lanterns by the door. "Watch your step," he cautioned. "Floor's a little uneven."

Diriem paused inside the doorway, taking in the log walls and patched roof. "May I?"

"May you what?" Alan asked.

He gestured, and a cluster of brightly glowing orbs appeared above us like impossibly large lightning bugs, though their light was white and steady. "Save your oil," he said as the orbs floated toward the rafters.

Alan extinguished the lantern without another word and hurried across the hall.

The interior of that building had never been so brightly lit, and I stood along the wall, taking in the cracks and dust and cobwebs fully exposed by the glow. The meeting house smelled musty and earthy, and the wood was dark in places with rot. Before, it had never been a beautiful space, but the shadows had smoothed over some of the imperfections. Now cast into clear relief, however, it looked tired and dirty, the rough-hewn benches and tables more primitive than practical.

Alan soon returned with a plastic box in his arms, a purchase from the store in Whitford, and cleared a space at one of the tables. Handing his gun to my grandpa, he gently lifted the oilcloth-wrapped record book out of its box and laid it down, then beckoned Diriem closer with a crooked finger. "This is it. Be careful."

Diriem briefly studied the brown leather cover, then opened the book to the middle and left it floating an inch

or two off the table, not fully flattened. "I have some experience with old books," he explained as Alan looked on.
"*This* one...I'm shocked that the binding is in such good
condition."

"We take care of it—"

"Certainly, but time and the elements degrade, regardless. Let's see..." A twitch of his finger ruffled the thick
pages from left to right as he turned toward the beginning
of the book. As he neared the front, he paused, then beckoned one of the hovering orbs closer and peered at the
text.

"You recognize that?" Alan asked.

"Is this the part you can't read?"

"That's it."

Diriem looked up at him with an expression of disbe-
lief. "That's High Elvish. The characters are slightly differ-
ent than those of the current script, but I know them."
Glancing back at the page, he said, "George Finn, born 5
September 1739. Stephen Willow, born 2 April 1740.
Charles Baker, born 15 April...Catherine Porter, died 17
April..." He chuckled low. "Strange to see names like
those transliterated."

"That's what that says?" Alan pressed, leaning closer.

He slid aside to make room, then pointed to the page.
"Look at this one that repeats. That's 'April' written pho-
netically. Whoever wrote this knew enough High Elvish to
use the script—and he or she knew the terms for 'born'
and 'died,' see," he murmured—"but the writer employed
the English names for months. Interesting."

"What does that mean?" Helen asked from further
down the table.

Diriem glanced up at her. "Judging by the dates alone,
you've got evidence of linguistic blending by the eighteenth century. Going back to the beginning, now..." He
waited while the pages turned, then bent closer to inspect
the faded ink. "This is in pure High Elvish," he said after a
moment. "Someone named Mary Amos states that she's

compiling a record of the community…it's dated 1750, but there's no month given. Perhaps those dates I was reading were added later." He turned the page, and his eyebrows rose. "Long blocks of text. I think this is a narrative. Would you give me a minute to read it over?" he asked Alan.

As Diriem worked, I stepped out into the warming morning to find my parents waiting, Dad with his arm wrapped protectively around Mom. "What's happening in there?" Dad asked, motioning me closer. "Are you all right, Maebe?"

"I'm fine," I insisted, joining them. "Diriem's reading the old records. He was right—they're in High Elvish."

"What does that even *mean*?"

"Possibly something big." I hesitated, then blurted, "I've been to the Pactlands, where he's from. Jane took me yesterday. It's a whole other world, and it's *amazing*. There's a huge city with buildings taller than the pines, and everything is so clean, and there's power and water and…and *elevators*—"

"And it's just about as flat as a pancake and can't grow trees worth a damn," Jane interrupted as she approached our trio. "But it's a hell of a lot safer for someone like Maebe." Nodding to my parents, she said, "I'm Jane. You've got a lovely daughter."

Mom smiled nervously. "Denise. And this is James," she said, glancing at my father. "You and Connor, uh…"

"We've been seeing each other for a while," she replied. "Could we sit down somewhere for a minute?"

I picked out one of the picnic tables near the meeting house, and Jane and I took the bench opposite my parents. "So," said Jane, "Maebe tells us she wants to explore her options beyond East Branch."

My parents traded looks. "It's not safe," Dad began. "Maebe's never spent any time out there."

"Granted, but this wouldn't be Whitford we're talking about. The Pactlands…it's a world unto itself, accessible only by magic. If we could get Maebe in school over there, she might have a brilliant future ahead of her."

But Dad shook his head. "The only safe place for her is *here*, with her family. We're protected—"

"To a point. And more importantly, Maebe's of age. You have no right to imprison her."

"No one is *imprisoning* her! We're protecting our child!"

"Who is a young woman." Spreading her hands, Jane said, "I get it. You don't trust anything outside of East Branch, and I understand why you'd worry. You don't want to be found out." Leaning closer to them, she said, "That's not an issue in the Pactlands. You saw Diriem— he's *normal* there. Plenty of folks there like me, too."

"You...know this place?" Mom asked.

Jane nodded. "My dad's native, but I was raised out here—well, in Ragged Gap. Close enough," she added with a quick grin. "I didn't really start spending time in the Pactlands until last February, when Diriem offered me a job, and...let's just say it's been an experience," she said, chuckling weakly. "School there goes to thirty-five. I'm twenty-eight, but I did all my education out here— homeschooled, then college, then I had my own busi- ness—so I'm a weird case with dispensation. And I was a pretty darn good sorcerer for my age when I started there—"

Mom cocked her head. "A what?"

"A sorcerer. Someone who looks like me but has a strong touch," she explained. "Anyway, so I go over, pret- ty confident, and Diriem assigns me tutors to work on the gaps in my education." She whistled low. "I've been *shocked* by what I don't know, and that's having grown up learning at the knee of a trained sorcerer, mind you. I mean, I'm actually ahead of my peers in some areas, but I'm way be- hind in others. What I'm trying to say is that Maebe could get a *much* better education than the one she's had if we can work something out in the Pactlands."

Dad started to speak, but Mom shushed him with a

hand atop his arm. "We've done our best—you know that, right?" she said, turning to me. "Just like your grandparents did for us, and their parents did for them. We couldn't risk sending you to school outside, baby, you understand—"

"No one is throwing blame around," said Jane, cutting short Mom's protestations. "But Maebe could have a chance now at something better. You know, last year, I came across a teenage girl who was born in the Pactlands but was spirited out and dumped in Whitford. She's, uh…well, her physique makes the flop look *mild*, and she had one hell of a time out here. Barely educated, period. She's home now and in remedial classes, and she's doing well. Thriving, really. If Maebe wants something like that, a boost to her standard education with some magical instruction thrown in…I bet Diriem could arrange it. He's got considerable pull over there."

Dad leaned in and lowered his voice. "How old is that guy, really? About Connor's age?"

She shook her head. "He wasn't lying. Elves—elvaniri, whatever you want to call them—they almost stop aging once they hit maturity. He's nearly seven hundred. It's *weird*, I know, but you get used to it."

My parents looked stunned. "Those of us in the community tend to live decently long lives," said Mom, "but nothing like *that*."

"Because he's full-blooded. That's the difference," Jane replied. "Look, genetics are weird. Diriem's got a great-granddaughter about my age who's ninety percent elven—both grandmothers were human, but she lucked into most of the elven genes. Apparently, she's got the longevity and the magical ability, but she looks as human as they come. Now, someone like Maebe, who's got a lesser percentage…I mean, there's no telling without specialist involvement, and that's way beyond my knowledge. But what I *do* know is that she could learn to do so much more with her touch. If Connor can improve, then so can Maebe." Giving my parents a small smile, she added, "Nothing has to be decided today, but you know, I go back and forth weekly. If Maebe wanted to try school, I'd be happy to look after her and give her rides home."

Dad's eyes narrowed. "And why would you do that?"

"Because she's Connor's family," Jane replied simply. "And because I know damn well what it's like to be the weird one."

I could tell my parents still weren't happy with this plan, but at least they weren't yelling. Mom sighed as she clasped Dad's hand. "I'm not saying this is a good idea at all," she mumbled, "but...could be it's for the best."

Dad's face twitched. "Denise—"

"This place is *dying*," she said to him. "You know that as well as I do." Turning back to Jane, she explained, "Right now, with Connor, there are only fifty of us left, elders to infants. It's so hard to have babies, and...you know, I wonder..."

"Elven birthrates are naturally pretty low," Jane told her. "You probably aren't doing anything wrong."

She forced a smile, but I caught the sheen in her eyes. "We tried so hard to give Maebe a brother or sister, but...well. I guess it's better that we couldn't. Not if we're going to lose East Branch."

I sat up straighter, shocked. "What do you mean, *lose* East Branch? What are you talking about?"

My parents shared another look, and Dad took the lead. "Darling...we've tried to keep this from you kids, but..."

"But what?" I demanded when his voice faded.

"We're in trouble," he said softly. "In the past, the county left us alone. We didn't bother them, they didn't bother us. But something's changed, and now they come every year, wanting money."

"Property taxes?" Jane asked.

He nodded. "That's what they say. I don't understand—we *own* this land. East Branch has been here for generations…"

"Even if you own property, you pay taxes on it. That's the way it works. Goes to roads, emergency services, schools—"

"All things we don't use," Dad pointed out. "Tom and Debbie—Connor's parents—they paid the taxes for us. Kept us together. Connor's picked up the burden since their deaths, but…but that ain't right," he muttered. "Ain't fair to the boy. Suppose we could sell produce, perhaps, but that'd be taking food out of people's mouths. And it's gotten harder to find somewhere to hunt that folks don't threaten the law and run you off."

"Connor's never said anything about the taxes," Jane replied, surprised.

Dad shrugged. "He's never complained, but we can't keep asking him to carry the load."

"When his parents left, there was a massive fight," said Mom. "Their parents said some horrible things. But looking back, their departure saved our home. They could have cut us off, but they kept this place alive." Turning to me, she said, "I don't want to lose East Branch, but if there's somewhere better for you, baby, somewhere *safer*…"

I reached across the table toward them, and she and Dad took my hands. "I just want to see what else there is," I whispered. "It's not forever."

Mom's smile didn't reach her eyes. "That's what you say now. Give you a season out there, and you'll be a town girl before you know it."

"Would that be so bad? I could help Connor."

"*Neither* of you needs to be shouldering that," Dad began, but he paused and looked around when the door to the meeting house opened and Diriem emerged, the record book in his arms and the elders behind him. Diriem seemed shaken, his face drawn.

"What'd you find?" Jane asked, sliding off the bench.

But he had eyes only for the crowd creeping closer, and he waited for a moment while folks drew near. As I rose to join them, he murmured, "I'm so sorry we failed you."

CHAPTER 9

Though mid-June wasn't the hottest part of the year, there was no breeze that morning, and it would have been uncomfortable to pack the whole community into the meeting house, even with the windows open. Instead, Diriem sat at a picnic table and waited while the stragglers were summoned in from the fields. By then, the guns had largely been put aside, to my relief—and Connor's, I suspected, noting how he kept close watch over Jane—but whatever had transpired in the meeting house, the elders stayed mum until the last of the adults had gathered at the tables and the little ones were off playing in the grass. I heard rapid murmurings as folks around me quickly filled in the latecomers, who eyed Jane and Diriem with deep suspicion.

In fairness, we never received visitors, and Diriem had yet to put his mask back on. But to me, at least, he didn't seem threatening just then—sad, really, or perhaps perplexed.

"All right," said Alan once the voices had died down to whispers, "he's read the old records. Got some information. Go ahead," he said, nodding to Diriem.

He didn't bother opening the record book, which Alan had by then rewrapped in its protective oilcloth but left out on the table. "I've got to start a bit before your records to give them context," he said, glancing around the crowd. "In the early sixteenth century—about two hundred years before this started," he added, lightly patting the book— "humans became a true problem for those of us who...aren't. We kept to our own territories for a long time, but they multiplied, and they spread out in search of new lands. When they crossed our borders, they were generally more inclined to go to war than to back off and move elsewhere." Briefly, he smirked as he shook his head. "They have a long history of doing it to each other, so why should we be any different? But add a fear of magic and some overly zealous priests to the mix, and we were reaching a tipping point. They weren't just stumbling onto us anymore—they were seeking us out to eradicate us."

He paused, but when no one spoke, he pressed on. "I knew we couldn't stay. I'm a farseer—I can see the future, to an extent. *Potential* futures, often enough. Sometimes, there's no obvious best future, or the potentials vary widely, but this was clear: if we did not leave, we would be destroyed. My people, Jane's people," he said, gesturing toward her, "and many others. Some of Jane's people thought they could build a separate world for us, a place humans couldn't find, where we could have peace. It took them more than a decade to do the work, but what they built was barely short of miraculous for us. And then they invited everyone in. But there was a catch."

"Isn't there always?" Alan muttered.

Diriem grunted. "The sorcerers who built our hidden world saw the potential for conflict. Some of the peoples invited in were more numerous, others were more gifted with magic...in any case, the architects wanted to avoid future problems by putting us more or less on equal footing. Those of us in positions of power sat down and negotiated the Pact. Ours is a representative government, and while it's not perfect, it's worked for almost five hundred years. But what became evident as we put together this agreement was that there could be no kings, no princes, no clan chiefs. The Forum we established had to be the sole authority. Now, that's not to say we started completely fresh," he continued. "Every troll I've met can tell you his clan and name several chiefs back in that lineage, for example, even those trolls born after the Pact. As for the elvaniri, we maintained our family Halls, and for good or ill, vestiges of that system remain today."

Beside me, Jane whispered, "More than vestiges, but I didn't say that."

Either Diriem didn't hear her or ignored the quip. "The Halls had joined into two kingdoms by that time, a northern one based in Scandinavia…uh…"

"Go east out of the mountains," said Connor, "and eventually, you reach the ocean. Cross that and go north."

As a few people nodded and others tried to piece that together, Jane pulled out her phone and nudged me. "Here," she murmured, showing me the screen. "This is a map of where we are. If we zoom out a little, that's Whitford, and there's Ragged Gap…and if we zoom out more, there's Central…"

"Uh-huh…"

She zoomed even further, until the land gave way to blue at its eastern and southern edges, then turned the picture and pointed to a place on the other side of the blue. "That's what he's talking about."

"How long of a drive is that?"

"You can't drive it—you've got to take a boat or fly."

I knew flight was possible—we did see the occasional airplane or helicopter over East Branch, though I'd never been close to one. "Have *you* flown?"

"Not to Europe," said Jane, "but yeah, I've flown a few times."

That she said that so cavalierly stunned me, but with the question of geography settled for the moment among the crowd, Diriem resumed.

"The southern kingdom had been based along the Mediterranean Sea…also across the ocean," he added before the questions could begin, "but they'd lost coastal territory by then and were being pushed inland. When the Pact was forged, I ruled in the north."

He dropped that *way* too easily.

"My vassal Halls knew my gift and understood that I wouldn't uproot us and abandon our lands and homes if I saw a way forward in this world. They came with me, as did a few of the Halls from the south. But the king in the south, Ivari ti'Ammaas, said we were fools. I sent envoys, tried to reason with him, but he'd be damned before he took off his crown and treated with a group of nymphs and fauns and such." Diriem's mouth tightened. "I've always suspected that he thought I was trying to do him harm. He sent assassins to murder my parents—it would have been fitting for me to avenge them—"

"I'm sorry, *what?*" Connor interrupted. "What happened to—"

"No fortress is impregnable," he replied with a bitter smile, "and my father took his personal security less seriously than he should have. He and Ivari were frequently at odds. But yes, Ivari rid himself of the Wolf of the North, and he got me, younger and presumably weaker. I've never had great martial prowess, and that was no secret then," he said, spreading his hands. "Instead, I inherited my grandfather's farsight. Ivari had no use for such, I suppose, but some of the old southern Halls were wise enough to listen to a ti'Dana farseer's warning. They lived. Those who stayed behind did not. Or so we've long thought."

His gaze dropped to the wrapped book. "I didn't want to give up on our people, so every few months, I arranged for scouts to return to southern territory and check on them. Even by that first trip, they'd lost land, but Ivari refused to reconsider. Within five years, the last of them were gone. Vanished. I used every trick in my arsenal, but the only conclusion I could reach was that they'd been slaughtered. But...I was wrong," he said softly. "Somehow, the heavens only know, the final refugees hid from me."

His hand rested on the book as he slowly scanned the crowd. "Your settlement's record was begun by one Mary Amos in 1750, when she was about forty-four. She died in

1836. *That* is not a human lifespan—"

I did the quick math in my head. A hundred thirty—she'd have been ancient.

"—and that alone would have raised questions," Diriem continued, "but that woman, bless her, explained where East Branch arose. She said there was a small village in northern England whose inhabitants were almost all killed in a bad winter—influenza, perhaps, but she didn't know. That spring—this would have been 1690—a band of eighteen elvaniri found them. The humans needed backs to plow and hands to work, the elvaniri needed food and shelter, and so they joined forces. In short order, each of the elvaniri had taken a human spouse, and they began repopulating the village."

"If they were from the south, then how'd they get all the way to England?" Jane asked.

Diriem could only shrug. "It had been decades—I can't help but wonder if they were looking for us while they were hiding. In any case, the last of the full-blooded humans in that village died in 1749, and the elvaniri and their children and grandchildren left for the colonies. Mary said they settled in Georgia, presumably here, and fought off any neighbors."

"Why?" I blurted. "Did they have the flop, too?"

"She didn't mention it, but it's possible that one or two of them showed it. What she said was that because their elders had been persecuted almost to extinction, they thought living apart was safest. Guess they didn't want to try their luck with another village."

"So, what happened to those last elves?" Jane asked.

"Suicide," he muttered. "According to Mary, East Branch faced a hard winter in their first years, one that came early and was particularly bad. After the harvest failed, they ran low on food. She said that one by one, the elvaniri wandered off into the woods at night, never to be seen again. They sacrificed themselves to save their children. And all of you are descendants of those eighteen families."

Carefully, he unwrapped the old book and gestured it off the table. As it opened to the front, he waited for the murmuring to subside, then said, "Mary recorded those earliest marriages and all the births and deaths from that point. The first in her list was that of her own parents, a woman named Mary Cole and Ivari ti'Ammaas himself. Their descendants took the name 'Amos'...and having perused the most recent entries in this book, I think it's safe to assume that most of you have a tie to that line. The other seventeen are all names I remember from the southern Halls. The English almost always gave their children their father's name, as I recall, and that tradition seems to have continued here. Jeniel ti'Non married Peter Church— I know that name is still alive."

Several people, mostly the scattered Churches, nodded.

"Farral ti'Pul married Henry Smith—that's another still extant. Any Tines?" A few hands rose, and he said, "A corruption of ti'Nallo. And the Black family...ah, yes," he said as more hands lifted. "John Black and Cammir ti'Tola."

Diriem turned then to Connor. "Your patrilineal line presumably goes back to Deriap ti'Catama."

"How do you figure that?" Connor asked.

One corner of his mouth twitched. "Ti'Catama—of willows."

"*Seriously?*"

Diriem nodded. "And I know for a fact that Deriap was that Hall's last lord. If I'm not mistaken, ti'Catama arose from a...what's the term? *Ah*, a cadet branch of ti'Ammaas. A very high-ranking Hall. Ivari actually sent Deriap to my father once as an envoy."

As Connor absorbed that, Diriem widened his focus to the rest of the community once more. "Obviously, I haven't had time to map your families with this book, but my understanding is that you've had no outside marriages in the last three centuries. Is that accurate?"

"Best I know," said Alan, and the other elders murmured their agreement.

"Well," Diriem replied with a little sigh, "that would explain the oddities in your community. The traces of High Elvish, the ear flop, and why Maebe—and I suspect many more of you—have talent."

"Practically speaking," said Helen, who'd perched on the edge of a picnic table with her arms folded, "what does this mean for us?"

Turning toward her, he answered, "It means I have work to do. You certainly aren't responsible for the mistakes your ancestors made, but you've been suffering for them."

At that, John piped up. "Now, I wouldn't say *suffering*—"

"Look around you," Helen snapped, cutting him short. "The canning fridge is out again, the white truck needs *everything*, little Maebe's desperate enough to run off without a word, and the only thing keeping this place intact is Connor's help. You know we're grateful, boy," she said, softening as she looked at Connor, "but something has to change. We need security."

"Helen's right," said my grandpa, and the latecomer elders nodded. "Though I can't say what's to be done, especially not if the county wants paid every year."

"Greedy beckim," Alan muttered.

Diriem's brows rose. "The original version of the consonant in the middle doesn't have a good English approximation, but I know what you mean."

I sat there stewing as the elders grumbled over things like generator fuel and horseshoes—important matters, sure, but small compared to the far bigger problems I could see after only a few days away. Fortunately, before I could explode, Connor beat me to it.

"I mean no disrespect," he said, focusing on his aunt and uncle, "but East Branch is worse than a slum."

Alan seemed taken aback by that pronouncement,

though Helen's only reaction was a tightening of her mouth. "Why would you say that?" his uncle demanded.

"Because it's the truth," Connor replied. "The cheapest apartments and the shittiest little houses in Whitford have electricity and running water, and certainly sewer or septic systems. I wasn't a great student, but hell, I can point to the damn Mediterranean on a map. Can any of y'all?"

Silence answered that question.

"You barely feed yourselves," he continued. "I know you're doing your best, but my parents used to tell me about days of old apples in the thin winters, and…" He struggled for a moment, then said, "My life's nothing fancy, but at least I've got a basic education, an insulated house, and an income. That's more than can be said for anyone out here. Don't you want something better, at least for the kids?"

"And what would that be?" Helen asked. "The first time a headband comes untied or someone slips up and uses their touch…"

"*I* never slipped up in school!"

"You got lucky, and your parents fretted every day you were in that place."

"I—"

"If I may," Diriem cut in, "there could be an alternative."

Helen glanced at him. "Go on."

"Your ancestors were left here to fend for themselves, only somewhat talented and ill equipped to survive in hiding, especially this long. The world has moved on, but…with all due respect, East Branch has fallen behind. It's incredible that you've lasted as a coherent community for so many generations. But even if only in part, you came from our people, and we owe you the option of something better, safer. What I'd like to do is go back and persuade the Forum to allow you access to the Pactlands. It would only be an invitation," he said as John started to speak. "Nothing forced. We have no right to do that. Still, you should have the choice."

"And what would happen to us, uh...there?" Alan pressed.

"With Forum backing, we could support you until you found your footing. Education could be arranged, either a normal course for the children or tutors as needed. Job training. We do have working farms, if that's where your interests lie, but if you wanted to explore, that could be arranged. Of course, that's *if* the Forum gives authorization, and...this may not be a task accomplished overnight. But I'm willing to try."

With that, he carefully closed and wrapped the book again. "I do have a request. Allow me to borrow this."

The elders looked at each other, and Alan again took the lead. "That's our only copy. The original."

"Precisely. I'm confident that I can be believed without it, but as an artifact, this is compelling...and disintegrating."

Alan winced but didn't argue. "We've done our best—"

"Oh, I don't doubt it," Diriem replied. "Considering your resources, it's in excellent shape. But if you want it to last another few centuries, preservative measures should be taken. I can have that done for you, use it to make your case, and bring it back."

Again, the elders huddled up, but they debated longer that time.

"If you're not comfortable with that, then I'll work around it," Diriem offered. "You don't know me, and I do understand not wanting to entrust a stranger with something irreplaceable—"

Almost before I knew the words were leaving my mouth, I blurted, "I'll go with it."

As my mother snapped, "*Maebe,*" the elders turned to me as a group.

"I'll go," I repeated, standing to be seen. "I've been there before and made it home, right? Let me go and protect the records. If Diriem thinks that book will help us..."

My grandpa gave me a long once-over. "You're willing, Maebe?"

"Sure," I said with feigned confidence. "I'll guard it with my life."

"It won't come to that. I will keep Maebe safe," Diriem insisted.

For a third time, the elders circled to discuss their options, and I ignored my parents' entreaties to reconsider while I awaited a verdict. After a moment, they reached consensus, and Alan cleared his throat. "You can tell your people about us," he said to Diriem. "For the children's sake. And you can borrow the records if Maebe goes along."

He bowed his head. "Thank you."

"This doesn't mean we trust you," Alan continued. "I sure as hell ain't leaving East Branch—I was born here, and I'll die here. But...well, Connor knows about the outside, and if he thinks you're honest..."

I cut my eyes to my cousin, as did most of the crowd, waiting.

Connor nodded. "He means what he says."

As I slowly exhaled, Jane leaned closer and whispered, "Probably a good thing that you left your stuff at my place, eh?"

The drive to Jane's house was as quiet as the drive to East Branch had been. I'd moved into the back seat, across from Diriem, and we'd wedged the plastic box holding the record book into the seat between us. He stared ahead, grimly focused on the windshield. Up front, Jane took Connor's hand as he drove into Whitford, and he flashed a brief smile.

We'd almost made it to Ragged Gap when she murmured, "You never told me you were paying their property taxes."

"Never came up, did it?" he replied.

"*Con.*"

"What? It didn't."

Jane snorted. "Will you let me help? I've got savings, and I still owe you big time for our cross-country trip."

"No, you don't, Firebug."

"I'm *pretty* sure I do. Let me help."

"We can talk about it later," he said, and I saw him squeeze her hand before he glanced in the rearview mirror. "All right back there?"

"Fine," Diriem mumbled.

"Need me to pull over?"

"No, but if you could avoid the scenic route, I would greatly appreciate it."

"10-4," said Connor, and picked up speed.

"Come again?"

"It's cop for 'understood,'" Jane replied, turning around, and grimaced when she saw her boss's masked face. "You sure you're going to make it?"

He grunted.

As soon as Connor pulled into Jane's driveway, Diriem slid out and leaned against the SUV, taking deep breaths. I grabbed the box and came around the back to find him. "Are you okay?" I asked as the others headed inside.

"I will be," he said, eyes closed.

"Don't like cars? I haven't ridden much…"

"Oh, I enjoy them, but from the driver's seat. Sitting in the back…have you heard the term 'motion sickness'?"

I frowned. "You're queasy?"

He nodded. "May you never experience it," he muttered, and pushed himself upright. "This morning's potion wore off too quickly. I'll live. Let's see what they're up to inside."

We found the others in the kitchen, Jane with a bottle of golden liquid in hand and Connor pulling glass cups from the cabinet. "Who's drinking?" Jane asked in greeting. "I don't care what the clock says—this is medicinal."

The men concurred, and Jane poured a little for me as

well. "That's my dad's aged 'shine," she explained as I gave it a sniff. "It's pretty smooth, but if you don't like it, you won't hurt my feelings…and that's a no," she said, chuckling as I screwed up my mouth at the taste. "This isn't a starter liquor. How about a Coke?"

The stuff in the red can was weirdly fizzy on my tongue and made me burp, but the sweet liquid was far better than the moonshine had been. Taking small sips, I pulled up the empty chair at the table, where the other three were drinking quietly.

As Connor threw back the last of his 'shine, Diriem murmured, "So, I understand you had the flop as well."

He swallowed hard, squeezing his eyes shut, then nodded. "Yeah. My parents had my ears fixed when I was a baby so I'd look normal…" His eyes popped open, and a guilty, slightly panicked expression crossed his face. "Shit, I didn't mean—"

Diriem, who'd unmasked again, smirked and raised his glass. "They *did* have them fixed, and frankly, it takes far more than that to insult me." He finished his drink in turn, then said, "Thank you for today. Driving me out and, uh…what you said back there."

"Yeah, sure."

"I mean it." With that, he glanced at the counter, where I'd left the box, and asked, "Jane, could I trouble you for paper and a pen?"

"No problem," she replied, rising and heading for a cabinet. "What're you doing?"

"Satisfying my curiosity," he said, and gestured the box onto the table.

Clutching my can, I mused that I might need to get used to seeing objects fly around the room.

She returned with a lined yellow pad and a pen, then brought over the moonshine bottle as Diriem unwrapped the book and left it hovering open above the table. "Refill?"

"Please." He turned to the back while she poured, then

began writing.

I didn't know what he was up to—his scrawl was illegible to me, the letters unfamiliar—and so I slipped back to the guest room to pack my things. When I returned about ten minutes later, having stowed my bag by the door, Diriem was just finishing his work, and he flipped to a clean page on the pad. "Want to see if this spell runs?" he muttered to the others, then made a complex gesture over the book.

Instantly, an image appeared in midair above the table like Jane's computer screen, with Connor's name and birthdate at the bottom and a pair of lines branching up to his parents, each of whom had two dates beneath their name. The lines branched again and led to four names—his grandparents—adding a dropped-down spot by his father for Connor's aunt, Tiffany Willow, who'd died unmarried, and one for Alan Black by his mother.

It was a family tree, I realized, compiling itself from the names and connections listed in the records. I'd peeked in the book once or twice to find myself and my parents, but I'd never gone back as far as the spell was going...nor so quickly, as it flashed another generation about every three seconds. In less than a minute, the tree was complete, and Diriem manipulated the view until the names at the top turned various colors, which bled down the branches. Next, some of the names at the top of the tree grew larger, and other names did likewise in a ripple running forward in time.

"That's me?" Connor asked, considering the image.

"Assuming the records are accurate," Diriem replied, "and at this point, I have no reason to doubt."

Connor's shoulders tightened as he studied the diagram. "I'm no genealogist, but I'm pretty sure that ain't good."

"Not...ideal, no—"

"Forget *ideal*. That's, what, eleven generations back? And how many *unique* ancestors do I have at that point?"

Diriem scanned the picture. "Thirty-six. You're descended from all of the founding couples."

"Thirty-six..." He covered his mouth and stepped away, then pulled out his phone. "One thousand twenty-four. I should have one thousand twenty-four ancestors at that distance. It's supposed to be a tree, not a bush..."

"It's okay," said Jane, wrapping an arm around his back. "Connor, honey—"

"I didn't know it was that bad!" he said to her, a note of pleading in his voice. "Swear to God, Janie, I didn't know—"

"It's okay," she repeated. "Sit down, hmm?"

Diriem waited until Connor had taken his chair again, then said, "If it helps, I don't see any sign of sibling marriages. Cousins, yes, but past a certain point, that would have been inevitable."

"Fuck," he muttered.

"And there's more. Assuming that these eighteen were the only survivors from the southern Halls, you actually have the best claim to headship of Hall ti'Catama *and* Hall ti'Un—you're the eldest of the eldest child to procreate all the way back." He zoomed in the picture on two of the larger names near the top, Richard Willow and Caroline Peters. "Richard was Deriap's eldest, and Caroline's mother was Madla ti'Un. Strange to see those Halls joining—ti'Catama was considerably higher, as I recall—but those were strange times, I suppose."

Connor looked at the picture again, then reached for the moonshine and poured himself another drink, which he downed in one long gulp.

"What about Maebe?" Jane asked, rubbing Connor's back.

Diriem waved Connor's tree away, then restarted the spell. I watched as my tree grew and changed colors, and once again, certain names began to enlarge. He examined the resulting diagram and chuckled. "Well, Maebe, you have the same thirty-six founding ancestors that Connor does, though they're one generation further back for you. And…again, assuming these were the only survivors from the south…your grandfather is the heir to Hall ti'Ammaas. Walter, yes?"

"That's my grandpa. My dad's dad, I mean. My other grandpa is a Smith—"

"Justin, I see."

"Wait—what does that mean?" Connor interjected. "If Walter's the heir to ti'Ammaas…"

Diriem regarded me with an inscrutable expression. "If there were a southern kingdom left to rule, it would be his by right, then his son James's as the eldest child, and then Maebe's."

Connor nudged him the bottle of liquor, and Diriem poured. Unlike Connor, he didn't gulp it all back, but he clutched his glass and stared at my tree for a long moment before speaking again. "We looked for survivors. I swear to you, we looked. When the scouts came back saying the southern Halls had vanished, I focused on Ivari and everyone else I knew from that kingdom. Everyone I'd even *seen*," he insisted.

"So, how did you miss those eighteen?" Jane asked.

"Not to be crass, but fuck if I know," he muttered, and drank.

"Blinding potion?"

Diriem shook his head. "They'd need a sorcerer's help to pull that off, plus the ingredients. To my knowledge, every sorcerer evacuated. But *how* they hid from me isn't the most important issue right now. They did manage to hide, and assuming Mary's right and they wandered off into the winter to die, their half-blooded children were left behind, unknown to anyone in the Pactlands and forced to fend for themselves…" He glanced from me to Connor and murmured, "I'm so sorry. If we'd known three hundred years ago…"

"Water under the bridge now," Connor replied. "So, what's the plan?"

He finished his drink. "Get the book back to DOI and down to our archivists—I trust them to handle an item that fragile. I'll have it analyzed and copied while it's being restored, just in case."

"Uh...I'm going with it," I interrupted.

He nodded. "Back to the Pactlands, absolutely, but you're not going to want to sit in a clean room with the archivists for days. Your book will be safe while they work—DOI hasn't suffered a successful break-in since the early eighteenth century. But looking beyond that," he said, "I need to build a case for East Branch and muster Forum support. That community won't last another two or three generations. Forget funding—East Branch doesn't have the people. Frankly, it's remarkable that you two are as healthy as you are."

Though Connor winced, he didn't argue.

"The safest plan, as I see it, is to bring the community into the Pactlands and take whatever measures are needed to help them adapt. Educate the ones who need and want it, train the ones with talent, and remove the risks inherent in maintaining a Georgian community of largely elven ex-traction."

I shared a look with my cousin, who shook his head. "Good luck with that," he said to Diriem. "You heard Uncle Alan—East Branch is home. That's family land, and we've been there for *how* many generations?"

"Eleven or twelve, the records suggest, but—"

"That's a *long* time, man. Perhaps not for you," he allowed, "but for my family, for that community...you're talking about old history. Our kin were born there, they died there, and they're buried in the big cemetery. Now, I might live in Whitford, and Maebe's figuring herself out, but a lot of those folks aren't going to leave willingly. East Branch is all they know."

Diriem waited until he finished, then said, "Understood. But sometimes, you must choose between senti-mentality and survival. Believe me," he added with a mirthless smile, "I've been there. Your ancestors chose poorly. Maybe we can begin to fix their mistakes before it's too late."

CHAPTER 10

We split up soon after that. Diriem announced he was going to return to the Pactlands straight away and have a quiet word with someone, but that left the problem of what was to be done with me. Jane, I learned, had a room within the DOI building for the nights she stayed in Beukal, and she offered to continue to host me. "The bed's plenty big for two," she said, "or the couch is decent."

Either option sounded good to me, especially if the furniture there was anything like Jane's furnishings in Ragged Gap, but Diriem had other plans. "Would you be opposed to staying with Maebe at my house?" he asked Jane. "I realize it's a bit of a drive, but there's no need for the two of you to bunk together in the agent quarters."

"Not turning that down," she replied. "And you're going to keep excusing me from my tutorials for now, right?"

He smirked. "I made your excuses for you before leaving this morning, girl. Meet you there," he said, and quickly packed the book back into its box. "Maebe, would you mind taking this with you?"

"No problem," I said, relieved that I hadn't had to argue with him over the book's custody.

"Great. And Connor, if you'd like to join us, I'll make the arrangements..."

But Connor declined. "Thanks, no. Duty calls."

Diriem cut his eyes to the bottle of 'shine on the table. "Don't take this the wrong way, but are you in any state to answer?"

"I'm not drunk, if that's what you mean. In any case,

I'll be fine once I go home and change clothes."

"They can make do without you," said Jane.

Shrugging, he said, "Yeah, but the best thing right now might be for me to focus on something…normal. And in case of emergency, someone should be here to communicate with East Branch."

Her brow furrowed. "Do you want me to stay?" she murmured. "All of this can wait—"

"Nah, I'm fine," Connor replied, though his insistence seemed forced. "Y'all go. Just do me a favor and look after Maebe, okay?"

Jane stared him down for a moment, clearly unconvinced, but relented. "Okay, if you're sure. Talk to you after you leave work tonight, eh?"

"Absolutely," he promised, then kissed her and headed for the door, calling, "Be careful, mitta," over his shoulder as he departed.

When the door closed behind him and his SUV's engine started up, Diriem and Jane shared a long look. "He'll be fine," said Jane. "You go on, and we'll be along behind you."

He masked again and took his leave, and Jane sighed as the sedan pulled away. "It's been a day, and it's not even lunchtime yet," she said, looking at the clock on the microwave. "You all right, hon?"

"I…think so. Yeah," I said, quickly taking stock. True, it *had* been a strange morning, and part of me worried that I should never have gone home with Jane in the first place, but on balance, I was excited for the possibilities ahead. "When do we leave?"

"Just let me close up the house," she replied, and pointed to my room. "Grab your bag, and we'll head back to Central."

I climbed up into the truck with Jane and buckled in, feeling more like a pro with every ride. Perhaps she'd be willing to teach me to drive, I mused. Back home, only a few people knew how to operate the trucks, and I hadn't yet been given the chance to learn. I was settling in for the ride, wondering how I might broach the topic, when Jane pressed a few buttons and a ringing sound came through the truck's speakers.

"Hey, girlie," said a man's voice when the ringing ceased. "How's work?"

"Weird this week," Jane replied. "I'm actually headed out of Ragged Gap now, and I've got a passenger."

"Oh?" He sounded concerned. "Agent?"

"No, one of Connor's cousins from East Branch."

He paused. "Dare I ask?"

"It's authorized, Dad," Jane assured him. "I had her over there yesterday, too. Keep this under your hat?"

"Uh, sure…"

"Short version, everyone in East Branch is quasi-elven, and Diriem's trying to figure out what to do about it."

"*What?*"

"Yeah, kind of a shock."

"Where the hell did they come from?" he demanded.

"Survivors who didn't opt for the Pactlands, looks like. Anyway, I don't know how the rest of this week is going to shape up, so I'll keep you posted when I'm heading home next."

"Okay, Janie," he said, though he sounded troubled. "You be careful, now, sweetheart."

She smiled as she drove. "Love you, too," she said, and ended the call. Before I could ask any questions, Jane dialed again, and a woman answered that time.

"Hey, stranger," she said. "What's up? You in town?"

"Hi, Tabitha. Just leaving, actually," she replied. "Could I ask you for a favor?"

"Depends on the favor."

"Fair. I'm concerned about Connor."

"Oh, no. Hang on, let me get this bottle labeled, and then you can tell me all about it."

Jane looked my way and whispered, "She's a friend of ours. Pharmacist in town, and she knows about the Pactlands."

"A sorcerer?" I whispered back.

"Not in the slightest—"

"Sorry!" Tabitha interrupted, returning to the call. "Getting my ducks in a row before the drama. Okay, what's he done? Tell me everything."

"He hasn't done anything," said Jane, "and we're not fighting. He just got some, uh...*weird* news in the last couple of days, and I have to get back to Neverland, so do you think you might have time to look in on him?"

"I'll make time," she replied. "Absolutely. But can you tell me what I'm walking into before I drop in on him?"

Jane kept her eyes on the road as we headed for the highway. "Yeah, but this is sensitive—"

"Is he okay?" Tabitha asked, concerned.

"I mean, he's going to work after a couple shots of 'shine. Not his best morning."

"*Already*? What the hell—"

"Diriem just left."

She snorted. "Well, *that* can't be anything good. What's going on with y'all?"

"Short version, Canna ran tests on one of Connor's cousins from East Branch, and Diriem looked over their old records today, and basically, everyone out there is part elf."

"Shit. You're serious?"

"Yup," said Jane. "Turns out the founders of that community were eighteen elven refugees and their half-human kids, so—"

Tabitha's tone sharpened. "*Eighteen*?"

"Yeah, and since the community's so closed, they've all come from the same thirty-six people, but, like, ten or more generations on."

She whistled on the other end. "That is...*very* much not good. I mean, all jokes about East Branch aside—"

"Connor's cousin is here with me, and you're on speaker," Jane hastily interjected.

"Oh, uh...hey, there," said Tabitha. "Sorry, didn't know..."

"Jokes?" I whispered to Jane.

"Tell you later." To Tabitha, she said, "Connor's aware of the problem. I don't think he realized how severe it was before today."

"Because *that* ain't a family tree," Tabitha replied. "That's a hedge. Listen...I'm no genetic specialist, but if there's someone with that sort of expertise in Neverland, then I would strongly suggest getting folks checked out. Even if they look perfectly normal, they might have health issues."

"Roger that. But for now—"

"Oh, I'll go check on Connor. Drag him out for dinner."

"If you do that, he'll know we've talked," said Jane.

"Shoot, that's barely a concern right now. If he's not distracted, he's likely to dwell on this. Remember the Banksy wannabe back in April?"

"Con did get a little obsessed," she allowed.

"*Right.* And putting aside the mess at East Branch, it's got to be a shock to get proof that you're not exactly human."

"True," Jane muttered, then groaned. "Hey, Tabitha, you're not hiding anything I should know about, are you?"

"Hardly," she scoffed. "Unless you want to count my incredible bowling ability, I'm pretty boring."

"You're anything but boring, lady. But if you wouldn't mind checking on Connor, I'd appreciate it."

"Sure thing. Come see me when you're back in town."

Once Jane hung up, I sat silently for another moment longer, waiting to see if she'd speak first. When she made no move, however, I asked, "What jokes?"

Jane sighed. "People who live in the towns around East Branch just know that it's a weird little community in a holler, y'all don't have utilities, and you run off strangers with guns. There are...*suspicions*...that the gene pool there is a little on the shallow side, and so folks joke about inbreeding. Which...isn't so funny now, I suppose. I mean, it wasn't funny to begin with, but those sort of comments abound in Appalachia."

"Oh." Flushing, I stared out the window to avoid looking at Jane. "We call it being close. Like, if your mom and dad have the same grandparents? We try to avoid that, but it's happened in the past. There's not enough people, and—"

"You don't have to explain, Maebe."

My guts clenched. "Do people in town make fun of us a lot?"

"I...wouldn't say a lot, but that's the kind of comment that comes up when East Branch is mentioned."

I recalled Grandpa and his horses, so carefully managed and traded away. "Y'all think there's something wrong with us."

She didn't deny it. "Things go wrong in communities that are too close. You see more genetic problems, sometimes intellectual deficiencies. There are known cases in Appalachia and elsewhere."

"The flop," I mumbled.

When I glanced over, Jane was nodding. "Exactly. Could be that some of those eighteen elves were carrying the gene for that, but since it's recessive, they wouldn't show it. You'd need two copies of the gene, one from each parent, for the flop to happen. But when those few elves with the gene had kids, and the kids started marrying each other, the odds of getting that double recessive gene shot up. Hell," she muttered, "you may all be carrying that gene now. Connor's parents didn't have the flop, and look at what happened to him."

I turned to the window again, then felt Jane's hand land on my knee. "Hey," she murmured, "I'm sorry. You haven't done anything wrong, and I know your folks have been doing their best."

"I don't want to be a freak," I whispered.

"You're fine, hon," she told me, but in my mind's eye, I saw Hirral, the healer, gawking at me with his mouth open.

Suddenly, exploring the wider world didn't seem like my greatest idea.

We made it into the Pactlands without incident, but once Jane cleared the portal building, instead of driving toward the glass spires of Beukal, she steered us toward a large stone building with a huge opening in the middle for vehicles. "Where are we going?" I asked.

"Internal portals. Nothing to worry about," she said with a reassuring smile.

The road into the building split into ten lanes once we were inside, each headed for a booth with a barrier arm much like the one in the portal building we'd just left. Here, however, there was a sign on each booth. The five on the right were lit with glowing characters—words, I presumed—and beyond each barrier hung a flashing portal. The other five booths were dark, but through the gaps between them, I could see cars emerging from the other side of their portals.

"We're going outbound," Jane explained, turning into one of the lanes. "Traffic can switch directions in here as needed, like at rush hour, but things are pretty calm at this time of the morning. See that sign?" she asked, pointing to the booth ahead of us. "'Viratta.' That's where we're headed."

"Where's that?"

"A few hundred miles away, best guess. If you map the Pactlands onto the outside world, Beukal is near Richmond, and Viratta is somewhere in central Pennsylvania." Seeing my bemusement, she added, "Hours by car. This is so much more convenient."

When she drove us through the portal, we arrived in a smaller building with only four lanes, and Jane guided us out into the sunlight. "Diriem's place is a bit of a drive from here," she said, lowering her sun visor. "He doesn't exactly have neighbors. The mansion's on a good piece of land."

"Mansion?" I echoed.

"It's a *big* house. You'll see." She left the portal area and turned onto a winding road that cut through gently undulating fields of tall grass. "I've been out here a few times, but not to visit Diriem. His great-granddaughter's become a friend in the last months, and she and her fiancé have an apartment in the mansion. Rose. I'm sure you'll meet her soon. The two of us and our friend Annie have had a handful of girls' nights at the ti'Dana manse. I don't really have space to entertain at DOI, and Annie lives with her husband and his dozens of brothers, so Rose's place is the best option. That," she continued, "and I've been helping her with preliminary wedding planning. Annie has zero patience for it, but I like looking at fabrics and flowers."

"Is she getting married soon?" I asked. Weddings in East Branch were community affairs, afternoon ceremonies followed by celebration late into the night, but I suspected traditions might vary elsewhere.

"She doesn't have a date yet, but she and Yven want to do it in the next year or two. That's her fiancé, Yven," Jane clarified. "Both of them and Annie work with Canna's husband at DPP."

"I see."

Jane slipped to the left to avoid what I initially took to be a woman out for a horseback ride until I looked more closely and realized there was no head on the horse, and the horse's legs were hers. "*What* in the world—"

"She's a centaur. Don't stare."

I forced myself to sit back in my seat but kept sneaking peeks at the side mirror. "She's part *horse!*"

"She's fully centaur, not part anything. They do *not* appreciate being called part horse."

"Sorry…"

"Hey, no, it's fine. Just us in here," said Jane. "But I

learned that the hard way, so I'm trying to save you from my mistake. You heard me when I told your parents about that girl I found in Whitford last year, yeah? She's actually half centaur—her dad's a sorcerer. Nice guy. Mom's a piece of work, but you can't win them all."

I tried to be delicate. "How does, um...how does that work for her?"

"Take the more equine half of a typical centaur and compress it into a single pair of limbs and a tail. She masks now—easier to find clothing, and she had a *really* rough time growing up outside, so I think it's better for her mental health. Her name's Sage," Jane added, slowing at an intersection. "She's a few years younger than you, but I think you two should meet up eventually."

We drove on past fields for a time, which gave way to a town at the center of a long stretch of houses—some about the size of Jane's, some larger, but all far nicer than my family home. Past the town, the fields returned, and I spotted the occasional house or cluster of buildings in the distance, wondering each time we approached if we'd reached our destination.

And then the biggest house I'd ever seen came into view over the treeless horizon.

"Here we are," said Jane, and turned off the main road onto a long, winding driveway.

I gaped for a moment, stunned by the sheer size of the place. "*That's* where we're going?"

"Yep. Personally, I think it's grossly oversized for three people and Diriem's staff, but I'm also not elven royalty, so..." She chuckled as she shrugged. "Let's just say he has room for guests."

The house was larger than all of our barns combined, a massive, multistory stone complex punctuated by towers. The morning light glinted off dozens of large windows, and fleetingly, I wondered how long it took to clean them. Around the house, the land stretched out in unbroken green, grass far too tidy and uniform to have grown naturally, but I couldn't help but think that a few trees would improve the effect. Without the protective mountains of home rising around us, the world felt far too open, like one might run right off the edge.

Jane stopped in a wide paved space in front of the house, then cut the engine. "Diriem's probably going to tell me to move to the garage, but he didn't give me the door code, so…"

"A garage? Like the one at DOI?"

"Kind of. See that low building with the big door up ahead? That's the entrance, and the garage goes down several floors. Dude loves his cars." Unbuckling, she said, "In all honesty, I'd just as soon leave mine out here. The thought of squeezing this truck between a couple of exotic sportscars makes me queasy."

We grabbed our bags, plus the box holding the wrapped record book, and I followed Jane up the steps to the tall double front door. She rang the bell and stepped back, and soon, the door opened to reveal a remarkably ordinary looking man—middle aged, thin, and of average height, with neat gray hair and blue eyes. The only thing odd about him was his attire, a sleeveless green robe like the ones I'd seen around DOI over a black shirt and matching trousers. He smiled at Jane and spoke, though I couldn't understand a word of it.

After their brief conversation, she turned to me. "Maebe, this is Scel Curain, the house manager. He says we're expected, so come on in."

I followed her through the doors and found myself in a high-ceilinged room with polished wooden floors. Directly ahead was a wide staircase, which split in half and landed in two places on the second floor. The rugs alone were fancier than anything I'd seen in East Branch, and a pair of wooden tables along the walls were decorated with generous sprays of cut flowers. I craned my neck and discovered a huge sort of multi-armed lamp covered in tiny glass pieces hanging overhead. "What…"

Noticing me, Jane said, "It's called a chandelier. Something like that would be a *little* big for my place—"

"*Hey!*" came a shout, and I spotted movement at the top of the staircase: a redheaded woman in gray leggings and a flowy purple shirt, who made good time as she descended. "Okay, I'm going to need *details*," she said—in English, to my relief—as she jogged toward us.

"Hey, Rose," said Jane, adjusting her bag on her shoulder. "Didn't know you'd be home yet."

"Eh, Pop called me with the short version, and I took the rest of the day. So, *what* is going on? And hi," she said, extending a hand to me. "I'm Rose."

"Maebe," I replied, gingerly shaking it.

"Nice to meet you." She looked back at Jane. "Start talking."

"Can we put our stuff down first? *Jesus*, I just drove in from Georgia," Jane groused. "Second trip in two days, in fact."

"Oh…*shit*, sorry. Of course." She spoke briefly to Scel, who nodded and went on his way, then told us, "Why don't y'all come to my apartment for now? I'll take you to your rooms in a bit."

Rose led us up the staircase, then down a long hallway pocked with wooden doors and decorated with more expensive-looking furniture and a rug I felt guilty walking on. "You'll be in the southern wing with us," she said, glancing over her shoulder. "The tower rooms have nice views."

The hallway ended in a semicircle of doors, one of which Rose opened to reveal a stone staircase that spiraled up and down. "This way," she said, beckoning to me with a smile, and we climbed two more flights to the fourth floor. "There *is* a way to get up here by elevator," she said as we stepped out of the stairwell, "but it's less direct."

"Good to stretch my legs," Jane muttered.

"Happy to help."

There were fewer doors in that floor's semicircle, only one on each side of the stairs, and Rose took the one to the left. "Come on in, and sorry about the mess. I wasn't expecting company when I left this morning."

I stepped through the door into a spacious vestibule with an ornate rug and a wood and brass table akin to the ones downstairs, on which sat a purse and a glass bowl holding a ring of keys. The vestibule opened into a den in which three plush leather sofas were arranged around a wide TV hanging on the wall. Shelves and side tables bore pots of the strangest flowers I'd ever seen, an indoor garden basking in the light that filtered through the trio of east-facing windows, each about eight feet high and filled with swirls of colored glass that cast rainbows on the floor. Paintings, mostly landscapes, decorated the walls.

Through an open door to my left, I spied a small room with an easel set up by a clear glass window, a half-finished painting awaiting, and a rack of paints and other mysterious items in pots and jars. The door beside it was closed, as were two on the right side of the den, but an opening gave way to a small kitchen in which a steel refrigerator hummed.

The apartment had to be bigger than my parents' house, and if I ignored the TV and the electric lights, it made me think of the palaces in my old storybooks.

"Y'all make yourselves comfortable," said Rose, ducking into the kitchen, and returned moments later with a blue package and a plate of cheese squares and crackers. "Sorry, nothing fancy," she said, putting them atop the low table in the middle of the sofas, "but it's getting close to lunchtime. Something to drink?"

"Hey, I don't turn my nose up at Oreos," Jane replied, opening the package. "Just water, if you don't mind."

Rose returned with bottles of water for all three of us, then pushed aside a laptop and sank onto the sofa cattycorner to ours. "So," she said, looking between us expectantly, "what's this I hear about elves in Ragged Gap?"

I lifted a hand as Jane opened her water and took a swig. "From what their records suggest," she said, wiping her mouth, "eighteen elves from the southern Halls who didn't evacuate back in the day ended up intermarrying with a group of humans, and they and their kids founded East Branch. Everybody there is descended from some of those couples...hell, probably all of them. Connor and Maebe both are."

"How'd you figure that out?"

"Found Maebe in the woods on Sunday, and I brought her to Canna for testing yesterday. She's about three-quarters elven, so..."

"Why am I just now hearing about this?" Rose griped.

"Because I called the senior ti'Dana first."

She huffed, then reached for the Oreos. "Okay, fair. Gimme."

Jane passed the package. "Anyway, Diriem said he's going to see about getting the East Branch crew access, but that could be a little tricky since they don't have established Halls here."

"Oof. Yeah," Rose mumbled around a cookie. "What happened to those eighteen elves? Are they still out there?"

"They killed themselves," I told her, and pointed to the box at my feet. "Or that's what the records say, I guess. *I* can't read them."

"Bad winter, food ran low, and they walked off to save their families," Jane added.

"*Yikes.*" She finished her cookie, frowning as she thought. "So...Connor?"

"Hasn't been tested yet, but Diriem put together his family tree this morning, and he's, like, the heir apparent to *two* Halls. Also, he neglected to mention to me until yesterday that he was born with this ear flop condition, so let's just say my working hypothesis about a sorcerer in the mix at East Branch is absolutely disproven."

"Ear flop?" Rose echoed.

"Uh...what did they call it..."

"Cifyent, I think," I said.

Jane snapped her fingers. "That's it. Ring a bell?"

"Sorry, no," said Rose, "but I'm no expert in all things elven. What are we talking about?"

"This," I said, reaching back to untie my headband, and pulled it off to show her. "See?"

"Oh, wow. *Huh.*" To my relief, she sounded more curious than horrified. "And you said *Connor's* were like that?"

"He had plastic surgery as a baby," Jane replied. "The thought is that the flop is a recessive trait found in some of the southern Halls, and since East Branch has been remixing those genes for quite some time…"

"Yeah. Genetics are *weird.*" Rose absently rubbed her chin for a moment as I turned to give her a full view of the side of my head, then leaned closer and offered me the package. "Oreos?"

"Um…sorry, what are—"

"Chocolate and cream," Jane explained. "Go for it."

Rose's brow wrinkled. "You've never had an Oreo?"

"We don't buy much," I mumbled, but accepted one and gave it a taste. Not bad, I thought, though sweeter than the treats I knew from East Branch.

As I tied my headband back on, I gave Rose a brief study of my own. She looked normal enough, a twenty-something woman with red hair that fell midway down her back and pretty gray eyes. She only had one piercing in each ear, unlike Jane, who wore triple studs, and she sported small silver hoops set with tiny purple crystals. Take away the earrings, elongate her ears, and raise her cheekbones slightly…and yes, I could see Diriem in her features, particularly when she looked at me. Having spent part of the last two days with him, I found some of her expressions familiar, though her accent was radically different. Rose didn't sound quite like the folks back home, but she was close enough to set me at ease.

"You've got the touch, right? Uh, magic, I mean," I said to her.

"Sure do." She flicked two fingers at the snack plate,

and a cracker and cheese slice sailed into her hand. "Pop said you do, too."

"It's not strong," I muttered.

"*Yet*. You're a lot further along than I was at your age—I didn't find out about this place until I was twenty-six. Didn't even know magic was a possibility until then. There's a learning curve, but you'll get there," she said, and fit the cracker stack into her mouth.

"What do I do for Connor?" Jane murmured.

Rose frowned and swallowed. "Tutoring would probably be a good place to start…"

"Well, yeah, but for right now. I…" She struggled for a moment, then said, "I've always known I was at least part sorcerer, right? You learned about yourself late, and Con…I don't know how he's taking all of this. Truth be told, I don't know what's more upsetting to him, the blatant record of inbreeding or the elf thing. So…you've been there. What can I do?"

She motioned another cookie from the package and twisted it apart while she thought. "I acclimated pretty quickly, but then I didn't really have time to dwell on it since Aunt Lily was on the run, and Yven was right *there*, and we got freaking arrested…not the easiest introduction to magic. After that, I was more concerned about finding someone to acknowledge me before Yven could take the fucking draught than about what it all *meant*. But if you think it could help, I'd be happy to call him…"

Jane made a face. "I'm not sure. Our friend Tabitha says she's going to distract him tonight—"

"This is Wiccan Tabitha?"

"I've got to introduce y'all one of these days. Yeah. But if he's not ready to talk, I don't want to make matters worse…"

"Hey, no sweat. I get it. It's a *lot*," said Rose, and turned to me. "Speaking of which, how're you getting on, Maebe? Any burning questions?"

I nodded emphatically. "*Many*."

"By the way, this one's in line for Hall ti'Ammaas," Jane said. "Practically royalty."

Rose snorted and rolled her eyes. "Yeah, join the club. That and five bucks will just about get you a grande latte."

"What's that?" I asked.

Her eyebrows rose. "Ever had coffee?"

"Uh…no, I don't think so…"

"Well, we can start by fixing that," she replied, going to her feet. "The espresso machine is in the big kitchen, but I've learned the basics from the Mangia Due crew. Come on, I'll hook you up. You can leave your stuff here—it's safe."

I stood and followed her. "From the…*what?*"

"Mangia Due is the café in the DPP tower, and they keep us well caffeinated. Definite agency perk," said Rose, and grinned impishly at Jane.

"You're aware of the DOI kitchen, right?" Jane countered. "Room service, hon."

She opened the apartment door with a flourish. "Which is all well and good, but Korek Shilg is a genius with espresso, and he's *ours*. After y'all."

CHAPTER 11

Instead of making me a latte, Rose whipped up something called a mocha, which she topped with a spray of whipped cream from a can and a drizzle of chocolate sauce. Both condiments came from outside, she and Jane assured me—the fact that I could read their labels was testament to the truth of *that*—but had they told me that the rich, frothy sweetness was the magical creation of some forgotten fairyland, I would have believed it. We kept bees in East Branch, and I'd had sweets from town on occasion, but never before had sugar been so omnipresent. Though delicious, the drink was almost sweet enough to turn my stomach, and I didn't object when Rose suggested chicken salads for lunch.

For that, she sought the mansion's cook, Ranarma Curain—Scel's nephew, as it turned out, a young, brown-haired sorcerer who'd been tending the tomatoes in the enormous greenhouse attached to the back of the mansion. He was happy to assist, even speaking to me in his strangely accented English when Rose explained my linguistic problem, though I'd stared at him blankly through about half of his recitation of the list of toppings on offer.

At least Connor could hide, I thought, settling in with my salad while Jane and Rose chatted. He looked normal, he never needed to reveal his touch, and he was familiar enough with the outside to get along. Had he wanted to, he could have fled the shadow of East Branch and never looked back, and no one would have connected him to the community. As for me, however, not only was I a walking freak of nature, but my unfamiliarity with things as apparently basic as craisins (delicious, incidentally) left me unable to function on my own. I'd known I was sheltered as an East Branch kid, but I'd had no idea I was so hopelessly *ignorant.*

I had no money and no useful skills, my community was dying, and my future depended on the generosity of others. Not just my future—if Diriem's plans failed, what would happen to my family, my cousins? Because they *were* all my cousins, weren't they? I couldn't let them down...

As I mulled that over, another thought struck me. Eighteen elves had founded East Branch, presumably the last survivors of whatever battles had wiped out their kingdom. *But what if they weren't the only ones?* What if there were other East Branches, isolated communities with weird abilities and weirder birth defects, unknowingly clinging to the last vestiges of a dead language?

If we'd been overlooked for so long, couldn't there be others left to discover?

I was picking at the bottom of my bowl when I heard men's voices approaching, and Rose perked. She called to them—or so I assumed, unable to understand her—and a few seconds later, Diriem walked in with another elf. He was short, no taller than me, and wore his dark hair fairly closely cropped. Oddly enough, instead of a robe, he sported frayed jeans and a long-sleeved gray T-shirt with a dozen unidentifiable stains splashed across it.

Rose waved from her seat. "Teolm?"

"Rosie. I understand we have a visitor," he said, his English decent but more heavily accented than Diriem's. Looking down the table, he nodded to Jane. "Agent Fortune, yes? Or is it Aniap?"

"Fortune, still a trainee, and 'Jane' is fine," she replied. "Uh...Lord ti'Cren, right?"

He grimaced. "Teolm."

"Rough morning at the office?" Rose asked.

Teolm glanced at his shirt. "Not horrible. Nothing's

being pollenated today, and the acid's been kept to a minimum...why, do I smell?"

"No, no," she reassured him, "just, uh..."

"The only time the robes come out at Dashom Brothers is for the investor meetings," he said with a dimpled smirk. "*Your* father should understand that," he added, turning back to Jane.

She grinned. "Oh, I've heard horror stories about the agency greenhouse."

"I expect you have. And this must be...Maebe?"

"Hi," I mumbled, and pushed my lunch aside. "Maebe Amos."

"This is my great-uncle, Teolm," Rose explained to me, then turned back to him. "What's going on?"

Teolm looked at Diriem, who murmured, "Maebe, if you wouldn't mind removing your headband..."

Steeling myself, I did as he asked, noting the shock in Teolm's dark eyes. He said something unintelligible to me, then shook his head. "Apologies, I...heavens," he said, turning again to Diriem, "you were not kidding."

"Not in the slightest," Diriem replied, "and if their records are to be trusted, she's a ti'Ammaas. A *living* ti'Ammaas."

Teolm pulled out a chair and sat opposite me, and though he stared, he seemed excited, not disgusted. "Ti'Cren is a southern Hall," he told me. "My grandmother, in her wisdom, followed Lord ti'Dana to this place"— he cut his eyes to Diriem, who'd also seated himself—"but we of the main line are kin to Hall ti'Ammaas. My grandfather was a ti'Ammaas—not their main line, but a cousin of Ivari's. So, you and I..." He twitched a finger back and forth between us. "Not the closest of kin, youngling, but kin nonetheless. How many of you are there?"

"In East Branch? Forty-nine, plus Connor—he lives in town," I explained.

"And how many of you descend from Ivari?"

"Quite probably a significant number," Diriem cut in.

"The Connor she mentioned is one of them. Eighteen families, and the youngest of them currently are of the twelfth generation..." Looking back at me, Diriem asked, "Could you show Teolm the record book?"

"It's in my apartment," Rose volunteered. "Come on, Maebe, I'll walk you up."

Once we were upstairs and out of earshot of the kitchen, Rose quietly said, "If you need to have a little freak-out, that's just fine."

"I'm okay—"

"If you're actually okay right now, I'll be shocked."

I said nothing further until we were in her apartment, and then I leaned against the wall and closed my eyes. "So much, all at once, and nothing's simple. I just wanted something more than East Branch, like...I don't know, a job in town. Not *chaos* and crazy family mess."

"You're really allowed to be overwhelmed," said Rose, and to my surprise, she hugged me.

I hadn't realized until that moment how much I needed one of those.

"Pop said you're eighteen?"

"Uh-huh."

"Shit, you're barely an adult as it is outside. Here, they look at you like you're a kid until you're thirty-five." She sat me down on one of the couches and took the spot beside me. "Pop means well, I'm sure he does, but it's been a *long* time since he was eighteen. He's going full steam ahead without stopping to ask whether you're ready—"

"He said I might be able to go to school, and that would be great—"

"Yeah, but how are you *feeling* right now?"

I paused and took stock. "Anxious...scared, I guess," I mumbled. "Uh, no offense—"

"None taken. And believe me, this place comes as a shock, even if you've grown up in a city. I don't know everything you're going through at this moment, but if you need to take a breather and scream, be my guest. The walls are thick."

Weak laughter seemed like a better idea than crying. "I just want to do the right thing, and I don't know…"

"Listen," Rose murmured, rubbing my arm, "Pop sees the future professionally, and even he doesn't always know what the right thing to do is. So, if you make a mistake, if you screw up, so what? You're a teenager doing the best you can in a *weird* situation, and that's all anyone can ask of you. Okay?"

Nodding, I pulled myself together. "That guy downstairs, who is he, again?"

"Teolm? He's my grandfather's big brother. Uh, on my father's side. Pop's my mother's grandfather."

I would, I feared, never be able to guess an elf's age. Teolm seemed barely older than Rose and Jane.

"He heads Hall ti'Cren these days," she continued, "and since that was the highest of the southern Halls to join up over here, I see why Pop's brought him in. He's not going to hurt you," she insisted. "Teolm breeds exotic plants. Floramancer. My greatest risk around him is letting him sneak off with my fiancé." Gesturing to the many flowers blooming in the den, she said, "It's not so much a hobby as an obsession. Those two can talk shop for *hours*. But in the grand scheme of things, Teolm's pretty harmless."

Somewhat reassured, I carried the box back to the kitchen and slid it onto the table. "This is it," I said. "Um, sorry for the delay…"

"No problem," Teolm replied with a little smile, and popped off the lid. "May I?"

"Sure, but it's kind of old…"

"So am I. No fear." Much as Diriem had done, he gently unwrapped the book, then gestured until it floated before him. "Yes, this does need preservation…"

"Turn to the front pages," Diriem suggested.

Teolm did so, and his eyes widened. "I see what you mean. And the rest is like this?"

"No, it switches to pure English fairly quickly, but the genealogical record is intact. Allow me to show you…"

I could tell he was triggering the spell again when the screen-like projection appeared above the book, but instead of starting with Connor or me, it began with the eighteen couples and rapidly worked its way down, the colored lines braiding and weaving around each other with the passing generations. When it finished, Teolm studied the diagram, his face drawn. "That is…sobering. And they have a heightened incidence of cifyent?" he asked Diriem.

"From what I can tell, but Maebe would know better."

"About three-quarters of us," I told them. "Most folks who have any, um, *abilities* have the flop, too. They usually go together."

"I see," said Teolm. "And your community has been hidden all this time?"

"We're not *hidden*. It's not like this place. But we do keep to ourselves, and if anyone goes outside East Branch, they cover up," I explained. Realizing I was still holding my headband, I hastily tied it back on. "Like that. Of course, if town folks already joke about us, maybe there's no point in hiding the flop. They'll just think it's part of us being too close, right?"

"No," Jane interjected, "covering up is a *very* good practice. Better for people not to ask even more questions about East Branch."

"They know about you," I retorted. "That guy at the restaurant, Tabitha—"

"A select group. There are a few in the area who know I've got real power, but that's not super-common knowledge, and most people outside that limited circle would poo-poo any talk of magic. But I can make this all a little easier for you," Jane continued. "I know how to create masking jewelry. They're not the most gorgeous of pieces, but they're functional pendants, so until you figure out how to mask on your own, you could use one to disguise your ears."

Recalling what Connor had told me in passing, I beamed. "Really?"

She smiled as she nodded. "Yep. Masking jewelry is one of the weird facets of magic I can handle reliably well. Give me a few hours with a necklace to put the spell together, and I'll teach you—"

"*Or* you could save time and allow me to pull something out of storage," said Teolm. "The vault has plenty of options." He paused, gauging Jane's expression, then asked, "You know about the family jewelry store, yes?"

"I didn't want to overstep…"

"Happy to raid our stash. It's bound to be easier to mask Maebe than it was to work on Annie Humphries during her Roulette days." Glancing at Rose, he asked, "She still likes her pendant?"

"Uses it all the time," Rose replied. "So, that's a start, then. We can get Maebe masked, and that should take some of the pressure off—"

"What about school?" I interrupted, looking at the two men. "Do you think you can get me in?"

Teolm turned to Diriem. "Surely we could manage that. I don't suppose I have grounds to *acknowledge* her, but…I don't know, could I sponsor her? Is that an option?"

"It's never been done," Diriem replied. "We've not had cause. This will take work behind the scenes at the Forum, which is why I want your support."

"You have it. I was meant to dine with Cirral tomorrow night, but if you would prefer to contact our contingent sooner, perhaps we could speed up the process of assimilating East Branch—"

"Hold it," I blurted.

Diriem raised his hands as if anticipating an argument. "*Assimilation* isn't the right word. No one will force your community—"

"What if we're not the only ones? There could be other places like East Branch, right? We just happen to be where eighteen of y'all landed. Couldn't there be more survivors or, like, kin of survivors?"

Teolm hissed through his teeth. "Youngling has a point. Unless you've seen something—"

"I've seen *nothing*," Diriem muttered, "which is how we landed in this mess. East Branch's progenitors hid from me. Perhaps they weren't the only ones."

"What about Ganti?" Jane asked. "He's got strong past-oriented farsight, yeah? Could you have him look back and check for rogue elves?"

"If they hid from me, they'll be hidden to him as well..." Grimacing, he looked at Teolm. "If we wanted to search, one possibility comes to mind."

"She's a *child*," Teolm protested. "You can't seriously suggest that—"

Jane perked. "A tracker? That only takes a little blood..."

Teolm's mouth tightened to a thin line. "No, not a tracker. It's called," he began, and finished that sentence with an unfamiliar word.

"'Bloodline,' more or less," Rose told me.

"*Highly* effective. You take it, and it identifies anyone who shares your blood: siblings, grandparents, distant cousins. Deploy a proper visualization, and you can find your kin worldwide."

Diriem spread his hands. "If any other children of those eighteen survivors also lived, or cousins, then Maebe might lead us to them. She's descended from all eighteen, yes? We could limit the results to elven lines outside the Pactlands. On the other hand, I did tell her family I'd keep her safe..."

"I'll do it," I said, nodding emphatically. "In case there's anyone else out there like us. Let me help."

"Don't be hasty," Teolm murmured. "I've not taken it, but my understanding is that it is an incredibly painful experience. Have you used it?" he asked Diriem.

"No, nor have I administered it. Now, I can *procure* it—"

"Or we could bring in an expert," he suggested, folding his arms over his stained T-shirt. "I have someone in mind."

"Oh?"

"Kelra Epannae," he said without hesitation. "Finest mind in theoretical potions in the city. She's one of our best customers. Teaches upper-level potions, but the bulk of her work is outside the classroom."

Diriem slowly nodded. "We've met. She could certainly brew it, but she'd need assistance for a visualization."

"I assume you or I could manage that. But before we agree to anything, I want her to speak with Maebe. Full disclosure of risks...*if* she's willing to give that potion to someone so young."

"That's wise, but, uh...you know Kelra decently well?"

"We do make it a point to know our customers before we sell them toxic plants."

"Reassuring," Diriem said dryly. "Tell me, does she speak English?"

Teolm made a face. "Uh...that seems unlikely. Not something she would need, and she doesn't have an agency background."

"That's what I fear. So, new plan: Maebe takes a language potion, and we bring Kelra in after she's adjusted."

It didn't bolster my confidence to catch Jane and Rose wince at Diriem's suggestion. "Does that one hurt, too?" I asked.

"Not necessarily," said Rose. "It hits everyone a little differently. You might feel like you have the flu, or you might puke, or if you're me, you might pass out for a couple days. But about a week after you drink it, you'll have fluency in whatever languages you were trying to acquire. It's convenient once you get past the initial side effects."

"I've taken it plenty of times, and I'm still standing," Diriem added. "Very commonly used in the agencies. Rosie's right, it hits hard, but it would serve you well."

The four of them looked at me—Diriem encouragingly, the others with greater reservation—and I pushed down my fear. "Sure," I said, forcing a smile. "Sounds...great."

What the heck was I thinking?

I sat in one of Diriem's many guest rooms that afternoon, staring out the window at the lovely yard and trying not to panic. The room was gorgeous, stone walls, graceful wooden furniture, a big fireplace, and a television hung at just the right angle to be viewed from the wide bed—I'd tried out the mattress and almost succumbed to a nap then and there—but left alone with my thoughts, I couldn't enjoy my luxurious surroundings for the anxiety that left my stomach in an impossible knot.

Two days prior, I'd have said that magic potions were elements of children's stories, nothing more. The closest thing to magic I'd ever seen in a drink was how Alan's homebrew could mellow moods and send grown men staggering. Now, I'd agreed to try an honest-to-God potion, one almost guaranteed to leave me incapacitated for a time, so that I could then try another one with far worse effects.

This possibility hadn't even crossed my mind when I ran away from home. Scrounging for summer berries in the mountains wasn't fun, but at least I knew what those berries would do to me.

And in a few hours, I'd know what the first potion would do, too.

Teolm had returned to the capital to have a quiet word with his expert, while Diriem had followed shortly thereafter to stop by the office and pick up the language potion for me. With them out of the house, Rose had resumed her unofficial hostess duties, showing Jane and me to our adjoining rooms and checking that we were settling in. Jane had left me to unpack, explaining that she needed to spend some time with her computer to catch up on messages she'd missed, and after ensuring that I was okay on my own, Rose had likewise slipped off to work in her apartment. With the click of the latch had come silence, and in that quiet, my fears had come screaming to the fore.

Someone had left a bucket of ice in my room, and I poured a few cubes into a glass and filled it at the bathroom tap. Cold water on demand in June was nearly magical enough for me on its own, but I tried to focus on the chill in my hand and on my tongue to anchor my scattering thoughts.

I was scared, yes. Of the unknown, of what my future could hold, of what the potions I'd agreed to drink would do to me. Scared for my family and my community. If my parents and Connor were right and East Branch was doomed, that was bad enough, but what had *I* done to everyone by sharing our secrets? Had I exacerbated the problem and hastened our destruction, or was this to be our salvation? And even if our future was in the Pactlands, what would the move do to us? Could we stay together, or would we be separated? In my desire to explore, I'd never imagined a time that I couldn't return to East Branch and find it much as I'd left it, full of familiar faces and the old buildings that constituted our town. No, it wasn't fancy, but it was *home*.

Could we lose our home because of me?

I hadn't mean to set off this impossible chain of events, but now here I was, alone in an opulent room of a mansion set away in a world built by *magic*, and I had no clue what I was doing.

Maebe, you fool.

Was I selfish or just stupid?

Putting my drink on the stone window ledge, I walked into the bathroom and stared myself down in the mirror. Same face as always—brown eyes, messy brown hair, the scratch on my forehead still red but healing up—and the headband I'd carried since childhood in case strangers came to East Branch. I untied it and set it aside, freeing my pinned ears, which promptly bent and fell over. Running my fingers through my hair, I fussed with it until my ears were covered, hidden once again.

The girl in the glass could escape notice, couldn't she? If she stood still, if her hair didn't move, if she didn't open her mouth to reveal the depths of her ignorance...

I didn't want to be that girl.

Surely I was born to be more than a skulking thing hiding in the shadows.

I could do this. I could be brave, take whatever potions they threw at me, and help East Branch. I'd give this expert what she needed to look for others like me, and then...

Well, I'd just have to cross my fingers and hope they wanted to be found.

Somewhat calmer, I returned to the main room and considered my abandoned drink. As I watched the melting ice cubes bob near the top of the glass, I had an idea: since I had time, why not practice? Perhaps just being in the Pactlands would make my touch stronger.

I fished a fresh cube from the bucket and set it on the window ledge, then stepped back and stared it down. "All right," I whispered, willing my power to wake, "*lift*."

No luck.

Trying to remember how Diriem had made the book float—or heck, how Connor had opened the refrigerator—I focused harder and waved at the ice cube, coaxing it to rise. But beg and gesture as I might, the stubborn thing did nothing but melt until I managed to convince a gust of wind to slide it off the ledge. It shattered on the floor, but even those shards wouldn't cooperate.

Groaning, I flopped back onto the bed and closed my eyes. Five minutes of rest, I told myself, and then I'd flex my wimpy magical muscles again.

That was when I discovered that the truly magical facet of my guest room was the mattress, as I crashed and didn't move until Jane knocked to rouse me for dinner.

Ranarma, who was a conscientious soul, raided the pantry that night to ensure there would be something familiar to me on the table. What he came up with was a box of Easy Mac, which Rose had brought home after a shopping trip outside the Pactlands. His effort at providing comfort food was wasted, as I'd never tasted macaroni and cheese, instant or otherwise, but I didn't care—that yellow-orange goop was delicious, and I could have made myself sick off it if given the opportunity. The rest of the spread was more recognizable to me—a dish of cubed root vegetables, a salad, a bean medley, and two whole roast chickens—though the seasonings were strange to my palate. I tried to be polite and took only a taste of the chicken, which was a special-occasion food at home, but Jane caught on and heaped my plate.

Diriem had returned in time for dinner, as had Rose's fiancé, Yven, a slim man with neat blond hair who, fresh from the office, sported a pinstripe robe at the table. Rose, I supposed, had warned him, as he didn't seem surprised to find Jane and me there that night, nor did he ask me about my headband. Midway through the meal, I learned that he was the person responsible for the flowers all over their apartment, which launched an enthusiastic discussion—well, more like a lecture—about orchid cultivation. By the end of dinner, Yven seemed primed to drag me off to the greenhouse to check out all the flowers he couldn't fit in their living space, but Diriem intervened. "Let's see to your potion first," he told me, "and then, if you're feeling up to it, I'm sure Yven could give you the tour."

I went back to my room and slipped on my nightgown, trying to prepare myself, and Jane kept me company until Diriem knocked. He brought with him a small glass bottle nearly full of a purple-brown liquid, which he held up for my inspection before unstopping. "I would say this is the slightly off-putting part, but the taste is also pretty bad, so…bear with me," he said, then stared into the bottle for a moment before spitting into the potion and muttering.

The liquid began to glow bright pink, and as the glow traveled down the bottle, he explained, "The way this works is through a donor system, if you will. The donor calls to mind the language or languages to be transmitted, and what follows is the least disgusting way we've come up with of making the transfer. You don't want to drink blood," he added, grimacing.

"Still kind of gross," I pointed out.

"But a necessary evil. If all goes according to plan, you should come out of this with Pactish and Low Elvish, plus whatever I recall of High Elvish. If I'm not fully fluent, I'm very close, and this will allow you to read your own records," he said, nodding to the plastic box in the corner. "Ready?"

He handed me the potion, and I gave it a test sniff, which told me nothing. Tilting the bottle revealed the thickness of the liquid, close to fresh milk. "Um...you said something about the taste?"

Jane and Diriem traded glances, and she said, "It's a weird combination. Fishy, kind of reminds me of canned tuna, but with strong strawberry overtones. Best thing is to hold your nose and knock it back, and I've got a chaser right here," she added, cracking open a can of orange-flavored fizzy water. "Bottoms up."

I steeled myself, took a deep breath, then did as she suggested. The potion coated my tongue, and even with my nose pinched, I could tell I wouldn't like it. Once the last was down my throat, Jane switched the bottle for the can, and I hurriedly swigged before the full taste of the potion could make me retch it back up.

"Well," said Diriem as I sat in bed, chugging my drink to clear the traces of the goop, "you didn't pass out immediately, so you probably won't. That's...not necessarily great."

As I drained the can, I began to shiver, lightly at first, then so violently that my teeth chattered and my hands shook. "What's going on?" I asked as Jane took the empty can from me.

"This is normal," Diriem assured me. "Chills, fever, nausea...all potential effects. If I were you, I'd forego the orchid tour and try to sleep it off."

"I'll stay with Maebe," Jane declared, then shooed Diriem out the door and tucked me in. "Are you just cold?" she asked.

I wasn't *cold*—I felt like I'd been dropped naked into a snowbank—but I managed to reply, "Uh-huh."

"Okay, you're chilling. We can make this better." She dug in a closet in the bathroom and returned with extra blankets, which she piled over me, then turned her attention to the fireplace. I hadn't paid it much mind on arrival, it being June, but someone had left a neat pile of split logs on the clean grate, perhaps intended as decoration until the winter months. Jane mumbled and twitched her hand, and a fireball landed on the wood and slipped into the stack, quickly setting it ablaze. "There, now," she said, pulling a metal curtain across the front of the fireplace, and felt my forehead with the back of her hand. "You don't seem feverish yet, but that may change. Get some rest, hon. I'll be here if you need me."

She'd brought her computer, which she set up on the small table by the window, and as she quietly typed, I closed my eyes and trembled, and eventually fell into fitful sleep.

The fever came in the middle of the night, and after bobbing up and down in unpleasant dreams, I woke around dawn Wednesday and ran for the bathroom, having not thought to place a bucket beside my bed the night before. In a moment of panic, I wasn't sure what to hit—the tub, the sink, the toilet—and I settled on the last just before the building wave of nausea crashed.

"Oh, *hon*," Jane murmured, flipping on the bathroom light, which sent a stabbing pain through my eyes. Clutching the bowl, I felt her pull back my hair and quickly braid it, keeping it clear of my face while I waited out the spasms. She grabbed a glass of water to rinse the acid from my mouth, then handed me a cold washcloth to wipe off my face.

As I cleaned myself up, she sent a quick text, and her phone chimed shortly thereafter. A few minutes later, while I sat on the cool bathroom floor, willing my stomach to calm, Rose knocked and let herself in. "*Shit*, I'm sorry," she said upon catching sight of me curled up by the tub in my sweat-damp nightgown. "This should help."

She'd brought two bottles with her, a squat white one that rattled and a much larger bottle of thick pink liquid, which only served to remind me of how I'd gotten into this mess to begin with. Before I could ask questions, she opened the small bottle and shook out two small white things into her palm—pills, I guessed, having once seen their like in a bottle brought back from town. "This is just aspirin," she told me, crouching to hand me the pills and my refilled glass. "I bought it in Richmond. Swallow them whole—don't try to chew, they're bitter."

I choked down the pills, and she poured the pink liquid into a tiny plastic cup. "Pepto-Bismol," she explained. "Not the greatest tasting stuff, but it's far better than the potion, and it'll help settle your stomach."

Too tired to argue, I slugged back the medicine and finished my water, and Jane, who'd already turned the pillows to the cool side, shepherded me to bed.

"Is this supposed to happen?" I mumbled, letting her put another rag over my eyes.

"It's not uncommon," said Rose. "I slept through it, but not everyone gets lucky."

Lying there, I cursed my miserable fortune. With the chills, fever, nausea, and a low headache threatening deep in my skull, I'd never felt so sick in my life.

Eventually, I dozed again, then woke to the smell of buttered toast. The cloth over my eyes had fallen, and I could tell by the light that it was decently morning. Jane sat at the table by the window with a tray of food, which did *nothing* for me, though the sight of it didn't send me sprinting back to the bathroom. Not wanting to disturb her, I feigned sleep, then heard the faint sounds of ringing before Connor's distorted voice said, "Hey, Janie. Everything okay?"

"Hey," she replied wearily. "Well, *I'm* fine. Maebe's sick as a dog from a language potion, but she's sleeping it off, poor kid. Got some drugs in her a couple hours ago, so here's hoping she's through the worst of it."

"*Yikes.*"

"Yeah, it hit her hard. There's no way to know until you drink the damn thing, so…" The clink of ice cubes told me she'd paused for water. "How are *you*?"

"Well, funny you should ask," said Connor. "Tabitha came by last night and wouldn't take no for an answer."

"Ravished you?"

"Dragged me out for pizza, actually. I do know an amateur conspiracy when I see one, Firebug," he added. "But thanks. It was nice of her."

"Tabitha's a good egg." Jane sighed. "I love you, Con, and I hope you know that. Just worried about you, that's all."

Connor hesitated before speaking, and when he did, his voice was soft. "I'm so sorry, Janie. I…I knew East Branch was close, and I should have been more upfront about it, but the fucking jokes—"

"*Stop.* It's all right."

"I should have been honest—"

"You can't help it, and I understand why you'd play down, you know…the *closeness.* The good news for us," she said, brightening, "is that I can now guarantee there's no overlap in our families. Absolutely none of your kissing cousins ever kissed mine."

Connor didn't answer that.

"You there?" Jane asked.

"Do you still want to be with me?" he asked. "Knowing all of…this?"

"*Con.*"

"If you don't, I totally understand—"

"Hear me: I love you," she insisted. "I don't give a damn *what* you are, whether you have a tail you've been hiding, how many extra fingers you may have had removed—"

"None. I've got the newborn pictures to prove it."

"Okay. And speaking of which, I don't care what your ears used to look like. Honestly," she said, a teasing note sliding into her voice, "the flop's kind of cute. Like a German shepherd puppy."

Connor snorted his incredulous laughter. "Did you…are you really comparing me to *Sam*?"

"He's a very good boy. Excellent K-9. Credit to the Whitford PD."

"True…"

"But honestly, I much prefer the chief."

"Oh, do you, now?"

As the two of them chatted and quietly laughed, I drifted off, still queasy, though my fever seemed to have subsided. At least my cousin and Jane were having a good morning.

CHAPTER 12

I dozed in and out all day Wednesday, taking sips of water and swallowing whatever pills Jane put in front of me. My fever surged that evening but finally retreated overnight, and by Thursday morning, I was feeling confident enough in my stomach's constitution to leave the room. True, I did so in Jane's bathrobe, with her walking by my side in case I should stumble, but we made it to the kitchen around seven. An early riser, Ranarma was already making bread, but he offered to put it aside and fix me something to eat. Jane said that wouldn't be necessary and slipped into the pantry to poke around.

Soon, she had a pot of chicken broth simmering and was chopping dried pasta into little pieces. "Should I ask?" quipped Ranarma, who was streaked with flour up both arms and across his apron.

"Pastina," she replied.

He frowned, then said something unintelligible. Obviously, the potion hadn't worked yet on me.

"Pastina," she repeated more slowly. "Italian chicken noodle soup. I'm going to need an egg, and what's your cheese situation like? Any parmesan?"

Ranarma sneaked curious glances as Jane cooked, muttering at the pot when it didn't cooperate to her satisfaction. Finally, she put a brimming bowl on the counter, where I'd perched on a stool to watch. "I learned this recipe online," she said, handing me a spoon. "Cures what ails you."

While I suspected that was an exaggeration, I took a

taste…and then, as my empty stomach recalled what food felt like and my tastebuds awoke, I shoveled down the hot soup. It was a little thinner than oatmeal, but creamy and salty and cheesy, and Jane chuckled and refilled my bowl when I came up for air. "Pace yourself," she said. "If you can keep that down, I'm happy to make more."

Ranarma sampled the leftovers and seemed pleasantly surprised. "Not bad. And this is…medicinal?"

"I mean, it's good for the soul," Jane replied. "If you want the recipe, I've saved it."

"Please." Pointing to a green binder tucked into a corner beneath a cabinet, he said, "I'll add it to the collection. Surprise Miss Rose, eh?"

"She'd probably like it. May I see what you've got?"

He handed over the binder, and as Jane opened it beside me, I saw that it was half full of copies of recipes in English—some handwritten, others perhaps pulled from books, considering the neat print. Jane flipped through while I ate and Ranarma got his bread into the oven, and then she said, "Going to let you in on a secret, all right?"

The cook perked. "What's that?"

"Rose *really* appreciates that you've been trying to make familiar recipes. The last thing she wants to do is hurt your feelings."

He tensed. "But?"

"But…gelatin salads had their heyday, like, sixty years ago. Want to put some fruit in one? Sure, but anything calling for vegetables or, like, *meat*…no."

"She always eats some…"

"Because she appreciates the effort," said Jane. "It's so sweet of you. But if it's all right, I'll have a look through this and pull out a few Jell-O dishes that you might consider skipping."

Fortunately, he didn't seem offended, and he looked over Jane's shoulder as she removed pages. "You know," he murmured, "I was wondering why humans liked seafood salad in gelatin."

"They don't, generally."

"So, the cookbooks lied?"

"The cookbooks are artifacts of their time, and some foods have just fallen out of favor. *Far* out of favor."

As the two of them discussed Ranarma's foreign recipe collection, I glanced at the refrigerator across the kitchen, recalling the ease with which Connor had commanded it. I'd been in bed for the better part of a day and a half—surely I was rested enough to open the door. Though I'd left Jane's wand in Ragged Gap, I picked up my butter knife as a substitute, aimed it at the appliance, and began trying to subtly flick my hand, hoping for magic.

Eventually, my gesticulations grew big enough that the others noticed, and Ranarma cleared his throat. "Uh...Maebe, what are you doing?"

"Nothing," I mumbled, my face burning as I put the knife on the counter.

Jane patted my back. "Give it time, hon. No one learns to cast overnight."

Easy for her to say. Jane made magic look as simple as walking, and even Rose, who'd known nothing of magic at my age, could accomplish wonders. I'd been wrangling my talent all my life, so why would it not work with me?

And if it didn't strengthen, would I be allowed to stay there?

Connor called again that night, at which time Jane broke the news that she wouldn't be home that weekend. "Maebe's still convalescing, and I need to be here," she explained. "Promise I'll make it up to you."

He didn't seem too upset, but I felt guilty at the news. When Jane ended the call, I said, "Go home—I'll be okay. They're not going to beat me when you're gone, right?"

"Negative. I'm not leaving you alone," she said, straightening my extra blankets.

"I feel much better," I insisted.

"Great. And you're still barely more than a kid, so someone needs to look out for you." With my bedding adjusted to her satisfaction, she tucked me in and flipped off the lamp on the nightstand. "Yell if you need anything. I'll be next door."

Though I was feeling considerably closer to normal, I woke late on Friday morning, tangled in a nest of linens, and spent a terrifying three seconds trying to figure out where the hell I was before my brain woke enough to remind me. Thus, I was washing my face at the bathroom sink when Jane knocked and entered, phone in hand. "For you," she said, passing me the device.

Frowning, I took it from her and held it to my ear, nudging the floppy bit out of the way with the top of the phone. "Uh...hello?"

"*Maebe!*" came a voice I'd have known anywhere.

"Mom!" I leaned against the counter, surprised and thrilled to hear her. "How did you find me?" There was only one phone at East Branch, a big, black cell phone about as old as I was that stayed plugged into a generator at the meeting house. Grandpa used it sometimes when he was setting up horse trades, but the rest of us knew it was there for emergencies—you dialed the three numbers taped onto the generator for reference, and the law would come, at least in theory. I'd never seen it used.

"Connor came by this morning with a new phone for us," Mom told me. "A *tiny* little thing. You can save numbers in this one, so he's added his for emergencies and Jane's so we can reach you."

From the way Jane grinned at me, I suspected she'd been in on this plan.

"How're you feeling, baby?" Mom asked. "Connor said you'd been sick..."

"*So* much better," I said, trying not to sound like I'd just crawled out of bed. My parents would have been horrified by my laziness. "People have been nice, and we're going to look for other communities like East Branch, in case there are more people like us hiding out there."

"Is that safe? If you go walking up—"

"I think it's all done from here with magic, but I'll be careful," I assured her. "I'm fine right now—and you should *see* Diriem's house. It's like a palace."

"Is that where you're staying?"

"For right now, but this isn't a permanent thing. With any luck, I'll be in school soon, so I don't know if I'd live there or somewhere else."

Mom softly sighed. "I'm sorry, Maebe. You know we did the best we could, don't you? It was good enough for our parents, and for us, and we thought it'd be good enough for you, but—"

"It's okay, Mom."

"No, it isn't." She struggled for a moment, then said, "East Branch has survived this long because it's *safe*. I know the outside has tools and luxuries that we can't touch, but we've been safe. That's what we wanted for you kids, and what our parents wanted for us, and their parents…it's not a perfect place, but it's been enough, you know?"

Mom had never been quite so frank with me, and I wondered what she must have been thinking about since my quick visit back.

"But I know it's not enough anymore," she continued. "I see Connor when he visits, and he's so *comfortable* with the outside, and…and I want that for you, Maebe. I do. I want you to have a sturdy home and ample food and the kind of life that makes you happy. I want love for you," she said with a hitch in her voice. "You know your daddy and I love you to pieces, but you're just about grown, and you should have a family of your own, and I…I don't know if you'd ever find that at home."

She sniffled into her phone, and I gripped Jane's as my throat tightened.

"So, if there's another place for you and the other kids, another *safe* place, then that's what you should have," said

Mom. "Now, I still don't know about that fellow Connor brought out with you, but Connor vouches for Jane, and I'm going to trust him."

"Jane's been taking care of me," I told her. "Honest."

"Good. That's good." Again, Mom paused as she sought her words, then said, "I'm sorry we didn't get you fixed like Connor was. Might have been easier for you. *Would* have been easier," she amended.

"Mom—"

"Tom and Debbie came back and told us it was a pretty simple operation, since Connor was so little. But they looked normal, and so the doctors outside thought Connor was a freak case. We talked about it as a community and decided we couldn't risk it. If I'd brought you in, with the same issue myself—"

"People would have asked questions," I finished. "It's okay, Mom. There's a guy here, *distant* cousin, but he says he's got jewelry that can let me change my appearance. Better than a headband on a hot day, right?"

"Do you trust him?"

"I see no reason not to. Diriem told him about us, and he's going to try to help." Conscious that Jane was standing by, I wrapped up the conversation. "Got to go, Mom, but I'll call, all right? Or you could call," I suggested, and Jane nodded. "Jane doesn't mind."

"We love you," she said. "Please be safe."

Jane showed me how to hang up, and I retrieved my discarded facecloth as she put the phone in her pocket. "Thank you."

"Of course. Con sent me their number, too, so you can call your folks whenever you like. Once things settle a bit, we'll get you your own phone," she added. "Don't ask me how cell service works in the Pactlands—the answer is probably 'magic,' and I don't pry."

I grinned as I scrubbed my face. "Now that they can call you, I bet my parents won't give you any peace."

"Eh, I'm used to it." Leaning against the long counter

beside me, she said, "Let me tell you about my first semester of college and the come-to-Jesus talk I had with my dad about calling me before eight on the weekends. Parents get nervous, but most of them learn eventually."

Diriem came home that evening in good spirits and smiled to see me loitering in the kitchen. "All better, Maebe?" he asked.

I shot him a thumbs-up. "Fever's gone, and so are the chills, but I don't think the potion's working yet."

"Hasn't been long enough. Patience, youngling." Nodding to Ranarma, he opened a small refrigerator under one counter that I hadn't noticed, which was loaded with tall bottles. Selecting one, he pulled a glass down and uncorked the bottle, then poured out the pale yellow liquid. "Wine?" he offered, tilting the bottle toward me. "Just grapes and yeast, nothing fancy."

"Thank you, but I'd better not," I replied, having already had my fill of strange drinks that week.

"As you like." He drank, grunted to himself, and recorked the bottle. "Ah, Jane, good evening," he said as she wandered in. "You should hear this as well. I've got promising news about East Branch."

"What's that?" I asked eagerly.

"Nothing firm quite yet, but moving in the right directions. Teolm and I met with our Forum representatives today to feel them out concerning the matter."

Jane, who'd grabbed a glass and was about to help herself to the wine, paused. "And?"

"They're shocked and beyond curious," said Diriem. "We've never anticipated a situation like this. They're eager to meet you," he added, glancing at me, "but they concurred with us that it would be best to wait until we've looked for other survivors before taking action."

"So...no school yet?" I mumbled.

"Give it time," he replied, not unkindly. "Once your

language potion is working, we'll start the process in earnest. I promise you," he said, then turned and sniffed the air. "Ranarma, what are we having?"

"Fajitas, sir," he said, pronouncing the word slowly. "I was going to wait on the meat until everyone's home, if that's all right…"

"Hm." Diriem seemed surprised, but pleasantly so. "We had the proper spices?"

"We have the internet and a list of substitutions," said Jane, holding up her phone. "But more or less, yes. I make no guarantees as to the salsa."

Having never had fajitas or salsa, I was no judge, but the kitchen did smell good—and judging by the look on Rose's face when she walked in a few minutes later, Ranarma had done well. "Oh, my God," she said, grinning, "*Mexican* night?"

I looked at Ranarma in time to catch the glance he shot Jane, who waggled her eyebrows and smirked in satisfaction.

Saturday was another lazy day around the mansion. I explored the grounds—beautiful lawns dotted with the occasional snarled plant that might have been a hip-high tree—and then I made the mistake of asking Yven about his flowers.

I'd never known anyone who loved plants as much as that man treasured his orchids. Skipping the apartment pots so as not to disturb Rose while she painted, he took me into the greenhouse and walked me through his massive collection. No two orchids were alike, and Yven knew the stats on each—common name, scientific name, origin, peculiarities. When Jane cut his lecture short around noon, I could barely recall what I'd seen, but I'd learned that orchids were a pain under ideal circumstances, which the Pactlands were not.

Since I still couldn't speak Pactish and Teolm hadn't

brought the promised necklace yet, Jane drove the two of us out to Green Lake, a nature park with trails, cabins, and boating. Headband firmly tied in place, I walked with her through the woods, which seemed fairly similar to those of home but for the relative flatness of the place. "I come out here during the week," she told me, "especially now that the days are so long. Nice break from Beukal. Green Lake's pretty, but it doesn't feel quite *right*, know what I mean?"

"It's not really wild, is it?" I replied.

"You feel it, too?"

We stepped aside, allowing a pair of jogging sorcerers to pass, then continued down the trail. "This place is like the farm zones—it's *heavily* anchored to the outside world with magic. That's the only way they can grow more than grass. The woods here look fine, I guess, and this is a popular park, but having grown up with real woods...to me, it's like there's a wrong note in the chord. Maybe a little sharp or flat, close but not quite."

"You're right," I said, "it's not perfect, but...it does remind me of home."

We walked on for a time, me stewing in my thoughts, until Jane asked, "Homesick, hon?"

"Kind of, I think. I've never really had a chance to be homesick before," I added, weakly laughing, "so that's one more thing to figure out."

"Hey." She stopped and pulled me to the side of the trail, where a well-placed boulder made for a natural seat. "It's fine. Feel what you're feeling, Maebe. You're entitled to."

I nibbled my lip as I sat and contemplated the trees. "It makes me sad, you know? They were outside with real mountains and forests and all, and they gave it up because it wasn't safe."

"Yeah." She wrapped her arms around her knees and pulled them in close. "My great-great-grandfather helped build this place."

"Green Lake?"

"The Pactlands. Diriem knew him back in the day. He was a pyromancer like me," she said, creating a spark at her fingertips that she just as quickly extinguished. "Born into a village of sorcerers, and they were so scared of him that they kicked him out when he was a teenager."

"But…if they were all sorcerers…"

She sighed. "Pyromancy is what's known as a wild talent. All sorcerers can cast, and most can work with fire, but I can do it so much more easily than your average sorcerer can. A well-trained pyromancer is pretty much on a level with a fire nymph, and that can be intimidating."

"What's a nymph?"

"They have power, but it only goes in one direction. Fire nymphs can manipulate fire, water nymphs can work with water, et cetera. That expert Teolm knows, the one he thinks can search for more East Branches? She's a nymph."

"You've met her?" I asked, surprised.

"No, but I've learned about nymphic naming conventions, and hers is obvious. I looked her up—she's an air nymph. Not the most common elemental alignment, but I bet it has its uses. Anyway, what I was going to say is that after my great-great-grandfather got tossed out, he moved into a human village and used his talent to protect them. Folks liked him, apparently, until they got a new priest in town who said he was evil, and so he lost his home for a second time."

"Why didn't his friends stand up for him?"

"Oh, hon," said Jane, and patted my arm. "Spend a few weeks in a world history class, and you'll see the kind of atrocities people have committed in the name of whatever god they follow. It's an *old* pattern. Like, during the witch-hunting days, if the community thought someone was a witch, they might haul her in, torture her for a confession, and then search her body for strange marks. An oversized mole could be deemed evidence against her."

"*Huh?*"

Jane smirked. "*Clearly*, that's where she suckles her familiar. Crazy in retrospect, but people died horribly."

If something as insignificant as a mole could lead to that, it was no wonder why East Branch had kept to itself. "I wish folks could just get along," I mumbled. "That we could be safe out there."

She nodded. "But don't go thinking everyone outside is horrible, eh? There are good and bad people everywhere." She paused, then said, "So, um...my dad is my *adopted* dad."

"Oh?" I'd never known anyone who was adopted— had my parents died when I was young, I'd have simply moved in with my grandparents. "Did something happen to your folks?" I asked, then froze as I realized how potentially loaded that question was. "I...that is, you don't have to tell me—"

"It's fine. I never knew my bio-parents—they had me outside the Pactlands, and they died when I was young, so no one in my extended family had a clue." She stretched her legs and rolled her shoulders. "Now that my mother's family knows I exist, they've been delightful—I've got aunts and uncles, grandparents, *great*-grandparents, a whole mess of cousins and kin like Canna. Then there's my bio-dad's father, who killed most of his children and came after me."

"You, uh...you mentioned something about that..."

"Yeah," said Jane, who sounded far too unbothered. "He's a real piece of work. Basically drained his family members' lives with a potion. My grandmother killed herself, my father ran, and had I not shown up here when I did, dear old Grandpa would be siphoning from his last daughter right now." She shook her head. "Like I said, there's good and bad here and elsewhere, and there are plenty of shitty sorcerers and decent humans. Neither group has a monopoly on assholery."

She stood and brushed off her pants, and we started on

again. For June, the day was remarkably pleasant, sunny and warm without drenching me in sweat, and in the shade of the trees, it was almost cool. We'd only made it a few yards before my curiosity got the best of me. "What happened to your aunt?"

"Who?"

"Your grandfather's daughter, the one he was attacking…"

"*Ah*." Jane chuckled. "Xila. Sorry, it's weird thinking of her like that. She's my half aunt, technically, and she's only about your age."

"So…more fun that way?"

"I wouldn't go that far." She picked a leaf off a low-hanging branch and twirled it in her fingers as we walked. "Four months ago, she had a pretty decent life—her father was a Forum rep, lots of money, whatever she wanted. Then we exposed her father in front of the whole Forum, and he was convicted and shipped off for what will inevitably be a life sentence, so now she's down to one parent, her dad's a proven murderer, and she's got to live with the fact that he was coming after her. I mean, that has to mess you up in all sorts of ways."

My parents' protectiveness suddenly didn't seem quite so onerous.

"I wasn't sure if she'd want to get to know me, seeing what I did to her father, but she's interested. We've been taking things slowly. Get together every couple of weeks, send messages and stuff. She's a nice kid, it's just…awkward."

"Sounds like it," I murmured. "Hey, Jane?"

"Yeah?"

"*Is* this a safe place?"

She stopped and cocked her head, then let the leaf flutter to the ground. "That depends on what you want to be safe from, I suppose."

I asked Jane to test me at breakfast on Sunday and was disappointed to find that I still couldn't understand anything more than English. "The potion *will* work," she assured me as I slumped in my chair. "There's nothing you can do to rush it, hon."

While I trusted that she was telling me the truth, I felt guilty nonetheless. I'd been staying at Diriem's since Tuesday, and I hadn't done so much as a single chore. He hadn't asked it of me, and when I'd offered to help Ranarma, he'd demurred and sent me on my way, which left me at a loss. In East Branch, if you spent the night at someone's house, you were expected to help out while you were there—cooking, drawing water, feeding chickens, sweeping, whatever was asked of you. That was part of being a good guest, and all of us kids had that lesson drilled into us via parental admonition to not embarrass them. If my parents knew I'd been lazing around all week, going for drives with Jane and begging my touch to work when left on my own, they'd have been appalled at my manners...but as far as I could tell, no one seemed offended. Jane hadn't exactly been scrubbing floors, and I'd gathered that the other people in the house besides Diriem, Rose, and Yven were paid to be on the premises. From stories, I'd learned that there could be folks outside of East Branch wealthy enough to have a staff to cook and clean for them, but I'd never anticipated *meeting* anyone like that.

Rose had just joined us with a cup of coffee and toast when Diriem popped into the dining room—and unlike the three of us, he was already dressed for the day. "Maebe, excellent. No plans this morning, I hope?"

I shook my head, and Jane said, "None yet. Why?"

"Because you should have a visitor around ten." Glancing at Jane, he explained, "I quietly mentioned the situation to Mirrik, and he thought Sage would love to see someone from home, so if that's all right..."

Jane seemed agreeable, so I didn't fuss. As Diriem left

us for his home office, Jane smiled and sipped her tea. "I haven't seen that kid in a couple of weeks," she said. "She's *shooting* up."

"This is the girl you found in Whitford?" I asked. "The one who's, um…"

"Half centaur, yes. Sage Voln. She'll almost certainly be masked, so don't mention it unless she brings it up. Her father's one of the sorcerer Forum reps, so if he's bringing her here today, I bet he'll support whatever Diriem and Teolm are cooking up. And Sage is a sweetheart," Jane added. "Don't worry."

Easy for her to say. I finished breakfast and made myself presentable, taking care that my headband looked neat and as normal as possible, and I'd joined Jane to wait in a sitting room near the entrance when the doorbell rang. Jane led the way, and as Scel opened the door, a skinny girl with long black hair and big green eyes slipped past him, beaming. "*Jane!*" she cried, and ran to hug her.

As Jane gave her a squeeze in greeting, I briefly studied her. Sage was a few inches shorter than me, only a bit above five feet tall, and all limbs. Her bare legs were pale below her shorts, but when she pulled back from Jane, I saw the dull red of a healing sunburn on her face and neck. When she noticed me, her smile widened. "Hi!" she said, her accent deeply—reassuringly—familiar. "Are you Maebe?"

"You must be Sage."

"*So* nice to meet you!"

A much taller, dark-haired man in khakis had followed her inside, and Jane extended her hand and spoke to him in Pactish, or so I presumed. As they conversed, Sage drew closer to me, her eyes crinkling. "Dad said you're from Whitford, too."

"Uh…nearby," I replied, hoping it wouldn't be a letdown. "East Branch."

"Oh! Like Connor?"

"He's my cousin."

"Fantastic!" Lowering her voice, she said, "He and Jane are still...you know?"

I laughed at her expression. "*Yeah*. Look, um...I don't know much about Whitford or Ragged Gap. I only left home a few days before I came here—"

"Shoot, don't worry about that," Sage replied, flicking her hand. "Until I got with Jane, I never left the property where I lived. It's just nice to be able to talk like this." Cocking her head toward the others, she murmured, "Dad took a language potion for me, and he does his best, but pretty much all I hear is Pactish on the daily..."

As Diriem arrived to greet the newcomers and steal the representative away, I asked, "So, you grew up on a farm? You said property..."

"Eh, not really. It was a farm once, but not by the time I came along. Just the old house and some outbuildings."

"Oh. Do you miss it? I can't get used to how *flat* everything is around here..."

Sage made a face. "I mean, I used to live in a barn, so this is a *major* improvement, but yeah, the scenery's not as pretty as Whitford. Ask Jane to take you to the Edolis," she suggested. "The mountains are bigger than the ones at home, but they still don't have any great trees—"

"Wait—a *barn*?"

"Uh-huh," she replied, nodding. "The asshole who kept me there told me I was a demon and left me chained up in the barn when he didn't need me, so..." She shrugged. "Whitford's nice, but I don't miss it too much."

Before I could fully process that, Jane appeared. "Let's take this to a sitting room," she suggested, nudging our shoulders. "Ranarma's making cookies."

Once we were situated, I turned to Sage and started to apologize. "I didn't mean to bring up something bad—"

"It's fine," she told me, sounding unbothered. "Look, I've had some *weird* questions over the last months, so you're going to have to try hard if you want to shock me." Grinning, she continued, "Did Jane warn you that I was masked?"

"I mentioned it," said Jane. "And look at you, doing it all on your own! I'm proud of you, hon."

Even with her sunburn, Sage flushed with pleasure. "I've got your pendant safe, just in case. Still wear it some days."

Jane's brow furrowed. "Not confident yet?"

"No, I just love the necklace."

"Shucks, you don't have to wear that. Your dad could get you much nicer jewelry."

"But yours was my first," said Sage, "and it's pretty, so…" Turning to me, she asked, "You can mask, right?"

"Um…no," I mumbled. "Don't know how."

Undaunted, Sage replied, "Neither did I. It'll click for you once you get a tutor to explain. But here, want to see how it works?"

Before I could mention that I'd witnessed it from Diriem, she already had her sandals off. "I'm just going to do my feet," Sage explained. "Don't want to tear my shorts…"

In the blink of an eye, her feet had been replaced by dainty hooves, and dark hair crept up her ankle.

"Good control," Jane told her. "Nicely done."

She smiled, then wiggled one hoof back and forth for me. "See? And I'll put the mask back…" Just as quickly as they had disappeared, her feet returned, toes and all, and she slipped her shoes on again. "It doesn't hurt, I promise."

Thinking I should reciprocate, I untied my headband and showed her what I was working with. "This is the problem—"

"Oh, that's *nothing*," said Sage, dismissing it with a wave. "You'll figure that out in no time."

At least she hadn't recoiled, I mused, warming toward the chatty younger girl. "Jane said you're in school?"

She nodded emphatically. "Just finished my first term."

"How is it?"

Her face screwed up in thought. "Weird sometimes, but I like it," she declared. "I never went to school before I moved here, so it's a definite culture shock. And people stare because I'm a stranger to the kids my age, and everyone knows I'm in remedial tutoring. But I'm glad to finally be getting an education. And I get to play sports now—I never had other kids around in Whitford, so this is new. Working on making friends. I've got one, but she's in another year, so we don't see each other all the time."

"Who's that?" Jane asked.

"Her name's Keef. She was assigned to show me around at the beginning of the term. People have been avoiding her because her dad went to a prison farm, but she's been really nice to me—"

"Is that Fellora's little sister?" she interjected. "A ti'Mal?"

"Yeah! Do you know her?"

"Sure. Fell's a pyro at DOL, and I go over there for training." Frowning, she added, "She never said Keef's having a hard time…"

"I don't know what Keef tells her sister," said Sage. "And people aren't *mean*, not that I've seen, but they don't hang out with her much. Aside from the rowing team—she introduced me to them, and she's going to help me with tryouts this fall, now that I'm starting to bulk."

Jane laughed as Sage flexed one scrawny arm. "You are anything but bulky, my dear."

"Stronger," Sage protested.

"And taller, I see. Eating your dad out of house and home yet?"

She grinned. "Doing my best. Oh, I almost forgot! Let me show you what I learned…"

Sitting in my chair, I watched as Sage levitated objects around the room, calling them to herself and returning them to their places with barely a wobble, then changing the color of the warm cookies Ranarma brought in. She made it look effortless, and Jane praised her for how well she was doing without a wand.

There was a confidence in Sage's bearing that I'd lost of late, and I wanted that security—in my talent, in my path forward, in myself. But for that moment, I applauded her tricks and ate my snack, swept up in her enthusiasm but wondering if I'd ever master the feats she displayed.

CHAPTER 13

I was hanging out in the kitchen with Ranarma on Monday morning, getting a lesson in knife skills while Jane worked in her guest room, when the moment finally arrived.

"Very nice, good cut—*ah*, knuckle forward, you don't want to catch your fingers," he said, watching me as I tried to make even tomato slices. The cooking styles favored in East Branch were of the "roast it over a fire" and "throw it in a stew pot" varieties, and while I had the opportunity, I thought I might as well expand my skill set. Ranarma knew all sorts of fancy cuts, but before he'd teach me, he insisted on knife safety.

"Keep that thumb back, let it anchor...good, *good*. You're getting it." He waited until I finished, then traded the sliced tomato for a cucumber and said, "Try it again. Let your guiding hand help you—"

Rapid footsteps interrupted us, and we looked up as Scel swept into the room, immaculate as always. Sometimes, I wondered whether the house manager bothered to sleep. "Ranarma, have you done the shopping yet?" he asked. "If not, would you mind picking up a few items for me?"

"I was going after lunch. Sure, just give me your list," Ranarma replied.

Something struck me as odd about their conversation...and then it hit me.

Scel couldn't speak English.

"Say that again," I demanded, wheeling on Ranarma.

His face broke into a wide grin. "Hey, your potion

worked! Now, that accent's going to take some practice, but—"

"Was that Pactish?"

"Listen to yourself. You're speaking it."

I paused, struggling to process.

"I know it's strange," Ranarma said gently. "Sounds that shouldn't make sense suddenly do, am I right?"

Nodding seemed like an easier response than speaking at the moment.

"Give it a day or two, and it'll feel normal. Or we can keep doing this," he offered, slipping back into English. "It's no trouble."

Though my mind was spinning as I tried to navigate two languages at once, I managed to find the Pactish words for my response. "No...no, this is good. I should practice, right?"

"I'll leave you to it," said Scel, and nodded to his nephew. "Thank you, and you'll have the list after lunch."

Once he'd walked away, Ranarma grinned and gestured toward the cutting board. "All right," he said in what my brain was beginning to recognize as Pactish, "let's try this, but if you amputate a finger, we're switching languages."

Apparently, Jane passed the news to her boss during the day, as Diriem came home that evening and immediately tested me—not just in Pactish, with which I'd almost grown comfortable, but in Low and High Elvish as well. Understanding wasn't a problem for me, but producing a coherent response in the correct tongue took some doing, and I flustered myself as I reached for my new vocabulary and pulled up words from the wrong buckets.

"Don't be discouraged. A multi-language potion isn't easy, especially if you try to use them all simultaneously," he told me after I'd answered in the wrong variety of Elvish yet again. "The potion is still taking effect, and you'll have much better control in a few days. For now, listen."

He tapped his ear, then his temple. "It's all in there, but the connections are crystalizing. Speaking from experience, the best thing to do at this point is to listen and give your mind a moment to catch up before you try to answer."

I nodded glumly, and he flipped back to English, to my relief. "I told Teolm the good news. He'll bring his contact out around lunchtime—and that masking jewelry he promised you," he added with a little smile. "If all goes well, we may have the locations of other East Branches by this time tomorrow."

Diriem may have been pleased, but I barely slept a wink that night. I spent Tuesday morning holed up in my room, trying to make my touch work before the expert arrived and saw what a failure I was, but it remained as weak as ever. Jane interrupted me midmorning with a call from my parents, but I kept it brief and fibbed with a feigned lightness in my voice. Everything was fine, I assured them. I felt great. I was keeping out of trouble, absolutely. No siree, nothing to worry about here.

When I handed the phone back to Jane, she surprised me with a hug. "You don't *have* to do anything," she murmured, holding me tightly. "Not a blessed thing. If you don't like this person, if you're scared, just say no."

But what use would I be then? If I could find other descendants of survivors and give them a chance at a better life but chose not to bother looking because I was *scared*, then what would that say about me? What kind of person would stand back and do nothing in those circumstances?

What was a little pain compared to so much possible good?

Thus psyching myself up—or shaming myself into action—I managed to eat a few bites of lunch without being sick. Though I put on a brave face, I suspected Jane knew what I was doing, as she brought her computer down during the meal and worked beside me while I pushed the remains of my salad around my plate.

Finally, the doorbell rang.

I stiffened in my chair, and Jane patted my back. "It's going to be okay," she said, closing her computer. "I'm right here, hon."

Footsteps in the hallway heralded the newcomer, but the person Scel ushered into the dining room was hardly the one whom I'd expected.

"Canna?" asked Jane, going to her feet to greet her cousin. "What are you doing here?"

The healer had come wearing her purple coat, and she carried a large black bag over one shoulder. "I'm on standby," she said, and hugged Jane. "On loan for the day."

"Oh?"

"Mitigating the risk," said Diriem, appearing behind Scel.

Pactish, I recognized, silently pleased with my new-found ability.

"I'd prefer to have a healer on hand, just in case," he continued, "and since Ms. Nerin is already involved in this matter..." With a nod to Canna, he added, "Thank you for coming...*again*. I fear that Kabno suspects I'm trying to poach you."

Canna spread her arms. "If she does, she's said nothing to me, sir, but then I seldom have facetime with our director." Looking from him to us and back, she asked, "You said Maebe's taking a potion with some potential side effects?"

"That's correct."

"Not to be rude, but if you'd been a bit less vague, I could have tailored this," she said, patting her bag. "Want to tell me what's going on?"

When Diriem hesitated, Jane jumped in. "Ever heard of a bloodline potion?"

Canna's eyes widened, and she wheeled on Diriem. "I'm sorry, *what*? That's completely irresponsible!"

"We're trying to find other places like East Branch," I hastily explained. "Odds are good that they'd be my distant kin—"

"That potion is a nightmare concoction. Let me put it like this: part of my training involved taking all manner of potions to learn the physical effects. That's one our instructors wouldn't give us, not even if we volunteered."

My stomach knotted, and salad suddenly seemed like a poor choice. "Is it that painful?"

"Pain's only part of it. That stuff can do terrible internal damage. Do you like your heart in its current condition?"

"We have an expert on the way," Diriem interjected, "who will tell Maebe what she needs to know before she takes anything. But if she's willing, I thought it wise to have you here."

Canna's mouth tightened as she eyed him. "Is this prudence talking, or is it farsight? Because if you *know* you're about to injure that child—"

"I don't. I'm too close to events to see the path clearly. So...please?"

When Canna wavered, I said, "If there are other folks out there like me and my family, hiding...East Branch isn't great. I want something better for us all. Maybe running water, to start with."

She frowned at that. "You don't have running water?"

"Nope. We're, uh..."

"Off the grid," Jane volunteered. "No power, no water, and not much money."

"So, if there are other communities like ours, I need to find them," I told Canna. "I got lucky, and Jane stumbled into me. What are the odds of finding another group like that?"

"And what if there are no others?" Canna countered. "Do you have any reason to believe that East Branch isn't unique?"

"No," I admitted with a shrug, "but there's a *chance*, right? Shouldn't we look?"

Clearly, Canna wasn't happy about this plan, but she

sighed and muttered, "Fine. If the worst happens, I'll do what I can, but this scheme is completely against medical advice."

"Understood, and thank you," Diriem replied, but paused as the doorbell rang again. "And that must be Te-olm. Let's take this into another room."

He led us into one of the mansion's many sitting rooms, a parlor with large windows and a thick blue rug. Four cream-colored sofas sat around a low circular wood-en table large enough to seat eight for dinner. Someone— Ranarma, I assumed—had left a tray of glasses and a pitcher of fruit-infused water on a side table, and the light passing through the set cast little rainbows on the wood. I ran my hand along the back of one of the sofas as if the smoothness of the leather could calm my nerves.

A moment later, Scel showed Teolm and his compan-ion into the room, then saw himself out. Teolm had dressed for the occasion, replacing his stained T-shirt with a pale green shirt, dark trousers, and a sleeveless green robe. The woman with him had opted for more relaxed attire—an oversized pink blouse hanging loose over baggy white pants—but that wasn't what caught my eye. She was about six feet tall, a full head taller than Teolm, and so thin that she seemed almost emaciated. Her skin was pale blue, and though she seemed no older than Jane, her braided hair was as gray as her eyes. Her ears were long and point-ed—no amount of hair fluffing would have hidden them—and while she wore no jewelry, she sported a pair of glasses with thick purple frames and even thicker lenses.

"Hello, everyone," said Teolm. "This is Professor Epannae—"

"It's Kelra," the nymph interrupted, striding toward me. "Now...*this* is who you want to anchor a bloodline trace?" she asked, and lifted my chin with two fingers. "Heavens, Teolm, she's a *baby!*"

"I'm eighteen," I protested. "I'm an adult."

"Oh? By whose reckoning?"

"In Georgia, she's of age," Jane offered.

Turning her gaze on Jane, Kelra retorted, "And here, she has seven years to go. Seventeen to full majority. She can't even legally consent to take this potion," she continued, folding her thin arms. "It's not approved for children."

"*Thank you*," Canna muttered.

Kelra meant well, I suspected, but something in her attitude rubbed me the wrong way. "See here," I snapped, my hackles rising, "Diriem's got the damn thing, and I'm going to take it, one way or another. Now, are you going to help us?"

She blinked, her eyes large behind her glasses. "I was informed that this was still up for discussion."

"It's not," I replied, my anger making me brazen. "You've got no idea where I come from."

"Outside…"

"My family's house is barely insulated. None of that fancy stuff like electricity. I can't even point to"—I paused, unsure of the proper Pactish profanity, and settled for a momentary segue into English—"fucking Georgia on a map, and I've lived there all my life. We don't have enough money to pay our *taxes*, and only my cousin's generosity stands between us and homelessness. *That* is East Branch," I said, getting up in her face—or as close as I could come, given our height difference. "Diriem and Te-olm said they're going to try to get us something better. But what if we're not the only ones out there? What if there are other communities with hungry winters and barely any schooling and…*these*," I said, ripping off my headband.

Kelra flinched, but she peered at me with interest. "What—"

"It's a damn birth defect, and it's one reason why my community has been stuck in isolation. Kind of hard to pass for normal when you can do this," I said, giving my head a brisk shake to make my ears flap. "We were fortunate—we were found. If there are others like me, then I owe it to them to find them, too." I could feel myself flushing, but I crossed my arms and stared her down. "So, tell me what I need to know. Please."

The professor considered me for a long moment before asking, "Are you not afraid, child?"

"Of course I'm afraid. I just got over a language potion, and I understand this is going to be worse. But I can handle it."

Again, she studied me in silence, then sighed. "Brave, perhaps, but ignorant and foolish nonetheless. Still, if you're set on this course…" Glancing at Teolm, she said, "I'll guide you, but I'm *not* happy about this plan."

"Thank you, Kelra," he said. "If you'd like to—"

"Stop. We do this my way." To me, she said, "Sit, girl. What's your name, anyway?"

I took a seat on the nearest sofa, resisting the urge to bounce my leg. "Maebe."

"Maebe. Very well." Perching on the table in front of me, she squinted and leaned closer. "The potion is short-acting. You say you've had a language potion?"

I nodded.

"That's a permanent potion. This one will only act for a few hours if you don't take the antidote first. Once you drink it, it will take effect within a minute. At that time, I'll instruct them"—she pointed to Teolm and Diriem with two long fingers—"to activate a visualization spell. You will serve as the anchor, and the potion will seek anyone who shares your blood. The spell will reveal their locations. I understand you're partly human?"

"Yes."

"That shouldn't be a problem. The spell can be tailored to weed out purely human lines."

"Sounds easy enough," I said.

"In principle, but I haven't come to the complicating factor. The potion *hurts* once it's activated with the visualization spell. It can attack your body, particularly your heart."

"Yeah, that's what I've heard—"

"You don't understand," she interrupted. "This will be excruciating. I've taken it," she added, holding my gaze. "For research purposes. It felt like my blood was on fire."

Kelra's mouth twitched while I considered that. "For this to work, you'll need to withstand the pain," she continued. "The spell isn't instantaneous, and it will only function while the potion is active in you. Once you end it, that will be the limit of any data-gathering we do here." Turning back to Teolm, she asked, "You *do* have the antidote here, yes?"

"Of course," said Diriem, pulling two opaque glass bottles from an inner pocket of his robe.

"And a healer, I see," she said with a nod to Canna. "If we're doing this—and again, I strongly counsel against it—then give her the antidote and let her ready it."

The others looked at me, waiting for a decision.

It couldn't be *that* bad, I told myself. I was tough, a mountain girl who'd fallen and burned herself and been kicked by a cranky old horse—I could handle this as well.

"Let's do it," I said, and clenched my jaw to hide its tremor.

If Kelra was disappointed, she remained stoic. "First, the spell," she announced, and beckoned toward the elves as Diriem handed Canna one of the potion bottles. "Here are the parameters…"

Jane sat beside me and watched as they worked, creating a translucent sphere that floated over the coffee table. "Nymphs can't cast," she whispered in English. "That's why those two are in this."

"What about you?" I whispered back.

She snorted. "I'm decent, but they've got centuries of experience on me. Better for me to sit this one out."

"Watch and learn," said Diriem in English, breaking his concentration just long enough to flash a quick smirk at Jane.

"Yeah, yeah," she retorted, waving him off. "This one ain't on the syllabus yet."

Kelra frowned at them, then asked in Pactish, "Something I should know?"

"Having a word with my trainee," Diriem replied in kind. "Nothing to worry about."

"What language was that?"

"English."

Her eyes widened behind her glasses. "Your trainee is *human*?"

"Georgian," Jane corrected, "but a sorcerer. I was raised outside, too."

"That's Gerem Aniap's granddaughter," Teolm muttered as he focused on the spell. "Did you not catch the blowup at the Forum in February?"

Her expression remained bemused. "No, that's panic season for my senior advisees. Why, what happened?"

"Tell you later," he replied, his face dampening with sweat.

Soon, the sphere took on color and definition, turning into a patchwork of blues and greens and browns, and Jane again came to my aid. "That's a globe. The outside world."

"The issue is the level of detail," said Diriem, who by then had flushed and was sweating as badly as Teolm was. "This will only help if we can pinpoint hits, so bear with us…"

It took another five minutes before they stepped back and Kelra deemed their work sufficient. "Very well," she said, and motioned for me to rise. "Come stand between those couches, get close to the visualization. Last chance to back out," she added, softening. "We can stop this, youngling."

"I'm fine," I lied, and took the bottle from Diriem. "So…drink this now?"

"If our healer is prepared…" he replied.

Canna nodded. "Ready," she said, holding up a loaded

syringe with a wicked needle. "Maebe, just say the word, and I'll hit you with the antidote."

I didn't want that needle anywhere near me, but I forced a smile and thanked her as she came over to join me. Before I could lose my nerve, I uncapped the bottle, peeked at the dark green liquid within, and gulped it back.

To my relief, it didn't taste terrible—sort of like chocolate and pumpkin, weird but not unpleasant. I'd barely swallowed the last of it when I felt a flush rapidly rising over my skin, like I'd stepped into the laundry shed when the fire was high and the water steaming. "Is this supposed to happen?" I asked Kelra.

She glanced at my face. "Yes, that's expected. A few more seconds..."

I was just beginning to acclimate to the unusual heat when she said, "Activate."

Diriem's fingers twitched, and my world exploded in agony.

The next thing I knew, I was on my knees between two sofas, digging my fingers into the rug and trying not to scream. Kelra was absolutely right—it felt like my blood was boiling in my veins, and there was no relief, no way to cool it, no outlet...

But this was the only way, so I scrunched my eyes closed and tried to hold on. I could do this, I told myself, fighting the urge to surrender to the pain. I could endure it. Every nerve sang with the exquisite torment, but I was stronger. I was an East Branch girl, and we were made to be strong...

Somewhere above me, I heard Jane say, "We've got hits. That's East Branch, and that one...can you give me state borders?"

"New York City," said Diriem. "Look at the coastline. Any others?"

"No," came Teolm's voice a few seconds later. "Just the pair."

I opened my eyes a crack to see the three of them clustered around the projected globe. Looking through it, I could make out two bright points of white light, but I didn't have the strength to waste on trying to comprehend what I was seeing.

"Can you zoom in or something?" asked Jane. "There's millions of people in New York. We need more."

Teolm gestured at the projection, and I saw the colors change for only an instant before the intensifying pain made me close my eyes again. The light hurt too much on top of everything else, but that left me alone in the dark with my burning body. Concentrating on my shaky breathing and on the feel of the carpet fibers beneath my fingertips, I tried to throw my mind elsewhere, like my grandma had told me to do when I dislocated my shoulder as a kid and had to have it popped back into place. If I could just distract myself...

"Closer."

The pain spiked again, ripping a cry from me, though I tried to bite it back. I was burning alive. Surely, if I could have opened my eyes, I'd have seen flames.

"We need more detail," came Jane's voice again. "I know this sounds ridiculous, but the population density is so high...this is a needle in a haystack."

"They can't go closer," Kelra snapped. "Narrowing the focus hurts her more. *Look* at her. She—"

"Do it," I muttered from behind gritted teeth. "Find them."

"Maebe, hon—" Jane began.

"*Do it, goddamn it!*" I screamed, and wailed anew.

After a pause, I heard Diriem: "We can make this quick, in and out. Jane, be ready."

I had time for a single breath before the pain doubled, trebled, pushing me far beyond the limits of my fragile control. I shrieked and buried my forehead against the rug, soaking the carpet with tears, and felt my heart pounding against my ribs like I'd run up a mountain.

Was I dying? Could I die of pain alone?

Above the unceasing, inhuman sounds coming from my throat, Jane called, "Got it! Landmarks, photos…any chance of street names?"

"*No*," said Canna.

Despite its size, I didn't feel the needle when she shot me in the arm. All I felt was a sudden coolness like winter runoff in a swollen stream, which flooded through my burning flesh and quenched the fire. The pain abated, receding like storm clouds over the hills, until I was left kneeling where I'd landed, a wet, snotty mess, hoarse from screaming and shaking as if I'd spent the night naked in a snowbank.

"It's all right, baby," Canna soothed, wrapping her arm around my back. "Can you stand for me? Let's get you to a sofa."

Leaning on her, I managed to find my feet, but I only staggered two steps before vomiting all over the rug.

Probably shouldn't have eaten lunch was my last thought before I passed out.

When I came to, I felt smooth leather beneath me, and my eyes were covered with a cold cloth. Groaning, I started to sit up, but a hand pressed me back down.

"Slowly," said Canna. "You fainted, dear."

She helped me ease myself upright as I removed the wet cloth, and I glanced at the place where I'd been…and, I recalled, where I'd regurgitated everything I'd eaten that day. The rug appeared unblemished, however, and when I caught Diriem's eye, he winked.

With the globe gone, Kelra sat on the table in front of me and waited as I clutched my spinning head. "That was impressive," she murmured. "*Foolish*, but impressive. How did you last so long? Painkiller in advance?"

I shook my head, then instantly regretted it and mumbled, "No. Just…toughed it out."

Teolm whistled softly, but before anyone could press

me for details, Canna swooped in again. "Maebe's on bedrest until tomorrow, understood? I'm going to start her on painkillers, and I'll be back in the morning to check her out. Where's her room?"

"Southern wing," said Jane. "I'll help you get her upstairs—"

"Wait," I said, "did we find them? The other group?"

"We've got plenty of pictures to work with," Jane replied, patting my shoulder. "Just need to compare notes with some labeled maps. You let us get down to a single block."

"So…what's the next step?" asked Teolm, rubbing the back of his neck. "Scour a map and go spying? Rosie can't look without a person to focus on, can she?"

"Precisely," said Diriem. "I suppose we could set up surveillance…"

"*Or*," said Jane, helping me off the sofa, "we could try the better option."

Diriem's brow furrowed. "Which is?"

"Call Annie. She was a private eye—if we need to look at deeds or whatnot, surely she'll have ideas."

He considered that, then sighed. "Much as it pains me to ask for intelligence assistance from DPP, I think you're right."

"And that's why you hired me," she said with a grin. "Come on, Maebe, let's get you to bed—"

"If I may," said Kelra, "since she doesn't seem steady on her feet…"

I gasped as a gust of wind swept me off the ground, cradling me about a yard above the floor. "What—"

"Air nymphs aren't the flashiest," she said, walking beside me as I floated along, "but we do have our skills. Now, could someone please guide me?"

"Just a moment," called Teolm, and jogged around the furniture to join us. "Here, Maebe," he said, putting a small cloth bag in my hand. "That's a masking pendant. Pinch it between two fingers and your thumb…"

But I was already on my way out again. Exhausted and cushioned on air, I mumbled my thanks and was asleep before I hit my bed.

CHAPTER 14

The sky beyond my windows was still glowing when I awoke, but the light had shifted much closer to sundown, and Jane was sitting at the table with a big tray of covered dishes. "Hey, sweetheart," she said as I cracked my gummy eyelids. "How're you feeling?"

I thought about that, taking stock of my body. While I was still in pain, it was a dull all-over ache, glowing embers compared to the afternoon's inferno. "Like I rolled down a mountain and hit every rock on the way," I croaked. "Is there any water?"

"Sure." She filled a glass at the bathroom tap and brought it to me, and I gulped at it until the ice cubes chilled my lips.

"Did everyone leave?" I asked.

"Teolm took Kelra back to the city. Annie's on her way out here," Jane replied, brushing my hair from my forehead. "Canna went home, but she's a phone call away, and she left you enough potions to get through the night. Want another?"

"What potions?" I asked warily.

"Painkillers. She injected you with one before she left so you'd sleep, but she said you'd probably want more to be comfortable. Here, I'll get it."

She returned from the bathroom carrying two small bottles, one full of a thin, pale green liquid, and the other with a burgundy brew. "This is good stuff," she reassured me, sitting on the side of my bed as she handed me the green one. "Tastes great, as potions go. It's not as strong as the prescription drugs back home, but it's a hell of a lot more effective than popping aspirin. Give it a try."

I opened the bottle and sniffed, but all I smelled was faint vanilla. Bracing myself for the worst, I took a sip…then relaxed. The potion tasted like vanilla and honey, sweet and warm, and I eagerly finished the bottle.

"We're going to keep those going down," Jane told me. "If your pain worsens, she left a sedative, too."

"What's that one?" I asked, glancing at the burgundy potion.

"This is a healing potion. Canna wants you to take one today and one first thing in the morning. We don't know what, if anything, the bloodline potion did to you, so just in case there's damage, this will help. Won't hurt you either way," she assured me.

Like the painkiller, the healing potion wasn't gross— vanilla and cinnamon, I thought, with a surprise lime aftertaste—and I took my medicine without complaint.

"Want some dinner?" Jane offered, nodding to the table. "Ranarma just brought it up for us."

Though I didn't trust my stomach, I crawled out of bed and slumped in a chair at the table while Jane uncovered the plates and bowls. Bless that man, he'd tried: a heaping helping of Easy Mac, several scoops of ice cream, even strawberry Jell-O cubes. Then I saw that he'd used Jane's pastina recipe and went for the soup, which, to my relief, seemed to settle.

As I scraped the bottom of the bowl, Jane said, "Teolm left a masking pendant for you. Want me to show you how it works?"

Eagerly, I followed her into the bathroom and leaned against the counter below the wide mirror while she fastened a gold chain around my neck. A tiny pendant hung from the delicate necklace, a little circle the size of my pinkie nail engraved with a curling *M*.

"Looks like he means for you to keep this one," she said, smiling as I admired the necklace—I'd never had anything so fancy. "This will be easy—you don't have to have any talent at all to make masking jewelry work. He said you put two fingers on top of the pendant and your thumb behind…yeah, just like that," she said as I moved my hand into place. "Hold on lightly and imagine what you want to change."

I eyed her reflection uncertainly.

"I'll show you. Be right back…"

She returned with her phone and pulled up a picture of Connor. "Okay, starting at the top. My hair needs to shorten and darken…"

As I watched, her shoulder-length blonde hair turned brown…well, the part that didn't vanish altogether. Her eyes and Connor's were about the same shade of brown, but the shape was slightly different, and his eyelashes were thicker. Her skin took on olive undertones, and the large mole near Connor's left temple popped into place as her triple ear piercings closed and the lobes attached to the sides of her head. Jane studied his picture again, comparing it with her reflection, then muttered, "*Aha*," and thinned her lips. Her chin rounded as a bristly five o'clock shadow sprouted—Connor always shaved, but he couldn't hide his stubble—and an Adam's apple popped out in her neck.

"I could make myself appear to be his size," said the ersatz version of my cousin with Jane's voice, "but this is enough, right?"

"That's *so* freaky."

"Tell me about it." In a blink, Connor's face was gone, and Jane flashed a thumbs-up in the mirror. "Now, I can do that on my own, and you *should* be able to do it eventually, but for now, let the pendant do the heavy lifting. Just imagine what you want to see. Take it one piece at a time. Ever wondered what you'd look like with green eyes, say? Or a shaved head?"

That might have been fun, and I intended to play later, but at that moment, there was only one thing I wanted to see.

Make them normal, I silently told the necklace.

Suddenly, my flopped-over ears were gone, replaced by a pair that looked much like Jane's, rounded and upright. I laughed aloud and reached up, assuming I'd feel my real ears, but the illusion worked on me as well. For all I could tell, what I saw in the mirror was what was actually attached to my skull.

"Ta-dah!" said Jane. "It's that easy."

"How...where did they go..."

"They're still there," she assured me, "just hiding. Hold the pendant and concentrate, and the mask will fall off."

Again, I followed her directions, and my ears returned almost as quickly as I could formulate the thought.

"It's easier to take the mask off than to put it on, but this will be second nature for you pretty soon," she said as I swiveled my head back and forth, checking for changes. "Want to do me a favor?"

"Sure."

"Mask again, but don't change the shape of your ears— just make them straighten."

With a moment's thought, they obeyed, and I chuckled as I tucked my hair behind them. "So, that's what they're supposed to look like, huh?"

"A little smaller than your typical elf ears, but they're not bad. They're *also* not bad as they actually are," she said, giving me a quick side hug. "Frankly, it's just a bunch of cartilage. But do whatever makes you feel best."

Briefly, I considered returning to the rounded version—the ears that looked like Connor's, that didn't have to be hidden if I walked around outside of East Branch. But for the moment, I decided to keep the ones I was wearing, the effect I'd only been able to achieve to that point by pinching the tips and pulling them against gravity.

As I examined my modified reflection, someone knocked at the door, and Jane opened it. "Hey!" she exclaimed—in English, I noted, and assumed it was Rose in the hall. But when I poked my head out of the bathroom, I found that Rose hadn't come alone. Standing there with her was a brunette who seemed to be about their age. I thought she was another sorcerer until I noticed her slightly pointed, albeit pierced, ears and amber eyes, which appeared to glow from the shadows as the bathroom light hit them.

"Okay, *why* am I the last to get the East Branch update?" the stranger groused, but hugged Jane. "Honest to God, people, this is why we have a freaking group chat. And you must be Maebe!" she said, noticing me as I skulked in the doorway. "Hi, I'm Annie. Not going to touch you—I bet you're sore—but nice to meet you."

Jane admitted them and closed the door, then gestured toward our dinner leavings and the available seating. "Make yourselves comfortable. And Annie, it was nothing personal. We've kind of been playing this close to the vest—"

"Yeah, yeah." She settled onto the loveseat against the wall and spread her hands. "Hit me. I hear you need a PI."

"Um," I began, venturing out of the bathroom, "sorry, who are you with?"

Annie grinned. "Professionally, DPP. I married into the Wild Hunt...it's complicated," she said, catching my confusion. "*Ancient* magic. My husband is...well, kind of like the current avatar of this cycle of predation and prey, I guess, but I can try to explain it better later. Anyway, I used to run in Rose's circles back in Richmond," she said with a nod to the redhead, "so I'm also complicated, you might say. But I was trained as a private investigator before I moved here, so let's hear it. What's going on?"

Rose gestured toward Jane, who took the lead. "You heard that Maebe anchored a bloodline potion?" she asked Annie.

"I got the short version. That's not one we typically play with in Interdiction..."

"Nor do we. Kid's a beast," she said with approval. "She hung on long enough for us to get the location of another possible East Branch."

Annie's eyebrows rose. "A second community?"

"That's what it looks like. And since that was the only other hit for her, we need to investigate. The problem is that these people are in New York."

"State?" she asked hopefully.

"City."

"*Fuck.* All right, what do you have?"

Jane opened her computer and put it on the edge of the bed, and the four of us clustered around. "I took these while Diriem and Teolm were trying to narrow in," she said, flipping through some photos of the globe visualization. See the glowing dot? That's our target."

"Any idea of a borough?" Annie asked.

"Not confirmed. This is as close as they could get," she said, turning to the final picture. "But I've been doing some cross-checking this afternoon, and I think I've found the location." Splitting the view on her screen, she pulled up a map with street names. "See how the roads converge? And those two aren't quite parallel?"

"Yeah, I see it," Annie mumbled, looking from the picture to the map. "Zoom out. Where are we?"

Jane pulled back to reveal the wider area. "Manhattan."

"*Manhattan*? And this...that's Wall Street running right there, and those are hotels," she said, tapping the screen. "That's the Financial District."

"Know much about it?" Rose asked.

"No, but I had a runaway who hid in the Village for a few weeks, and I got better acquainted with Manhattan. There *are* residential areas in the Financial District, but it's largely business. Maybe they're in condos or something."

"Hopefully not living in the subway or the sewers," Jane muttered.

"Let's assume they're above ground for now. I'll do some digging tonight, see what's in the buildings in this block," said Annie, pointing to the glowing dot in the photo. "Shouldn't be incredibly complicated. Send me your stuff," she told Jane, rising from her seat, "and y'all tell Diriem I'll come by in the morning with my findings."

As Rose was escorting her out, she glanced at me and smiled. "See you got your necklace."

"Necklace?" asked Annie as I nodded.

"A masking pendant from Teolm."

"Oh!" Reaching under her shirt, she pulled out a silver disc on a chain. "Twinsies, then. Play around with it—you can do some *wild* tricks with masking."

Experimentation would have to wait, however, as Jane ordered me back to bed once they'd left. "You can watch TV," she offered, "or there's a nice library here, but you need to *rest*, Maebe."

I wanted to complain, to tell Jane I was grown and she wasn't my mother, but honestly, she was right. Full, weary, and magically doped, I crawled back into bed with my new necklace and drifted off, wondering about my distant cousins in faraway New York...wherever that was.

I took a fresh painkilling potion in the morning and managed to make myself presentable for breakfast. Rose and Yven had left for work by the time I got downstairs, but Diriem remained, dressed and sipping coffee while he read on his computer. "And how are we feeling?" he asked as I pulled up a chair.

"Better. Still kind of sore."

"I'm not surprised. Canna should be here in half an hour or so..." He paused, then chuckled. "You're getting the hang of the pendant, I see."

"Jane helped me," I said, reaching for the basket of toast.

"She's quite good at masking jewelry, especially given her age. Have you seen her today?"

"She said she got a text—"

The doorbell rang, and Diriem grunted. "That would be Annie. You know, it's funny," he murmured, putting his computer aside. "She's almost always polite and knocks, but unless I arm the defenses on the house, she can let herself in. Ever heard of teleportation?"

"No, sir."

"It's a power unique to the Wild Hunt, as far as I know. They simply envision the place they want to be, and there they are."

"That's pretty neat," I said as I buttered my toast.

"It's useful, I'll grant you that. But you know how I fare in the back of the car? It's worse when Annie's in control."

Before he had time to get into the details, Jane swept in with Annie, whose puffy eyes suggested she hadn't seen sleep all night. "Hey," she grunted, lifting a hand in greeting as she headed for the table. "Do me a favor and make my excuses with my director, will you?"

"I've already informed Pateme that you're indisposed," said Diriem, glancing toward the kitchen door as Ranarma poked his head in. "And good morning. Coffee?"

"Oh, my God, *yes*."

As she unpacked, Ranarma returned with a large mug topped with milk froth. "Latte, double shot, and foam to be fancy," he announced, sliding it in front of her. "How's that to start?"

She took a sip and smiled gratefully up at him. "You're *good*, man."

"There's plenty more if you need it," he said, and slid the toast basket toward her. "Hungry?"

"No food until I'm sure the caffeine's in my bloodstream, but thanks."

In short order, Annie had her computer open and several folders of papers stacked neatly on the table before her. "All right," she said between sips of coffee, "I did a little snooping last night. The good news—or maybe the strange news—is that none of the buildings in your target block are condos. We're not dealing with a residential area, which means that all of Maebe's New York cousins are working in the same building."

"If they're not mole people," Jane muttered.

"Yes, *if.* I haven't ruled that out yet, but that's not something I can confirm with deeds. Anyway, we have five buildings in the block. Number one is the biggest, and it's going to be a doozy because of the mixed tenancy. You've got a bodega at street level, and then you've got thirty floors of office space and one spectacularly overpriced gym. Here's what I can find about the tenants," she said, passing Diriem the fattest of the folders.

He opened it and riffled through the pages. "Thorough work for one night."

"Not my first rodeo, but thanks."

"What about the other four?" he asked, putting that folder aside.

Annie groaned. "One is a hotel, but it's very expensive and not an extended-stay sort of place, so either Maebe's kin are all in housekeeping or that's not the one you want." She slid the next folder toward him, then opened the third. "This one's half empty. Big tenant moved out a few weeks ago, so we've got fewer leads in here. Number four is my *absolute* favorite because it's empty and about to be renovated."

"They could be squatting in there," said Jane.

"Possibly, but I visited last night to check it out, and it was dead inside. Which brings me to number five," she said, opening the final folder. "Smallest of the bunch, and an old building, but there's a lot of money in this one. It's owned and entirely occupied by a brokerage firm—not one of the big players, kind of niche, but wealthy. I hadn't heard of it, so I poked around...ah, here we go. Rush and Sons."

Jane shrugged. "No clue, but I don't exactly have a portfolio."

"Well, I figure this one should be easy to rule out," said Annie. "I printed a good chunk of their website. Obviously, this doesn't show many of the employees, but here's the

C-suite. The CEO's actually pretty young..." She shuffled through the papers and pulled one. "Here we go. Irving Rush the sixth. Looking at the firm history, he's the latest in a line of—"

Diriem's palm slammed on the paper as if trying to pin it to the table, and he jumped out of his seat to look closer.

"Uh...you okay, there?" asked Annie, startled.

Even I could tell the answer to that was *no*—the blood was draining from his face, his breathing had quickened, and he was staring at the picture like he'd seen a ghost.

Jane rose to view the image. "What's wrong? Do you know that guy or something?"

He nodded, his gray eyes wide with disbelief. "That...*that* is Ivari ti'Ammaas."

"Are you sure?"

"He had my parents murdered. That's not a face I'd easily forget...and he's barely masked," Diriem murmured, his gaze fixed on the clean-cut man in the charcoal suit. "Used to be blond, but it's like he's not even *trying* to hide."

"I don't understand," I said, looking between Diriem and the other two women. "Mary Amos said the elvaniri walked off that winter to save their families, didn't she?"

Diriem nodded. "Perhaps she was mistaken. That's Ivari, I'd stake my life on it."

"But he's not an Amos," I pointed out.

"Listen to the words. *Ti'Ammaas*. It's High Elvish."

Of rushes.

"Rush," I mumbled, and scooted past Annie to see the picture for myself.

Ivari looked human enough: ordinary features, a healthy tan, rounded ears that most certainly didn't flop over. His dark brown hair, barely graying at the temples, was thick and neatly styled with a side part, and his eyes, greenish brown, almost seemed to twinkle. He had dimples, which took a few years off his face, but he seemed to be about my parents' age, maybe forty or so. His slim-cut suit jacket hugged his shoulders like a glove, and he wore a crisp white shirt and deep blue necktie beneath it.

"Who else works there?" Diriem asked Annie.

She laid out a few more pages, which featured smaller pictures of men and women. "These are the execs on the website…"

He bent over them and scanned the text. "Farrah Grassley, that's Farral ti'Pul. I know her face. Paul Sand…probably Paril ti'Tola, just going by his name, and Cammie Sand, that's his sister, Cammir. Now *that* one is familiar: Kevin Knight. Caven ti'Elta, absolutely."

Ti'Pul, of grass. Ti'Tola, of sand. Ti'Elta, of night…

"Maebe, you didn't find another East Branch," said Diriem, who sounded almost dazed. "You found your *ancestors*."

"And if they're running a brokerage firm in Manhattan, they're probably loaded," Annie added. "That building is worth millions."

As she said that, a thought flashed in my mind—an alternative way forward. "If we can't stay here, or if folks in East Branch don't want to leave…do you think he could help us? If he's rich…"

"I mean, the *firm* is wealthy, but he's probably not hurting," said Annie. "I can do a title search on the C-suite, but assuming we're dealing with a group of people who have to periodically reinvent themselves when they get too old, I bet they're using shell companies. This could be a mess to untangle."

I tried to put the pieces together into a form that made sense. Mary had written that her father and the other elves had left to keep their community from starving…but maybe they'd found help out there in the wilds of Georgia. Someone could have taken them in, fed them, given them shelter…but then why hadn't they returned? Did they believe the worst had befallen East Branch? Bad information?

Surely that had to be the case, I told myself. So, if I

could get to this Ivari—my...eighth great-grandfather? I was still fuzzy on the family tree—and tell him that East Branch needed help, wouldn't he come running? If Diriem's suspicions about our intermarriage were accurate, then it could be that *everyone* in the community was his descendant. He'd help his family—why wouldn't he? That way, even if Diriem and Teolm couldn't get us into the Pactlands, we might be able to pay our taxes and repair our trucks. If we could get masking jewelry for everyone with the flop, then the little kids, at least, could go to school...

He could save us. I just had to find him and make our case.

"Can we go see him?" I asked, tapping the picture of Ivari. "I...I understand that you don't like him," I said as Diriem looked at me, "and I'm not trying to hurt your feelings or anything, but could you drop me off? Let me talk to him?"

"My feelings have nothing to do with this," he replied, "and I, too, would like a word with our mysterious Mr. Rush. But walking in right now wouldn't be the wisest course of action." Glancing at the other papers, he said, "I don't recognize all of these faces. Some may simply be masked, but I'd prefer to have a southerner take a look. Annie, is there any chance you could procure an employee directory?"

"Uh...I'll see what I can do," she told him. "And if you want *southerners*..."

"Someone from the southern kingdom," he clarified, briefly smirking at her. "A person who might have known the survivors before the Pact."

She grimaced. "How many five-hundred-year-old elves are walking around, especially from the southern Halls? You've got ti'Vir...oh, ti'Grell..."

"There are very few of us left, period," he murmured, "and you're forgetting ti'Cren."

"Teolm predates the Pact? I knew he was old, but—"

"No, he was born here. I remember the party."

Annie hissed through her teeth. "Are you thinking…"

"Unfortunately, yes. If anyone here knew the southern aristocracy, it's Inade. He came of age long enough before the Pact to have been socially active. Didn't inherit the Hall until the seventeenth century, but he'd have known the major players in the south."

By then, Jane appeared to have caught on, as her expression mirrored Annie's. "You really think he'll talk to you?"

"Sorry," I interrupted, "who's Inade?"

Diriem's mouth tightened into a grim line. "Inade ti'Cren. Teolm's father, former lord of the Hall…and another of your distant cousins. Gifted floramancer, talented jeweler, and murderous drug baron. We couldn't pin him for decades, but thanks to Rosie, he's spending the next three centuries on a penal farm. Oh, there's no great love lost there," he added as my face scrunched. "He'd have killed her if given the opportunity, so I doubt she's losing sleep over his fate."

"Again," said Jane, "do you think he'll talk?"

He snorted. "To me? Not for nothing—he loathes me. But I may be able to bribe him. Annie, if you could look for names, pictures, anything from the firm, I'd appreciate it. Whatever you can find, regardless of age," he said, and headed for the door.

"Going somewhere?" she asked.

His smile seemed more predatory than pleased. "My office. I believe a quiet word with Laws is in order."

CHAPTER 15

I didn't know car brands. Our two trucks at East Branch were sturdy but nothing fancy, a Ford and a Chevy, both older than me and held together with home welding, rope, and prayer. Jane's Ford truck was a newer model, still not particularly shiny but produced in the last two decades, while Connor's personal vehicle was something called a Hyundai, which I couldn't have begun to spell at the time.

Diriem thought we needed a comfortable vehicle for the drive that afternoon, something conservative but roomy enough for four, so he opted for the Mercedes he'd driven to Ragged Gap.

"Ah, yes," Jane teased as she saw us off, "the perfect car for a prison outing. Will you need a chauffeur?"

"I'll be driving, *thank you*," Diriem muttered, and shot her a scowl that earned a cheeky smile.

Teolm, who'd arrived wearing a dark purple robe and seemed far more subdued than usual, grunted. "It's not like we'll be driving it up to his dormitory. There's a shuttle on the grounds."

I felt bad for him. Though I knew little of the circumstances that had landed his father in prison, I imagined it couldn't be pleasant to see him locked away. Sure, Diriem had said the elder ti'Cren had done horrible things, but still, that was Teolm's *dad*.

I wasn't sure how I felt about going to a prison. I knew what they were—at least back home—and I'd never had any great desire to see them for myself. But I was in this mess too deeply to sit back, and though Diriem had suggested I could stay behind and get the report later, I'd declined. He didn't argue with me, for which I was grateful. I was still sore from the bloodline potion, even with painkillers, and Canna had only reluctantly cleared me for the outing after her morning visit—given my state, if Diriem had tried to persuade me to stay at the mansion, I might have caved. But perhaps my performance the day before had shifted something, and if he still didn't see me as a full-fledged adult, maybe I no longer seemed like such a completely helpless kid.

The fourth member of our group wasn't Jane, as I'd anticipated, but rather a white-haired woman the size of a little girl. Though her face seemed young, there was a shrewdness in her pale blue eyes that suggested she was much older, and she carried herself as if she were the biggest person in the room. This was, I'd been told, Kabno Erenani, the director of the Division of Laws. Per Jane, folks underestimated her at their peril. She was a gnome, Jane had hastily explained, not talented in magic but phenomenally strong and fast. Unlike the men, she'd opted for a black T-shirt and loose trousers, eschewing a robe and any trappings of formal attire. When Diriem had made the mistake of commenting on her wardrobe, she'd snapped, "It's a penal farm. If you're wise, you'll wear something that will let you run in case of emergency."

Not owning a robe myself, I felt better about my casual clothes as I slid into the back seat of the sedan with Kabno.

She was pleasant company on the drive, curious about my background and East Branch but polite. "I can't believe you *missed* them," she said, leaning toward the front seats. "How have you not seen that there are elves out there?"

"You know, I'm not actually omniscient," Diriem replied, slowing into a turn.

The penal farm was located several miles from a town called Cavimet, which Diriem told me was close to Wichita before he recalled that I had no sense of geography. Cavimet was tiny, and there was no direct portal access to Beukal, so we had to go through several sets before arriving in the district. On either side of the road rolled wide fields green with summer produce, and I was surprised to see a neat apple orchard before Kabno explained that this was all farmland, anchored to the outside world with complex magic that allowed their crops to flourish. "We have three penal farms, all in agricultural districts," she told me. "Most people convicted of crimes serve their sentences in places like Cavimet, where they can give back to the community they've wronged."

"How?" I asked.

"Farm labor. The facilities grow food sent to institutions across the Pactlands—schools, hospitals, and such. Now, that's not to say the only thing our inmates do is manual labor," she continued. "We have classes, both in the facilities and by correspondence, we offer handcraft workshops, and of course, there's therapy. Mandatory, and plenty of it."

"The point," Diriem added, "is for a person's first stint in custody to also be his last."

After a few minutes more, I saw the air in the distance shimmer like a heat mirage in August—strange, as the Pactlands was fairly cool for summer. "What's that?" I asked, pointing to the anomaly.

"That," said Kabno, "is our destination. Cavimet Farm."

"Is that a barrier spell? Like at DOI?"

She chuckled. "Correct. That's the boundary fence, my dear. Much simpler to maintain a few spells than to deal with a wall."

The road ran along the boundary for a time, and then Diriem turned off onto a narrower access road. At the border of the fence sat a small building about half the size of my family home, and a sorcerer in a black shirt and pants stepped out as Diriem stopped the car. "Afternoon," she said as he rolled down the window. "If I could see some...*oh*! Uh, Director ti'Dana?"

"Good afternoon," he replied, and thumbed one hand over his shoulder. "The lady in charge is behind me."

Kabno lowered her window and nodded to the guard, who straightened to attention. "Here for a visit, Sergeant," she said. "The superintendent is expecting us."

"Yes, ma'am. Certainly. Right away," the guard replied, and retreated to the building. A few seconds later, the shimmering barrier vanished over the road, giving us passage onto the grounds.

"Thank you!" Kabno called as Diriem slowly drove through, then raised her window and shook her head. "Honestly, I've ruined more younglings' days..."

"You didn't yell at her," said Teolm.

"No, but tell me, is a surprise visit from the boss *ever* fun?"

He snorted. "Point taken."

As we drove through the fields toward the central complex of buildings, I spotted people of all descriptions working around us: driving machinery, carrying spray cannisters, weeding. They all wore brown, and most sported hats with long flaps over the back of the neck as protection from the cloudless sky. Pop-up tents were placed at intervals between fields, where black-uniformed guards sat with water. No one was armed, as far as I could tell, which gave me pause.

"How do you keep the prisoners in here?" I asked Kabno.

She gestured behind us at the boundary fence. "Permeable to gas and water, but that's about it. Also, if you touch it, you'll get a nasty shock. No successful escapes yet."

"But you've got sorcerers and elves and all here, right? How do you keep them from breaking the spells?"

"It's called a dampening potion," she replied. "Temporarily decreases talent. They can't cast, and nymphs lose their elemental abilities. It's not perfect—it won't stop a naga from secreting lust pheromones, and it can't mute a siren—but it addresses the most pressing threat."

"And...they all take it?" I asked incredulously.

Kabno smirked. "Not willingly. It's given in long-lasting injections, and believe me, those are *carefully* scheduled."

We parked in a small, nearly empty lot a distance from the buildings, and we'd barely exited the car when a door-less vehicle—in retrospect, having seen them, I'd compare it to an extended golf cart—drove up beside us. "Good afternoon, ma'am," the nymph behind the wheel said to Kabno, then nodded to Diriem. "Sir. The superintendent says the visiting room is ready if you'd like to proceed there directly."

"Thank you," said Kabno, hoisting herself into the front seat beside the guard. "That would be ideal. No disrespect to your superintendent, but this is not a social visit."

The guard grinned. "She thought you'd say that, ma'am, and she sends her regards."

The rest of us climbed aboard—Diriem slid onto the middle of the first bench and braced himself—and our driver bumped over a packed-dirt pathway around the complex.

The best word I could use to describe the place was *institutional*. Aside from the central building, which was three stories tall, and the barns in the distance, everything was single-level and made of the same gray stone. Several buildings sat in a neat row with grassy strips between them and guards stationed at the doors—the dormitories, perhaps, since their signs only bore single letters. A cluster of larger buildings set apart had signs for classrooms and medical facilities. An even bigger one was marked as the dining hall. As we drove past, the trio of brown-clothed inmates snapping beans on a patio outside the back doors barely looked up.

Our driver brought us through the winding paths to the

central building, then parked and ushered us inside. Down a hallway, past some offices, and around a corner, we came to a door marked Visitation, outside which a sorcerer sat with a computer. He stood when he saw Kabno approaching and nodded to the rest of us. "Ma'am. He's waiting inside. Would you like security?"

"That won't be necessary, Officer," she replied with a tight smile, then swept past him and pushed open the door.

The visitation room wasn't exactly homey, a white-tiled windowless space large enough for half a dozen round tables and a few scattered chairs. The only inmate in the room was an elf, who sat with his elbows propped on his table, studying the door. Sporting the sort of tan only acquired from long hours in the fields, he wore his limp brown hair in a low ponytail, and he didn't appear to have shaved for a week. His thick eyebrows drew together when he saw us, and he lowered his arms to cross them, one hand covering a hairy birthmark on the other forearm.

"Teolm," he said with a quick glance at his son, then stared at Diriem and slipped into Low Elvish. "What the fuck do you want?"

"Good afternoon, Inade," said Diriem, pulling out the chair opposite him, and put a folder on the table. "You're looking well."

"Go jump in a fire, whore-get."

"Lovely to see you, too." Switching back to Pactish, Diriem said, "I'll be brief: I'm looking for information, and I believe you may be the easiest source."

"Me?" said Inade, following his linguistic lead, and laughed incredulously. "Why would I help you?"

"Because I'm willing to barter for it."

Diriem said nothing while the rest of us sat, letting Inade stew. Finally, Inade asked, "And what's on offer?"

"Here's the deal. I've brought pictures and names with me," he said, patting the folder. "If you look through them and tell us whether you recognize anyone, then Director

Erenani has agreed to take five years off your sentence."

Inade's gaze shifted toward Kabno, who nodded curtly. "A small request, really," she said. "I'm sure he could get the information he seeks elsewhere. But Director ti'Dana thought you might be knowledgeable and asked me to cut a deal if you cooperate."

His dark eyes narrowed as he considered the proposal. "Counteroffer. You wouldn't have come to me if you had an easier source of information," he said to Diriem, "Five years, plus twenty-four hours with my wife."

"Oh, please," Teolm scoffed, "since when have you given a damn about Mother?"

"I've had two years to think," his father replied. "To reflect on certain matters. And...truth be told, I miss her," he said quietly. "Liventi and I won't be permitted communication for another three years," he continued, looking at Kabno. "Give me a day with her and five years off my sentence, and you'll have whatever answers I can provide."

She mulled that over. "What if Ms. ti'Tam is unwilling to see you?"

"Don't force her. But if she *is* willing..."

"Very well. Five years off, and if Ms. ti'Tam is interested, I'll arrange for her to be brought here for a twenty-four-hour period. The regulations concerning intimacy will still apply."

The corner of Inade's mouth twitched. "I sincerely doubt that will present a problem. Very well, you have a deal," he said, and turned his attention back to Diriem. "Show me."

Diriem opened the folder, which was stuffed with Annie's frantic findings from that morning. She'd set up camp at the dining room table and worked until lunchtime, searching and printing, then packed up when Teolm arrived, announced she was going home to crash, and simply vanished. But she'd done good work, and her few printouts from the night before had been joined by photos from charity events, news stories, and something called

LinkedIn.

"Do you recognize this man?" Diriem asked, sliding the topmost photo across the table to Inade.

He reached forward to take it, frowning, then jerked in shock. "Is that…that *cannot* be…"

"Look at the name. Irving Rush…the sixth. He's been remaking himself for a while. Head of a financial firm."

Visibly stunned, Inade shook his head. "That's either Lord ti'Ammaas or someone who knew him well enough to mask as him. But he's been dead for *centuries*, hasn't he?"

Diriem grunted. "Perhaps not."

A flash of amusement crossed Inade's face as he looked up from the photo. "You don't know?"

"I'm assessing."

"Wait, now, let me be sure I understand: Diriem ti'Dana was *wrong*?" he asked, his voice thick with sarcasm. "All that talk of destruction if we didn't sign the Pact, and…what, a misunderstanding? An unclear vision? Perhaps we're more nearsighted than farsighted?"

He waited for a break in Inade's jabs, then murmured, "It appears there were eighteen survivors from the south. Total."

Inade's mouth snapped shut.

"In the last week, we've found records revealing their fate…to a point. Ivari and the others made their way to England, intermarried with a human community, and brought their half-blooded children to Georgia. Do you know where—"

"I'm aware of the region. What are these records?"

"One of Ivari's daughters wrote an account of their community's founding, and the descendants of that group still live together and keep that book. Here are the rest of the photos," he said, passing Inade the folder. "Anyone you know?"

Inade sat in silence for a few moments while he leafed through the printouts, pausing occasionally to look more closely at pictures. "I can't swear to most of these," he finally said, "either because they're masked too heavily or because I don't remember them that well, but I've got some likely identifications."

"Who?" asked Diriem.

"Farral ti'Pul—she hasn't masked much," he replied, going through the pages. "And these are probably two of the ti'Tola siblings, Paril and Cammir. There were four of them, as I recall, but I only see the pair here. Anna Marin—that's Anvali ti'Merin. She's aged herself, but the name's a giveaway. Caven ti'Elta," he said, tapping the next picture. "Michael Salt…that's *probably* Mima ti'Gol, but I'm not entirely convinced." After another pass through the stack, he grunted. "Eighteen, you said?"

"I did."

"Obviously, there are more here than that," said Inade, passing Annie's hastily compiled list of employees back to him. "I don't recognize every name or face, so either those eighteen have procreated and grown creative with their masking or else the firm has hired humans to fill out their ranks. Now, how the hell did you find them?"

Diriem gestured toward me. "This is Maebe Amos—"

"*Amos?*"

He nodded. "She's descended from all of the eighteen survivors, but her grandfather is Ivari's heir. Maebe's third in line."

Inade studied me for a second, and then his laughter burst forth. "*Her?* You're telling me *that* is what's become of mighty Hall ti'Ammaas? A damn half-breed?"

"Technically, she's closer to three-quarters elven, but that's not important. She took a bloodline potion, and that's how we found Ivari and his people."

He wiped his eyes as his fit of mirth passed. "Barely looks the part. Her features are human, and those ears…indeterminate, aren't they? Turn your head, girl."

Gritting my teeth, I obliged.

"Undersized. If that's Ivari's line…pathetic."

I was grateful that I'd masked, as I suspected Inade's

commentary would have been no kinder had he seen my ears as they truly were.

"Appearances really aren't everything," said Diriem, sliding the papers back into their folder. "I mean, Maebe looks more elven than Rose does."

Inade's mood soured immediately. "That girl is a disgrace, and you're a fool for sullying your Hall with her."

The corner of Diriem's mouth curled into a smile. "She's at DPP now, or had you heard? They finally have their own farseer on staff. Your brother-in-law is exceedingly pleased with her progress."

"That sniveling bureaucrat is nothing of *mine*," he snapped.

"He seldom has cause to mention your relationship, so I believe the feeling is mutual," Kabno quipped.

Inade glared at her, then turned his attention back to Diriem. "So, what now? You plan to reach out to Ivari, welcome him in, act the hero again? As per usual?"

"You know, Inade," he deadpanned, "aside from dismantling your criminal enterprise, I've done nothing to earn your animosity."

"You and that brat—"

"Our great-granddaughter is an accomplished young woman, and you might have appreciated that had you…let me see, what's the phrase she uses…ah, pulled your head out of your ass."

"*Boys*," Kabno warned.

"She's walking proof of your idiot son's betrayal of *everything* this place stands for," Inade snapped, then muttered, "And my idiot son's as well. Yet you flaunt her. *Acknowledge* her. As if she were something to be proud of."

"Because she is," Diriem replied. "And incidentally, I've seen Fradin's work from his DPP days. He was no idiot. *Principled*, now, rather unlike his father—"

"He threw everything away and spat on my Hall, and for what? Some human bitch—"

"Fradin adored Miranda," said Teolm, interrupting his

father's rant. "And she loved him in return. Ask Liliol if you don't believe me."

Inade waved that away with a snort. "Love, *please.*"

"It's more than you and Mother ever had," he retorted. "My brother died young and poor, but he had something even you couldn't buy."

Ignoring him, Inade said to Diriem, "You haven't answered my question. What's your plan for Ivari?"

"That's yet to be determined. Thank you for your assistance," he said, taking the folder as he rose. "I'm satisfied, Kabno. Much appreciated."

"Is that truly all you wanted?" Inade asked, standing in turn. "That's five years' worth of information, is it?"

"Today, it is. But…" He paused, then cocked his head. "I do have one more question, if you'll humor me."

One of Inade's eyebrows rose.

"Satisfy my curiosity. I knew you wouldn't use the bloodline potion or a tracker to find Rose when she went on the run, but I still don't know *why*. What stopped you?"

He folded his arms. "Seeing as Pateme had his fingers all over that affair, I assumed a tracker would be useless."

"Mm. Yes, there are certainly potions that will block a tracker, but you didn't try."

"Was I mistaken?"

He chuckled. "Absolutely. She was wide open. But that's the tracker—why not the bloodline potion? It's far more difficult to block."

With a shrug, Inade replied, "That stuff is poison. Painful, damaging…frankly, I didn't think she was worth the trouble or expense. I assume you were hiding her and that damn agent, anyway."

"*Me?* No, I never spoke with her directly until the night before your trial."

Inade seemed taken aback. "Then where was she?"

"Maine. They found a house far from a portal, and Rose spied on you for weeks. All I did was give her a map of portal locations," he said, and barely smirked. "By the

way, you might be interested in knowing that your grandson would have made a talented jeweler. He rebuilt pocket
watches for fun—Rose has a few. I dare say that of all
your children and grandchildren, Henry came closest to
matching your skill in that domain. I'd have introduced
you if you wouldn't have murdered the poor boy and my
granddaughter, but…well, nothing for it now. Have a good
day."

Inade was still sputtering as the four of us departed,
and I stayed close to Kabno until we were on the shuttle to
the parking lot. As I buckled up in the back of the Mercedes, Teolm murmured, "You had to mention Rosie,
didn't you?"

"He was annoying me," Diriem replied, pulling out of
the lot. "Interesting request he made."

"What, to see my mother?"

"Yes. What about his children?"

Teolm leaned against the door. "Otun is here with him.
Jomin and Kilch are elsewhere. Kilch is with Mother, as I
recall…"

"You don't visit often, do you?" said Kabno.

"I have little to say to them."

"And neither does Inade, it seems," said Diriem. "A
pity. Your mother's primary contribution to his empire
was a blind eye, but your brothers and sister were his lieu-
tenants."

"Not useful to him now, are they?"

We rode in silence until we left the penal farm grounds,
and then Diriem quietly said, "Perhaps he'd like a visit
from Rosie."

"Perhaps you've lost your mind," Teolm countered.
"But the old fool did have a point: what are we to do
about Ivari and his band?"

"Leave that to me," said Diriem, "and keep your
schedule flexible tomorrow."

Teolm didn't press him, and soon, the two of them and
Kabno were discussing scores for a game I'd never heard

of, played by teams I'd never seen. I let their conversation wash over me as I stared out the window with Inade's voice echoing in my head.

Pathetic.

Yes, we were poor and under-educated in East Branch…and probably too close…but pathetic?

All I was, all I might become, all that I'd taken from the people before me who'd held our community together…and he'd dismissed me with barely a minute's contemplation.

At least I'm not locked up, my mind helpfully suggested hours after the fact, once the time for retorts was long past. *At least my family loves me. At least I can do magic…*

Well, the last was a stretch, but I was going to fix it.

Spurred by my wounded pride, I sat on my bed with a stack of paper napkins I'd begged from Ranarma after dinner and concentrated, trying to still my mind and focus on what I wanted.

From what I'd witnessed in the last few days, the trick to the touch wasn't yelling at objects, but rather gesturing at them. Maybe the problem with my touch was that I'd never intuited what motions to make. If Connor could make his work, then surely I could, too…right?

Pathetic.

I placed the stack of napkins a few feet away from me, giving myself plenty of room to gesticulate, then crooked my fingers and stared at the napkins.

They refused to budge.

Okay, not that gesture. I turned my hand sideways and repeated, then switched hands, but they didn't so much as twitch.

Again and again, I tested different gestures, desperately fighting to ignore Inade's voice in my head, until finally, my frustration boiled over, and my reluctant power shot forth as a gust of wind that blew the napkins into the air and sent them fluttering all over the place.

"*Shit*," I muttered, but before I could pick them up, someone knocked at the door.

I scrambled off the bed and started retrieving my napkins, then called, "Come in," assuming it was Jane.

Instead, Yven poked his head into the room. "Hi, Maebe," he said with a grin. "I got a new orchid today. Want to come up and see it?"

"Oh, um…" I paused, napkins crumpled in my fist. "Uh…"

"If you're busy, no worries." Noticing the napkins scattered around me, he asked, "Did you spill something? Need a hand?"

"No, I…" I sighed and crouched to collect the rest. "I'm trying to make them move, but my touch barely works."

He stepped into the room and closed the door. "I don't know, *that* looks pretty effective. Want to show me?"

I put the napkins on the bed and stood back, hugging myself. "Don't laugh, okay?" I mumbled.

"I won't."

That time, I used a little more control with the puff of air I stirred, and the napkins rose and dropped again. "Best I can do. No one's ever taught me the motion to make if you want something to come to you."

Yven gestured with two fingers, and the napkins flew into his hands, straightening themselves out as they settled in a neat pile. "There is no set motion," he said, putting the stack back on the bed. "Just like there are no true magic words. The idea is that you learn to associate actions with particular movements or sounds. A lot of us use similar gestures because there's a standard set, if you will, but you can do whatever feels best. And…that didn't help, did it?" he asked as I looked glumly back at him.

"If I was just moving my hands wrong, I could *fix* that. Nothing works right." Sitting at the foot of the bed, I said, "The best control I've ever had was when Jane loaned me her wand, and I was still just moving air—more effectively, but not what I should have been able to do."

"So, let's find a wand for you, then," he replied. "They're not expensive."

"She said she outgrew hers."

"Yeah, sorcerers typically do. They're focusing tools. Most of them start on wands in school until they get the hang of spellcraft."

"And elves?"

Yven hesitated. "*Typically*, we don't need them. Magic tends to be somewhat more intuitive for us in that respect. But there are exceptions," he said as I groaned, "and tools are designed to be used, Maebe." He pushed the napkins away and took a seat beside me. "Look, there are some spells for which even trained sorcerers need focusing help. You've met Canna, right?"

"Sure…"

"Her husband, Pars, was my best friend in school. *Big* guy. We both ended up at DPP," he added with a wry smile, "but there's a reason that I'm in Regulatory, doing greenhouse inspections and checking potencies, and he's over in Interdiction, breaking down doors and smacking skulls together. Anyway, Pars is very good at his job, and he casts beautifully, but he keeps a staff around for field-work."

"Like…a walking stick?"

"Probably thicker and longer than what you're thinking of. He can use it as a weapon, but it also works as an over-grown wand in a pinch. All that is to say there's no shame in needing a boost, particularly since you're starting late."

"*If* I have real power," I muttered. "I mean, if I can't even make napkins do what I want…"

Yven lowered his voice. "I'll let you in on a secret. Not all of us have the same abilities."

"Wild talents, I know—"

"Beyond that. By way of example, I'm *terrible* at defensive magic. Yet another reason I try to avoid Interdiction," he said, chuckling softly. "I know what I need to do, but it just doesn't click with me. Now, I *am* pretty good at this," he continued, and held out his hand. A green headband much like mine suddenly appeared, draped over his palm, and he passed it to me for inspection. "Object manifestation comes to me easily. I don't know why. It's not a wild talent—just about any elf can learn to do this—but for whatever reason, I'm unusually good at it." Pointing to the floor, he said, "Diriem's almost obscenely talented as a farseer, but he'd be the first to tell you that object manifestation isn't his strength. We vary. So, rather than sit in here alone, kicking yourself all night, recall that you haven't truly been trained, and you may have strengths you have yet to explore. All right?"

"Okay," I said, and rubbed my shoulder. "It's just…we went to the penal farm at Cavimet today to talk to Inade ti'Cren, and he said I was pathetic—"

"*Maebe*," said Yven, "Inade's an asshole on his best day. He's never had a kind word for Rosie, either. Don't let him bother you."

Feeling slightly better about my uncooperative talent, I asked, "Can I see your new orchid?"

"Of course. Come on upstairs—Rosie's painting, so she won't mind if we're quiet." He led the way out, then walked me toward the door to the tower staircase. "Why don't I have a word with Pars about getting you a wand? He'd know the good ones."

"You wouldn't mind?"

"Not at all," he replied, and opened the door. "Remember that every master started at the beginning."

CHAPTER 16

Diriem had warned me only to dress comfortably before retiring Wednesday night, so I didn't know what I'd be walking into Thursday morning. Ranarma had set the dining table for seven, and I smiled to find Yven already halfway through his meal when I ventured in. But he wouldn't be part of Diriem's scheme, he explained—he was heading outside for a couple of greenhouse inspections, and he'd be gone until Saturday. Rose, however, was along for the ride, and she came downstairs in gray leggings and a loose blue top, ready for the summer heat.

Naturally, Jane was in as well, but unlike Rose, she'd opted for dark jeans and carried a crinkly black jacket to the table. Rose eyed her getup, then chased her toast with a sip of her latte and frowned. "You want a windbreaker in *June?*"

"Have you looked at the weather?" Jane countered.

"No..."

Jane snorted. "You live here long enough, I guess you start forgetting that the real world isn't quite so climate controlled. The radar for New York this morning is *ugly.*"

Rose's face fell. "Rain jacket?"

"Rain jacket. And if you've got a spare, I'm sure Maebe could use one."

As Rose ducked out of the room, I said to Jane, "So...New York?"

"That's the plan. Going to pay Ivari a visit and have a little *chat.*"

"No one told me—"

"Because Diriem thought you wouldn't get any sleep if you had forewarning." She turned at the sound of footsteps and raised her juice glass in salute. "Speak of the devil. I see we're slumming it today."

In lieu of a robe, Diriem wore black pants and a gray pinstripe button-down, which he'd left open at the collar. "Thought a tie might be overkill. Why the jacket?"

She looked at him incredulously. "You run an intelligence agency, and you didn't bother checking the weather? It's going to be, like, monsooning."

He muttered a brief string of profanities in Low Elvish but settled in to eat.

I wasn't surprised when Teolm arrived—and in a T-shirt, no less—and the sixth member of our party was shown in a few minutes later. Like Jane, Annie had opted for jeans and sensible shoes, and she carried a blue jacket over her arm. "I saw the forecast," she said as she pulled out a chair. "Sheesh, Diriem, we could have waited for the front to move through."

The plan, I learned, was simple and somewhat flexible. We would go to this Manhattan place, locate the Rush and Sons building, and see if we could get in to meet with Ivari. Precisely how this was to be accomplished was the vague bit, but the others seemed relatively confident that it could be done.

As Diriem finished his coffee, he asked, "How do we want to drive? The closest portal is probably Woodland."

"Woodland…" Jane prompted.

"New Jersey. It's in the Pine Barrens. With luck, it's a two-hour drive, but we could be looking at a three-hour trip. I do have a vehicle large enough for all of us—"

"Or we could do the smart thing," Annie interrupted, and pulled a small cardboard box out of her pocket. "Put one of these on and give the meds a chance to work."

Diriem balked. "Wait, now, that's—"

"Picked it up from Canna last night. Seasickness patch," she explained to Jane, "but on steroids. Whatever potion they use here *works*."

"That's not necessary," Diriem tried, but Annie was having none of it.

"I can get you into the building next door, the empty one being renovated. There's no need to drive in from freaking Jersey. So, suck it up, buttercup," she said, nudging the box across the table toward him. "Stick one behind your ear and give it half an hour, and maybe you won't puke your guts out this time."

While he didn't seem to be on board with this plan, Diriem did as Annie ordered, and Ranarma brought him more coffee as consolation.

By the time we'd finished eating, dressed for the weather, and masked as appropriate, Annie deemed the patch effective and motioned us closer together. "Okay, this the weird bit. Everybody hold hands. I can only transport what I'm touching, so link up."

"Uh," I ventured, joining hands with Jane and Teolm, "transport *how*, exactly?"

"My little trick. And for the benefit of the first-timers," she said, addressing Teolm and me, "it's going to feel odd. Best advice is to close your eyes, take a deep breath, and trust that you're not actually falling into the void."

"Come again?" said Teolm, a high-pitched note of uncertainty creeping into his voice.

"It'll be over in seconds. Right, hold on, close your eyes, get a good breath...and *now*."

The floor suddenly wasn't there.

A twinge of pain shot through my hands, and I barely had time to realize that my partners and I had tightened our grips before the ground returned. I gasped and stumbled, but Jane held me up. Teolm, who wasn't so lucky, fell to his knees with a grunt.

Opening my eyes, I saw that Diriem's mansion had vanished, replaced by a cavernous space that smelled odd—a bouquet of wood shavings, mold, and something chemical that I couldn't name. The floor beneath us was now rough grayish-white stone, while the interior walls had been removed, leaving framing and translucent plastic sheets. Someone had strung bare lightbulbs overhead on orange cords, but these were dark, and the only illumination came from the gray world beyond the dirty windows.

"Took it down to the concrete, huh?" said Jane, tapping her foot against the floor.

"Yep," Annie replied. "They've made more progress downstairs, but work seems to have stopped temporarily. Wonder if there's a money problem," she mused, and glanced at Diriem. "All right, there?"

"Fine," he muttered, and exhaled slowly. "I'm fine."

"Are you positive about that?" asked Teolm, dusting off his knees. "You, uh…"

"*Fine.*"

He lifted his hands in placation. "Sure, sure. Annie, where to?"

Pointing toward a stairwell, she said, "The street is two flights down. Let's roll."

"And how did you get us here?" he asked, hurrying after her.

"It's a Hunt thing, and no, I can't teach you."

"But *how*—"

"Talk to Wylan, man. I'm still figuring everything out myself."

We descended to the ground level, and though Diriem brought up the rear and clung to the banister, he appeared to be less green by the time Annie poked her head out of a door to peek around. "Convenient that they forgot to lock up," said Rose.

Annie turned and smirked. "The broken chain in the alley suggests this wasn't an intentional oversight."

"*Ah.* Your handiwork?"

"No, but I'm not complaining. All right, hoods up. It's gross out here."

One by one, we filed out the door and into a narrow, paved lane between the building and its neighbor. The immediate blast of sensations was almost overwhelming: the pounding rain, the stench of garbage in the big blue bin nearby, the rush of cars on the wet road and honking of horns, the percussion of feet as people hunching against the storm or sheltering beneath umbrellas jostled each other on the edges of the street.

I couldn't see the horizon. All around me, stone and brick buildings rose to heights I would have deemed incredible had I not visited Beukal. But unlike that city, with its wide roads and well-spaced structures, this neighborhood was cramped, its towers pressed together like too many seedlings germinating in a small pot. Wind whipped down the road ahead of us, a breeze churned into a gust by the artificial canyon walls.

Jane gripped my arm, jolting me back to the task at hand, and I trailed her down the road toward the next building. It wasn't as impressive as its neighbors—the building was shorter and fashioned of brown bricks, a style less sleek than the towers around it—but it still rose a good eight or nine floors above the street, and as we drew near, I could see a sign in glowing white letters mounted over the tall double doors, bright against the watery gloom: RUSH AND SONS.

I scurried up the brick staircase toward the entrance and shook myself off beneath the black awning while Teolm held the door open for us. "Here," he murmured, making a quick gesture toward my legs, and my rain-soaked pants were suddenly dry. I smiled gratefully, and he winked and nudged me inside.

The lobby was every bit as nice as the marble-covered entrance of DOL or the warm wooden foyer of Diriem's home, a high-ceilinged room with bluish-gray slate floors and white limestone plated over the brick. Above us hung three large brass chandeliers—smaller than Diriem's, but still enormous to me—and they followed the gray runner from the doorway toward an imposing wooden desk between us and two brass doors that I suspected were elevators. Behind the desk sat a dark-haired man in a brown and white outfit, who peered at us and frowned.

"Security guard," Rose whispered. "*Great.*"

The guard was built like he tossed boulders for fun, and the look on his face suggested he wouldn't mind tossing us back out into the storm. "Can I help you?" he asked, his accent strange to my ear.

Diriem strode across the lobby toward the desk. "Good morning," he said. "I'd like to see Mr. Rush. Is he available?"

The guard smirked. "Do you have an appointment?"

"No, but I'm an old friend."

"*Sure* you are, buddy. Tell you what, you go on your way and give your friend a call, and if he agrees to meet you, he'll let me know—"

That was as far as he made it before Annie vanished. "What the—" he started, leaning over his desk toward the place where she'd been standing…which was precisely the wrong thing to do, as Annie, who had by then appeared behind his chair, pulled a syringe from her jacket pocket and jabbed it into the guard's neck.

He barely had time to register the injection before he slumped to the floor as if he were boneless.

As she recapped the syringe, Teolm gestured at a pair of wall-mounted cameras focused on the guard's desk, and both exploded with a hissing pop. "Too little, too late," he lamented. "If I knew where the tapes were kept—"

"Don't trouble yourself," Diriem interrupted, unclipping a plastic card from the unconscious guard's belt. "This should do the trick. Come on, let's find our elusive CEO."

Once the elevator door opened, he scanned the card at a black panel inside before punching the button for the top floor. "How do you know where to find Ivari?" I asked.

"One of the perks of senior management is often the view from your office," he replied. "I doubt there's much

to see these days from the top of this building but concrete, but surely he wouldn't have relinquished the big
corner office to an underling."

My ears popped just before the elevator finished its ascent, and the doors opened into a much more intimate
space than the lobby. The floor was covered with thick
white carpet, and the lights, hidden in the ceiling, seemed
warmer than the chandeliers below. On the far side of the
room was a glass wall with a door built in, demarcated by
gold-colored hinges and a handle. Between us and that
door were a pair of tan leather sofas and a glass-topped
desk, behind which sat a pretty blonde in a form-fitting
lilac dress. She glanced up from the large white screen of
her computer as the elevator chimed its arrival, and her
posture stiffened.

Diriem, as calm as if we'd opted for a stroll in the
woods, strode out and made a beeline for her. "Good
morning," he said. "I'd like to speak with Mr. Rush. Is he
in?"

Her feet, clad in pointed purple high heels, tucked
themselves beneath her chair as she sized him up.
"Uh...do you have an appointment, sir? And...do you not
have an escort?"

"No need to worry about that. I don't have an appointment, in fact, but if you'd be so kind, tell Mr. Rush
that Mr. Storm from Norway has come to talk with him
about a matter of importance."

"Mr. Rush has several appointments today," she said,
her eyes flicking from him to the screen and back. "It
would be better if you set up a time—"

"I am *confident* that he'll see me," Diriem replied. "Call
him, please."

Her pink lips pursed, but after a moment's hesitation,
she picked up her desk phone and pressed a button. "Yes,
sir, I'm sorry to bother you," she murmured, "but you
have an unexpected guest. A, um...Mr. Storm? He said
he's in from Norway, and he brought, um, some associ-

ates."

"Generous of her," Jane muttered to me.

"Yes, sir," she continued after a pause. "They're here now. No escort. I..." Her voice faded as she stared at her screen. "Sir, there's been a security incident in the lobby, and—"

The pause was longer that time.

"Uh...yes, sir. Are you sure? I can call...okay. I'll inform him," she said uncertainly, and hung up. Looking back at Diriem, she said, "Mr. Rush will see you shortly. You can have a seat."

"Thank you. Incidentally, your guard will be fine," he told her as he sank onto one of the sofas. "He's merely taking a little nap."

"Please don't hurt me," she whispered. "I'm just doing my job."

Diriem's expression softened as the woman watched us from behind her desk, tense as a compressed spring. Her eyes seemed watery, and she chewed on her lip as she gripped the sides of her white chair.

She was terrified, I realized, and trying not to show it. Then again, considering how much larger the guard downstairs was, she must have known she'd have no chance against his assailants.

"We're not here to harm you," he said. "Or your boss. But..." He faintly smiled. "If there's a pressing matter to which you need to attend elsewhere in the building, we'll wait here until Mr. Rush is ready for us."

She sniffled, regarding him warily. "What do you mean?"

"Perhaps you would like to check on your colleague while he...sleeps it off. I suspect he wouldn't mind terribly if he woke to see your face."

She was torn, I could tell, but she slowly released her chair and rose. "You...you promise you'll wait here?"

"You have my word," he said, settling back and crossing his legs.

With a nod, she skirted her desk and speedwalked toward the elevators, the spike heels of her shoes digging deep into the carpet as she made her escape. As soon as the door opened, she darted inside, and I heard her slam a button before the door slid closed again.

As the elevator descended, Teolm asked, "You think that was wise?"

"Scared people do stupid things," said Diriem. "Better for her to be out of the way."

Jane grunted. "And what's the plan for when the cops show up, again?"

"They won't."

Her eyes narrowed. "So says the oracle?"

"No, that's my calculation. Ivari has a good thing here," Diriem quietly explained. "If he's aware of the situation downstairs, then he knows better than to call in the local police. After all," he added with a cold smile, "he doesn't know what I'm willing to do. We haven't seen each other in centuries."

I sat on the opposite sofa, fighting the urge to fidget and keeping watch over the glass door as I tried to process our position. Yes, it was difficult to see Ivari, but perhaps that was normal for wealthy people—after all, in the fairy tales I used to read, kings certainly had guards. And Ivari *was* wealthy. The building wasn't gilded, but it whispered about old money. Considering what the blonde had been wearing, I appraised my brown summer-weight trousers and white homespun shirt, and found them lacking. In East Branch, as long as your clothes were clean, mended, and decent, you were sufficiently attired. Here, though, I suspected more would be expected of me to pass muster.

But Ivari would understand. He'd founded East Branch, so he shouldn't be surprised by our ways. Besides, we were kin, even if a few centuries and a dozen generations separated us, so I told myself he'd appreciate the effort I'd made, weak though it was.

My only jewelry was my masking pendant, which I kept

tucked beneath my shirt. I'd rounded off my ears before leaving Diriem's place, so I looked as normal as anyone else in our group. Granted, I was young, and I definitely could have used some polish, but once I explained the situation back home to Ivari, he'd help us. The man in the picture had seemed friendly enough, and surely he wouldn't want his distant grandchildren to lose their home or starve.

I sat there and stewed for about ten minutes before a youthful brunette in a dark gray pantsuit opened the glass door from within. Her brow furrowed as she noticed the empty chair behind the desk. "What did you do with Tiffany?" she demanded, locking on Diriem as the likely culprit.

"She had pressing business elsewhere in the building, and we didn't want to detain her," he replied. "Don't worry, we didn't need coffee. Now, are you Mr. Rush's assistant or his bodyguard?"

Her rouged lips curled into a smirk. "Head of Administration, actually, but I've come to fetch you…and your entourage."

Though her English was flawless, her bearing told me she wasn't truly a twenty-something human.

"You're 'Mr. Storm,' I take it?" she asked, a note of challenge in her voice.

"I am," said Diriem. "And you?"

"Matilda Ravensworth."

"*Ah*. Lady ti'Un," he said, and slipped into High Elvish. "I have not had the pleasure of making your acquaintance."

That startled her, though she quickly regained her composure. "I would not have thought that one such as you would know the old tongue," she replied in kind.

"Indeed? I learned it at my mother's knee, though I admit I've seldom had cause to use it since."

"How did you know who I am?"

He laughed softly. "Yours was not a difficult name to

decipher, and I do recall something of the southern Halls. Will you take me to Ivari?"

She nodded curtly, turned on her heel, and opened the door with a wave of her hand. Diriem followed her, and as the rest of us fell in line, I glanced at Teolm. "You look confused," I whispered.

"I got about every third word of that," he whispered back. "My knowledge of High Elvish is fairly spotty. Did Diriem give it to you?"

"Uh-huh."

"Mm. Appropriate."

The brunette—Matilda, Lady ti'Un, whatever she called herself—led us down hallways keeping in theme with the waiting room, all thick white carpet and soft lighting, though the walls were hung with large paintings at regular intervals, scenes of a sprawling city nestled against a broad blue expanse I took to be the sea. I didn't have time to give any a close inspection as we walked—our escort set a brisk pace—but I thought we'd reached the far side of the building when she stopped before a wooden door. Most of the others on the floor had borne brass nameplates, but this one was unmarked. She knocked three times, then opened the door and poked her head into the room. "Sire," she murmured in the foreign tongue, "I've brought them."

"Show them in," came a male voice from beyond the door.

She stepped aside but eyed Diriem as he brushed past her, his expression placid.

The room beyond the door was nothing like I'd expected. Instead of minimalist white and gold, it was plastered and paneled in dark wood. The furniture reminded me of that in Diriem's office at DOL: six blue leather chairs with cherry legs situated around a coordinating table and atop a patterned rug, a pair of overburdened bookshelves, a side table lined with glass bottles of what I assumed to be alcohol. Instead of hidden ceiling lights, this room bore a pair of brass floor lamps with cream-colored shades, both darkened, and lit silver candelabra on the side tables. At the back of the room was a massive desk with another candelabrum perched beside a pair of computer screens, behind which the windows were cracked open, admitting a breeze that ruffled the ornate draperies and carried the smell of the pounding rain.

And leaning against that desk, his arms folded over his white button-down shirt, was the handsome man from the picture—well, a variant of him. The green-brown eyes were the same, but his hair had lightened to blond, his face had lost about a decade, and his features had turned distinctly elven.

Rose, who'd brought up the rear, closed the door, and Diriem barely nodded toward him. "Ivari. I must say, I'm surprised to find you alive."

He smiled back at Diriem, but it wasn't kind. "Well, well," he said in High Elvish, "the wolf pup finally crawls out of hiding and shows his face. Took you long enough, boy."

"You know, I don't believe that either of us has been a boy in quite some time," Diriem replied, following his lead, then gestured to remove his mask. Teolm followed suit, as did Annie, though I left mine in place.

"I apologize for the unexpected visit," Diriem continued, "but in light of our history, I had doubts that you would have agreed to meet otherwise."

Ivari grunted his laughter deep in his throat. "And who might these be?"

"This," he said, gesturing to Teolm, "is Lord ti'Cren—"

"*Lord*? What happened to Davanal?"

"She...uh...she..." Teolm tried, flailing, and Diriem came to the rescue.

"Davanal drowned about a century and a half following the Pact," he explained. "Her son inherited the Hall, and this is her grandson, Teolm."

"He doesn't understand this tongue," said Ivari, which, given the slightly panicked look on Teolm's face, wasn't far from the truth. "Does he understand his family's treason, at least?"

"Hall ti'Cren and its vassals survived when their king was too stubborn to act in their best interest," Diriem countered. "As for the rest of our party, these three are Pact agents."

Rose's expression gave nothing away, but I was briefly offended for her until I recalled the bad blood between the two former kings. That Diriem still didn't trust Ivari was beyond question.

Ivari's gaze slipped over Rose and Jane, but it lingered on Annie. "That one is…half-blooded?" he guessed.

It was Diriem's turn to laugh. "That one is a Huntsman. Delightful young woman. Excellent aim."

That, I suspected, was a threat.

"And we can discuss the youngling in a moment," he said, pointing to me. "I have questions first. We sent parties out of the Pactlands to search for survivors, but all they found was destruction. I looked and saw nothing of you or your people. How did you hide? And why?"

Ivari lifted his right hand and rubbed the gold band on his third finger. "A little something developed under my watch. Keeps filthy spies like you in the dark."

Diriem shrugged. "A useful tool under other circumstances, but had I seen you, we would have offered assistance *centuries* ago."

"I don't need your charity," Ivari spat. "And what conditions would it have carried, hmm? Bow and grovel before your band of cowering castoffs?"

If he'd wanted a rise out of Diriem, he was disappointed. "Joining us from the beginning would have saved your people."

"*I* saved my people."

"You saved *eighteen*," he snapped, the veneer of civility chipping. "While I certainly commend your tenacity

and…*creativity* in forging a path toward survival, you pre-
served only a tiny fraction of your subjects. What happened to the rest?"

Ivari smirked. "Don't you know?"

"I can guess, especially as we've found no trace of
them. But I'm not here to chastise you for decisions that
can't be changed," he continued. "I want to discuss—"

"How *did* you find me, boy?"

Diriem's hand landed on my shoulder. "Through this
lady."

His gaze turned on me, hard…but nervous? Was I im-
agining the wariness I thought I saw? Still, this was my
chance.

"Hi, I'm Maebe," I said before Diriem could stop me,
and took a step closer. "Maebe Amos. I'm from East
Branch—"

Ivari jerked in surprise. "What—"

"In Georgia, you know? In the mountains?" Could he
have forgotten the place in the last few hundred years?
"We, uh, we've kept Mary's record book going. Your
daughter, Mary?"

With the initial shock past, he peered at me like I was a
ghost. "You're still *there*? Speaking this—"

"No, Diriem taught me," I clarified. "Er, uh, well, there
was a potion involved. We've kept a few words, that's all.
Folks forgot—they didn't know anything about you until
he visited and read the book," I said, nodding to Diriem.
"But we're right where you planted us," I added, and
smiled.

To my dismay, he didn't seem overly enthusiastic about
this news.

Diriem slid in. "I had no idea that any of you had survived until about ten days ago, when Maebe was brought
in for genetic testing. She's three-quarters elven."

"Is she masked?"

"Slightly."

"Drop it," he ordered.

Diriem seemed poised to object, but I murmured, "It's all right," and gripped my pendant.

I could tell when the mask had fallen, as Ivari's face twisted. "*That*—"

"Apparently, cifyent is common among your descendants," said Diriem. "Often paired with talent. Maebe's not well tutored yet, but she has the knack."

Whether that was farsight or manners talking, I couldn't tell.

"I'm sorry for barging in like this," I said to Ivari, "but, um…thank you. For what you and the others did." When he looked blankly at me, I said, "Mary wrote that you left East Branch so that your families would have enough to eat. That must have been awful. But it worked—the community survived that winter, and we've been on the land ever since…" I faltered, trying to find the right words as he continued to stare at me, then said, "We're pretty self-reliant. Always have been. But times have grown hard. The community's not as big as it once was, and there aren't many children, and…and now they tell me that we don't have enough to pay the taxes. Diriem and Teolm are trying to get some of us into the Pactlands to get educated, but I know not everyone would go, even if given the chance. East Branch isn't much, but it's *home*," I said, holding his gaze. "The elders wouldn't leave unless you dragged them out, and I don't know how they'd start over or where they could go. I hate to show up on your doorstep and ask for charity, sir, but is there any way you could help us again?"

I held my breath, hoping.

And then Ivari laughed.

"Is that what Mary said?" he asked me. "That we left to save the others?"

"She…she said you wandered off into the woods at night," I replied. "When the food ran low. She thought you died so that your families wouldn't starve."

He rolled his eyes. "Mary was always a sentimental fool. Tell me her line was extinguished."

"Not at all," said Diriem. "Maebe is one of her descendants."

"Fitting," he muttered.

"If she was mistaken, then enlighten us. Why did you leave?"

Ivari looked incredulously at Diriem. "Why did we leave a primitive farm in the damn wilderness? Are you seriously asking me that? What, you think I'd keep scraping the soil any longer than necessity dictated? Don't be stupid."

The flame of hope in my chest, which had been sputtering for the last few minutes, went cold at the absolute disdain in his tone.

"Do you have any idea how *dull* life was in the mountains?" he continued. "Nothing but hardship and privation, plus the half-breeds' litany of complaints. They were getting older, graying, breaking. Some of them kept whining about leaving England, as if matters were any better in that dump that spawned them."

"That's...debatable," said Diriem. "Colonization is seldom a bloodless enterprise."

"We left them in good condition in that regard. A few displays of power, and no one bothered East Branch, native or settler. But the situation was unsustainable. We'd spent more than sixty years among those creatures—"

"Your *children*, you mean?"

"Bah." Ivari waved as if swatting a mosquito buzzing around his head. "Useless things."

"You *made* them!" Diriem protested. "You married their parents—"

"For protection. Security. No one attacked us while we lived among those peasants, and the half-breeds were the logical end of our...partnership," he said with distaste. "But none of them could truly weave the subtle energies, and they aged almost as quickly as full humans did. What use were they? We did them a kindness by giving them a place to live."

"And faked your deaths?"

"We left and allowed them to believe what they wished," Ivari replied with a light shrug. "Did it over the course of three weeks so they wouldn't grow suspicious, then assembled at a location I chose in advance and made our way toward the coast. Too many humans there, of course, but at least there were entertainments and gold to be made. Eventually, we settled on this teeming island and made a place for ourselves. Built the firm." He smiled slyly. "It's easy money. So many of them are terrible with their finances, and having had a few centuries to study the markets, I do well by our clients. And there you have it," he said, crossing his ankles. "New identities every few decades, carefully managed transfers of money and property, and we can exist in perpetuity. Heavens know we have the forgeries perfected."

"And I congratulate you," said Diriem with less than full enthusiasm, "but there remains the matter of your descendants in East Branch. Maebe speaks the truth—they have very little. And unless you have children older than your Henry…"

His mouth tightened. "You know of him?"

"Correct me if I'm mistaken, but John was born first and died young and childless, leaving Henry and his two younger sisters—or so I recall from Mary's work. Yes?"

"That's accurate."

"Very well. Do you have living children older than Henry?"

By then, some of the cockiness had drained from Ivari's voice. "No. They were slaughtered. Their whole lines. The only survivors are the seventeen of us."

His head tilted. "Eighteen, don't you mean?"

"Seventeen. Deriap ti'Catama never made it to New York."

"I'm sorry to hear that. Highwaymen?"

"No, the fool fixated on the idea of going back for the half-breeds. I couldn't have him showing them where to find us, so I handled the matter."

I might have been an ignorant country girl, but even I knew damn well what *that* meant.

Diriem must have understood as well, but he let it go. "I see. In any case, you have my sympathy for the loss of your children—I know something of that," he murmured. "But Ivari, I've seen East Branch's family trees down the generations. This girl's grandfather is your heir," he said, touching my shoulder again. "As is she through her father. Given the intermingling of the families, it's quite possible that everyone in East Branch carries your blood. And they have been *abandoned*."

He shook his head. "Don't be ridiculous, they're not my *heirs*. I've had true children since leaving—"

"You know the old succession laws as well as I do. Primogeniture. Should harm befall you, Hall ti'Ammaas passes to its quasi-human branch. But that's not important today," he added, speeding up as Ivari started to object. "As Maebe said, Teolm and I are trying to arrange educations for anyone at East Branch who desires one, but those who stay behind could use your help. Not millions, just enough to keep the taxes paid. Or, if you would consider being especially generous, you should know that they live without electricity and running water. Utilities and newer homes would make an incredible difference."

Again, Ivari laughed. "Why would I waste the money on useless half-breeds like *that*?" he said, jabbing his finger toward me as I tried not to cry. "They're not my problem, boy. Let them die off and be done with it—that's all that humans are good for."

I bit my lip, hoping the pain would distract me so I wouldn't embarrass myself.

Beside me, Diriem sighed deeply. "I'd hoped you had changed," he said to Ivari. "Reading Mary's account, I truly thought you had become a better man. But even now, you're concerned with no one but yourself, though your grandchildren's grandchildren are struggling and facing eviction into a world they are not equipped to navigate."

"Not my responsibility."

"How can you *say* that? They're your blood!"

"They are *nothing* of mine," Ivari growled, "and had I known before now that they lingered, I'd have corrected the problem."

A chill ran up my spine as those green-brown eyes coldly appraised me again. I stood frozen on the expensive rug, rubbing my sweaty palms on my pants, and murmured, "Please. If we're asking too much, would you consider a loan? Give me a few years to figure out magic and learn to support myself, and I'll see that it's repaid. I just don't want my family to lose everyth—"

His finger twitched, and I went flying head over heels across the office, stopping only when I slammed into a chair. Stars flashed behind my eyes, and I groaned as I slumped on the ground, almost too shocked to feel the surge of pain.

"You see?" said Ivari, raising his voice over the others' protestations. "Useless! And more than that, a stain on my Hall."

Hope might have gone out within me, but a different fire was growing in its place, one much hotter and brighter. Distantly, I recognized my touch, but this wasn't its usual fluttering. It licked at my limbs, flickering in my fingertips, and urged me to get up.

"What sort of fool would bother with castoffs like that? Why waste the time trying to educate them?"

Despite the pounding in my head, I managed to get my feet under me and pushed myself off the ground.

"And you know what inbreeding does to human populations. Frankly, I'm surprised the girl isn't drooling."

My touch stirred to awareness and fixated on the open windows. Not great for cross-breeze purposes, but...

"Useless as they are, it's a wonder those creatures haven't starved yet. We should have taken more of the food when we left. At least *we* did something with our resources."

But.

Pain and anger fueled the fire—my aching skull, my humiliation, Ivari's casual insults and refusal to assist us despite the luxury all around him, his not-so-veiled threats. My eyes fixed on him, and as he finally noticed me wobbling by the table, I lifted my fists and slammed them down on nothingness.

The air around me came alive, the energy spreading from the point of impact like fast-moving ripples in a creek when a rock falls in, and joined with the wind blowing through the windows. Within seconds, gusts swirled around the office, toppling candles and sending papers flying. Diriem braced himself as he struggled to stay upright, and Ivari crawled behind his desk to take shelter, but I found myself in the eye of a raging storm, untouched but blazing with power.

The alcohol bottles flew off the side table and soaked the carpet, which ignited when one of the tossed candles rolled too close. Smoke joined the whipping wind, and I smiled. Good. Let Ivari choke on it, let it set his eyes watering and steal the breath from his lungs.

Someone was calling my name over the screaming wind, but I ignored it as I made my way toward Ivari, bringing the tornado with me.

"Useless?" I yelled, slipping back into English. "You want to see *useless*, you ass? Say it to my face! Come on out of your damn hole!"

Suddenly, a hand clamped on my wrist, and I turned to see Jane beside me, disheveled, coughing, and bleeding from a cut on her forehead. Her other hand was locked on Teolm's, the end of a living chain through the storm around us. "Maebe, hon," she managed, hacking, "we've got to go."

With my concentration broken, the wind died, and I saw that two walls of the office, including a bookcase, were on fire. The sprinklers had popped on at some point, and I hadn't even realized I was soaked.

An alarm blared through the building, and Jane's grip tightened. "Annie, *now!*"

The world went dark, and I was falling...only to land in a pasture with warm sunlight streaming from above. I sank to my knees and clutched at the tall grass, centering myself with the familiar scents of earth and green things and...

Horses?

Looking up, I saw a trio of black mares watching us from a few yards away, ears pricked with curiosity and tails flicking.

"So," I heard Rose say behind me, "were we not feeling up to firefighting?"

Jane grunted and straightened her clothes. "I mean, I could have made it *worse*, but I think Maebe had that covered."

"Yeah, sumbitch had it coming for throwing her," said Annie, and offered me a hand. "Feeling okay? You didn't land in horse poop, did you?"

"I, uh..." I took her hand and let her help me upright. "I don't think so..."

"Lucky kid," Teolm muttered, and I glanced over in time to see the dark stains on his jeans vanish.

I blinked, my brain struggling to process the last minutes, and turned in search of something familiar. A massive building made of logs and stone rose beyond the pasture fence, and a man sporting a rack of antlers like a buck stepped out onto the porch.

"Hi, Derat!" Annie called in Pactish, waving. "Off today?"

"Committee meeting was postponed," he called back. "Um...should I fetch Wylan?"

"Nah, just needed a landing pad."

Jane waved as well. "Hey, there! Remember me?"

He shielded his eyes with his hand and grinned. "Ms. Fortune, of course. Or is it Aniap yet?"

"Still Fortune. Sorry to impose, but do you think we

could get a glass of water or something for this one?" she asked, throwing an arm around my shaking shoulders.

The antlered man peered at me for a few seconds, then motioned us closer. "Why don't we take this inside? Can she walk?"

I wasn't sure—part of me felt like it was buzzing, while another wanted to puke where I stood—but Jane and Rose sandwiched me between them so I wouldn't fall as we made our way up the porch and into the oversized log cabin. Within, instead of the rough boards and patched walls I'd have expected, the place was immaculate: polished wooden floors that practically gleamed, white plastered walls hung with tapestries, paintings, and a wicked-looking sword, and high ceilings from which descended iron light fixtures. There was no need for their illumination at that time, given the wide windows that bathed everything in the glow of morning.

As Derat escorted us deeper into the building, I caught faint whiffs of sweat that struck me as unquestionably male. Annie sniffed deeply and muttered, "Whose turn is it to clean?"

"Tholla," said Derat. "He went out with a hunting party last night—"

"Right…"

"And returned shortly after you left today. Broke his leg chasing down a moose. He's in bed."

"*Yikes*. I'll get Wylan to handle the funk while Tholla's off the rotation."

Derat shook his head. "You're the only one who complains of a smell, Annie—"

"Because the rest of you are nose-blind to your own stench! *Men*, I swear."

Given their almost joking tone, I assumed this wasn't their first such discussion of the topic, and it gave me something to focus on besides my shock and discombobulation. I said nothing and held on to Jane and Rose until we emerged in a kitchen that could have easily contained

East Branch's meeting house, had one removed the long island and the breakfast table built for a couple dozen. A cooking fire crackled at the far end of the room, over which something that smelled like beef stock simmered in an iron cauldron. One wall was lined with cabinets—some holding dishes, others food—which terminated in three steel refrigerators, much like Jane's but larger.

I was directed onto a stool at the kitchen island, and after taking a closer look at me, Derat opened a cabinet and extracted a bottle of golden liquid. "Here," he said, pouring at least a half cup into a glass goblet, "try this."

While I didn't recognize the taste, I knew the burn of alcohol and coughed as it filled my mouth and nose.

"Ooh…" said Annie, "do you not drink?"

"Wasn't expecting that," I told her, and sipped again. "Better."

As I drank, Rose turned to her great-grandfather and demanded, "What the hell just happened? You two were talking too quickly for me to even try to follow."

He looked disheveled, his formerly neat ponytail cock-eyed and tangled. "The short version is that he'll be no help at all. The survivors abandoned their children to their fate and set off for a better life unencumbered," he said with distaste. "Ivari killed the one of them with a sliver of conscience, ti'Catama, but the rest ran away for a less tedious life. He was surprised but thoroughly unimpressed to learn that East Branch endures. I…" He paused, frowning into space. "I fear this visit may have done more harm than good. The matter bears monitoring."

"What does that mean?" asked Teolm.

"Just what I said. I don't have answers for you today. But in light of that group's existence, I believe it would behoove us to have a few more people on hand fluent in High Elvish. Rosie, Teolm?"

"Sure," she said as he nodded. "I'll clear my schedule with Pateme—"

"Hold up," Jane interrupted, "priorities. What happened to Maebe back there?"

As the others' eyes turned to me, Diriem slowly smiled. "That was her touch, of course."

I shook my head. "It's never been like that. Whatever that was—"

"Your talent is awakening. Faced with danger and everything Ivari was saying, you reacted. *Dramatically*, perhaps, but yours is the sort of talent that should have been noticed and cultivated from early childhood, and your imperfect control is understandable."

"I…I don't…"

"You're an aeromancer," he murmured, leaning closer. "That's a wild talent, Maebe. Rare in elves but useful…and also potentially *very* destructive. So, finish your drink, youngling. Steady your nerves. You have work to do."

I had no idea what an aeromancer was or what this meant for my future. I didn't know whether Ivari would pretend I didn't exist or hunt me down for setting his office on fire. Hell, I still had no idea what I was drinking.

But I swallowed hard and took another sip.

CHAPTER 17

The weekend was anything but restful.

By the time we returned to Diriem's house on Thursday afternoon, he had already begun placing calls, and a guest awaited us. "Ah, Agent ti'Gata," said Diriem as the man in black rose from his chair in one of the parlors, nervously playing with the strap of the messenger bag over his chest. "Welcome. Thank you for coming on such short notice."

The man, an elf with cropped black hair and large eyes, nodded. "Of course, sir. Director Erenani told me to come straight here. What can I, uh…do for you?"

"At ease," he replied with a little smile, and motioned me into the room. "This is Maebe. She discovered a talent for aeromancy…oh, about two hours ago—"

"Indeed?"

"Yes. No loss of life, but let's just say it's a good thing sprinkler systems exist. Now, Director Erenani informs me that you're a talented aeromancer, Agent."

"Um…I have experience, certainly," he said, gripping his bag, "but I suppose 'talented' is a relative term."

"From what she's told me, you're being modest," said Diriem. "I appreciate that this is an imposition in the middle of your day, but might you spare a few hours to help the youngling?"

Though uneasy, he agreed, and Diriem showed us upstairs to the well-padded room he called a gymnasium. Once he'd left us, my drafted tutor asked me for a demonstration. Anxious and possibly still a little tipsy from my time at Annie's place, I summoned a wind so strong that it picked up a stationary bicycle and threw it through a window. As glass tinkled to the floor and the equipment thudded into the yard, I covered my mouth and whimpered. "Sorry, I'm sorry, I didn't mean to—"

"*Damn*," said the agent, picking himself up off the mats, though he sounded more impressed than horrified. "I see why I'm here."

"It was an accident, I don't have anything under control," I babbled. "Not a darn thing. I'm awful at magic, and I probably still am, only now I can do *that*, and—"

"Hey." He gently gripped my arms and hunched to be closer to my eye level. "Maebe, was it?"

I sniffed. "Yes, sir."

"I'm Orten. Why don't you sit down and tell me what's going on?"

So, I did. He listened, jaw progressively descending as I recapped the strangest week and a half of my life, then snapped his mouth shut and rubbed his chin. "To be clear, you're eighteen and have no formal training in magic? And you've never done anything like *that* before today?" he asked, pointing to the broken window.

"Uh-huh."

"In that case, it's a good thing I don't have any plans this weekend…and as of now, neither do you."

With his director's blessing, Orten returned to the mansion on Friday, Saturday, and Sunday, giving me a crash course in spellcasting basics and safety before turning to the problem of my wild talent. He worked with me from early in the morning until late at night, a patient but demanding instructor. By dinnertime Sunday, I was still miles behind where I should have been in magic, but I'd learned to modulate the breezes I created from tornadic winds down to drafts. My control wasn't good, and neither was my aim, but as I only broke one of the gymnasium's windows that day instead of the half dozen I'd smashed on Thursday, Diriem deemed my emergency tutoring sessions a success.

I had another matter to attend to that night: my wardrobe. Diriem announced at dinner that the Forum had agreed to take up the issue of East Branch, at least in a preliminary state, on Monday morning—good news, if nerve-racking for me. After the meal, I called my parents to update them—well, more specifically, I called to assure them that I was alive after another day of training. My family was just as surprised at my aeromancy as I was, and they fretted from afar while I tried to work through that unexpected development. Once they were satisfied that I was whole and largely unbruised, I turned my attention to the morning's appointment with the Forum. As I rooted through the drawer in which I'd stowed my clothing, looking for something presentable, Jane and Rose stopped by and pulled me up to Rose's apartment. "It's too late to shop tonight, but you're about my size, so we'll make do," Rose told me, and before I could say more than hi to Yven, I'd been swept into her walk-in closet.

I goggled. Never had I seen so many clothes in one place—shirts, pants, skirts, dresses, a hanging canvas shelf unit stocked with sweaters. She had at least ten pairs of shoes, a staggering number to my eyes, and multiple coats and jackets hanging at the back. As I struggled to comprehend the notion of having an entire room just for clothing, she headed for a portion of the right-hand rack about two-thirds of the way in and began examining her options. Jane joined her, and I sidled closer to see what they were going on about.

Having been working in the Pactlands for about two years, Rose had amassed a number of formal robes for the office and other occasions—some in thin cotton, others in stouter wool, a handful in silk. She favored greens, blues, and purples, with the odd gray and black thrown in. After a moment's debate, she and Jane pulled a turquoise-colored robe from the rack and showed it to me. "What do you think?" Rose asked. "Doable? Hate it? You'd look great in red or pink," she said apologetically, "but I just don't wear much of either."

I let her help me slip it on, then stepped to the long mirror at the back of the closet. The robe was light, probably cotton, and it swished when I walked. I didn't see any buttons, but I ran my fingers over the silver embroidery around the collar and down the open edges of the front.

"It's a little short on me," said Rose, smiling at me over my shoulder, "but I think it fits you well. How about it? Or I've got other options—"

"This is gorgeous," I said, shifting slightly to make the robe twirl. "You don't mind?"

"Shoot, no. Glad you like it. Now, let's figure out the rest..."

Rose only had about an inch on me, but her tailored pants were too long, so she opted instead for a knee-length cream dress with long sleeves, summer-weight but conservative in its cut. "Very nice," she said as I turned for the two of them. "What are we doing about shoes?"

After much trial and error, we settled on a pair that were open-toed for comfort and flat so I wouldn't kill myself. Satisfied, Jane stepped behind me and pulled my hair back. "What do we think? Half up, half down? French braid?"

The debate continued Monday morning as Jane and Rose fussed over me, settling for a braided partial updo before turning to makeup. I'd never worn any, but Rose had a steady hand and a few fresh supplies, and soon, I barely recognized myself in the mirror: my eyes looked larger, my lashes darker and thicker, my hair wavy but tamed—and thanks to my masking pendant, my ears were actually perky. Though I wanted to learn to mask on my own, Orten had decided we'd needed to prioritize.

"Thank y'all," I said, smiling at Rose's and Jane's reflections. "This is...wow."

Jane gave me a quick hug, and Rose said, "You're very welcome. Here, stand up, let me check for wrinkles..."

Soon, the two of them had joined me in Diriem's Mercedes for the ride to Beukal, Rose up front with her great-grandfather and Jane in the back to periodically squeeze my hand in reassurance. I carried the record book on my lap in its plastic box, and I tried to focus on the scenery to keep myself from throwing up with nerves.

As we reached the portal building and the line for capital-bound traffic, Diriem caught on and glanced back at me in the mirror. "You're awfully quiet, Maebe."

"I'm okay."

I met his gaze in the glass, and he winked at me. "Don't worry."

Easy for him to say. Now that my talent had burst forth, I was uncomfortably conscious of its presence, a low-burning fire always on the edge of flaring. My anxiety was doing nothing to calm it, and though it didn't feel nearly as hot as it had in Ivari's office, the flames were creeping higher.

"What if I lose control in there?" I blurted.

Diriem inched the car forward as the one at the front passed through the portal. "You won't."

"But what if I *do*? What if I freak out and, like, break more windows?"

"When you feel it building, you take a deep breath," said Jane. "Remember that you control your talent, not the other way around. Draw it back in. Fear can make it spike, but it's usually anger that makes mine misbehave."

"What do you mean?"

She grinned as tiny flames began to dance over her sleeves. A few seconds later, they vanished. "Sometimes they pop out on their own. Just stop what you're doing and try to think of something calming until you feel more centered. Or at least that's why my dad always told me."

Rose turned around. "I thought your dad's a *floramancer*."

"Sure, but he had a whole career at DPP. I wasn't the first pyro to cross his path."

"There are a variety of control techniques," Diriem offered. "Assuming we can get you into proper tutoring, Maebe, you'll learn several."

"Assuming," I mumbled.

Jane patted my knee. "Worst-case scenario, if Dad could train me, then he could train you. I bet he wouldn't mind."

"Really?"

"Absolutely. He needs a challenge. Actually, he's offered to work with Connor, but Con's still taking baby steps into the shallow end, so to speak."

"That *is* understandable," Diriem murmured, and glanced back at Jane once the cars paused again. "A suggestion?"

"Hit me."

"Tempting as it may be, don't push him. Let him come to it in his own time."

"I just want to help him—"

"Of course you do. But there's an inherent caution in the boy. Not a bad thing, certainly. He wants all the facts before he makes a decision, yes?"

"Yeah…" Jane allowed.

"So, if Connor isn't convinced about a course of action, he'll drag his heels. Give him options, but give him space to consider them."

She huffed a sigh.

"Jane, this is experience talking. Do you have any idea how many agents I've overseen?"

"A few."

"Few thousand, more like. Part of doing that well is learning personalities. In that respect, Connor's far from a closed book." He paused, then added, "You have good taste, you know."

"We are not having this conversation," Jane muttered.

He chuckled. "Come on, he's obviously smitten."

"All right, then," she said, a note of challenge in her tone, "so when's he going to propose, huh?"

"How long have you been dating, six months? Seven?"

"*When?*"

"You know I can't tell you that."

She snapped her fingers and leaned forward. "Ah, but you just did. You didn't say he *wouldn't* propose."

"I didn't say anything. You're making assumptions, Trainee," he replied, but I caught his little smile in the mirror and kept my secrets to myself.

Jane had given me a brief primer to the Pact Forum, the Pactlands' governing body. Each of the member races, from the numerous sorcerers and fauns to the handful of sirens and the few dozen members of the Hunt, was entitled to three representatives, chosen as each group saw fit. The elves sent their lords and ladies to the Forum on a rotating basis, one of the vestiges of the old Hall aristocracy…with the addition of the heads of the two newer Halls of commonfolk, ti'Gata and ti'Van. Diriem was not currently on the Forum, but the three elven representatives—Arana ti'Ansha, Cirral ti'Pon, and Hemar ti'Dir—generally took his calls. There were, after all, certain perks to being the unofficial first among equals.

The Forum representatives served on various committees, each with its own member-selected head, but when the full Forum convened without a committee request, the proceedings were governed by the Overseer. For the past century or more, that position had been held by Ketling Tiramae, a metal nymph. The Overseer was not elected, but rather served at the pleasure of the Forum and could be fired by majority vote. As Jane told it, Ketling was good at her job, apolitical and concerned only with the rules of order, and so she'd become a fixture on the Forum floor.

Jane had told me a bit about the Forum's building, but I still gawked as we parked in the lot beside it. A far cry from the meeting house at home, the structure was circular and made of smooth limestone. A low dome served as the roof about a hundred feet above the lush grass and well-weeded flowerbeds. Around the building was a covered walkway, the roof of which was held up by columns, and people in robes bustled around singly and in small groups.

I clung to the box as I got out of the car, and Jane joined me. "It's prettier inside," she murmured. "Check out the ceiling in the lobby—it's painted to look like the sky."

Though I was nervous, Diriem seemed to be at ease, and he lifted a hand in greeting as Teolm walked toward us. Teolm had dressed for the occasion, though his fingers were stained with purple streaks.

"I hope we haven't kept you waiting," Diriem said as he drew near.

"No, I just arrived. Traffic?"

"Unfortunately. And, uh…dare I ask?" Diriem prodded, glancing pointedly at Teolm's hands.

Teolm wiggled his fingers. "I pollinated covanis lilies on Friday. You can wear the tightest gloves you like, and you'll still inevitably end up with pollen streaks. The only thing that removes them is vigorous scrubbing and time."

"Or you could mask," Diriem suggested.

Teolm smirked. "In my line of work, this is a badge of honor. Do you have any idea how difficult it is to get co-vanises to maturity? I'm *breeding* them."

"Fair enough. Shall we?"

The five of us headed into the building and past the security checkpoint. Jane was right about the ceiling—it looked like a summer sky, complete with scattered puffy clouds—but far more impressive was the main meeting hall, the ceiling of which was designed with glowing stained glass. Two balconies curved around to meet the straight walls, from which a platform protruded before a huge green curtain and the biggest hanging screen I'd ever seen. Atop the platform sat a modest wooden desk and chair on the left-hand side, a wooden podium in the middle, and a long table to the right of the podium. The balconies were filled with padded benches for visitors, but on the floor, split by three aisles, were the representatives' seats. Each trio had its own section of tables and chairs sufficient for the representatives, a few assistants, and their guests...or rather, *most* did. Some of the sections had thick mats instead of chairs, which puzzled me briefly until I saw a robed centaur walk in and make himself comfortable.

A polite assistant led us down to the very front of the room, where a selection of chairs had been arranged at the foot of the platform. Diriem sat and motioned for us to do likewise. "Get comfortable," he murmured. "These things seldom start precisely on time."

Sure enough, it was almost ten minutes past the hour when Ketling, a gray-skinned woman with piercing blue eyes and a tight brown bun, banged a small mallet—a gavel, I would later learn—on the leather mat atop her desk on the platform. When the room quieted, she said, "On this the twenty-seventh day of June in the four hundred eighty-fifth year of the Pact, I call this meeting of the Pact Forum to order."

The hanging screen illuminated, showing a close-up of her face and torso behind the desk.

"Good morning," she said, and smiled at the assembled.

The representatives and balcony observers murmured a reply.

"Since no committee has asked for dedicated time, today's will be a general session," Ketling continued, folding her hands in front of her. "Is our secretary prepared?"

Another nymph, who was sitting at a desk a few feet away from our group, nodded. "Yes, Madam Overseer."

"Thank you." She paused to consult the computer before her, absently tucking a stray strand of hair behind her long ear. "The first order of business this morning comes to us from Representatives ti'Ansha, ti'Dir, and ti'Pon," she said, and nodded to the elves. "And it seems Director ti'Dana will be speaking to it." Glancing over her desk toward the floor, she found him and crooked a finger. "Welcome back. The podium is yours."

"Thank you, Madam," he replied, standing, "but I don't speak alone. Lord ti'Cren has graciously agreed to join me today."

She inclined her head. "Then gentlemen, you may come up. Anyone else?"

He touched my shoulder, and I rose on quivering legs. "Just one."

Ketling peered down at me. "A child?"

"And a visitor, in fact."

The room rumbled while we took the stage, me with my plastic box and Teolm with his arm around my back, steading me. At his whisper, I put the box on the long table, and Diriem carefully unpacked the record book and set it aside. Taking the podium, he said, "I do not come before this body lightly. Nor do I come on behalf of the Division of Intelligence today. First, I have news. We were mistaken about the fate of some of the southern elves who did not join us here."

The mutterings resumed, dying only when Ketling rapped her gavel.

"Eighteen survived," Diriem continued. "Of *all* their number, eighteen. Including their king, Ivari ti'Ammaas. How do I know this?" Pointing to the record book, he said, "The survivors crossed Europe and made their way to England, where they intermarried in a human village. Eventually, they and their half-blooded children settled in the wilds of Georgia...west of the Central portal, if that helps," he added. "After a time, the survivors tired of their situation. Their children thought they had wandered off into the winter to leave more food for their families," he said, and paused to flip to the front of the book. "Madam Overseer, is there a spare projector?"

She pulled one from her desk, and Teolm speedwalked across the stage to take it from her. Diriem fiddled with it for a moment, and then the screen behind us filled with a picture of the time-yellowed page.

"High Elvish," he said. "And I have no reason to doubt the veracity of the account...well, the veracity of the *writer*, who believed this to be the truth," he amended. "Mary, the fourth of Ivari's half-human children. She mistakenly believed that her father and his followers had sacrificed themselves. In truth, they abandoned their families and returned to the coast. Today, the remaining seventeen work in finance, hiding in plain sight, and by all appearances, they have done well for themselves."

"Seventeen?" asked Ketling.

He nodded. "One apparently wished to go back for their children, and Ivari killed him to prevent it. I know this because I spoke with Ivari last week...myself, Lord ti'Cren here, and several agents."

Rose smirked up at him.

"I'm not unduly concerned about Ivari and his band continuing to live outside the Pactlands," said Diriem, scanning the room. "It's evident that they know how to hide themselves. What I *am* concerned about is their descendants." Glancing over his shoulder at the screen, he said, "This did not come from thin air. Those children and grandchildren abandoned in Georgia managed to survive. The youngest of their number are now eleven generations removed from the surviving eighteen...and to this point, they have not intermarried with the humans around them. A mere fifty remain, many of them with talent...like this young lady," he said, looking my way.

I gripped the edge of the table as the room's eyes turned to me.

"This is Maebe Amos. Behind Ivari, she is the third heir to Hall ti'Ammaas. Eighteen, largely untutored...and an aeromancer of surprising ability, as it so happens."

My cheeks flushed beneath the Forum's stares, and to my horror, I saw that the screen had switched to my reddening face. Deep inside, I felt the stirring of my talent and forced myself to breathe. I could do this. I would *not* embarrass myself.

For East Branch.

"A healer has already analyzed her genetics," Diriem continued. "Seventy-three percent elven."

"Barely looks it," called one of the centaur representatives, earning a gavel rap from Ketling.

Diriem spread his hands. "That may be, Representative Berek, but these things are variable—"

"Is she masked?"

"Slightly, but—"

My power, swelling as my fear and discomfort grew, struggled to break free, but I gritted my teeth to hold it back. I would *not* create an uncontrolled tornado in front of the Forum. Still, the representative's tone, which reminded me of Inade's and Ivari's, was doing my control zero favors.

But I could do it for East Branch.

And if this was our one shot...

"You want to see?" I interrupted, stepping out from behind the table. I held my pendant until the mask fell away, then stared down at the representative and gave my head a brisk shake. "Good enough?"

His eyes widened. "What...I'm sorry, what...uh..."

"It's called cifyent," said Teolm, joining me. "Much more common in the southern Halls than in the northern."

"And most of us have it," I said. "That, plus talent...I mean, you see why we've kept to ourselves, yeah? This raises a *few* questions," I added, jabbing my finger toward my ear. "So...if you've had your fill of staring, mind if I mask again?"

The representative raised his hands, his expression shifting toward contrition. "Not at all. I, um...I apologize..."

As I triggered my mask, Diriem said, "You may have noticed that Maebe is using masking jewelry. Her community is grossly undereducated concerning magic."

And other matters, I thought, but kept *that* quiet.

"But if she is a fair representative of that community's potential, then they *should* be educated. The number of windows I've repaired in the last days thanks to her wild talent is proof enough for me," he added, and glanced toward the floor at a soft chuckle. "I trust you know what I speak of, Representative Peolid."

The pink-skinned nymph sitting near the front grinned. "*Far* too well."

"How many children, now?"

"Seven," the representative replied. "All of them air-aligned."

"Congratulations?" he said, and the other representatives laughed.

The nymph waved them down. "That's roughly what my parents told my spouse after the seventh. But yes, reinforced glass is a wondrous thing."

"So I've heard. But returning to Maebe," he said, sobering, "I've seen the community. They're not destitute, but they're edging closer by the year, they risk losing their land...and Ivari has made it plain that their ancestors will do nothing to help them." Nodding to Teolm, he continued, "We've agreed to support them, at least for a time. As the situation is unsustainable in the long-term, however, what we propose is bringing at least the younger members here and educating them, with the goal of eventual integration."

"*How* many half-breeds, again?" asked a woman below us—a sorcerer, I assumed. "*Fifty*?"

Diriem picked her out of the room. "That is the total population, Representative Carinar. My understanding is that not all would be willing to relocate."

"Legally, how would you keep them here? On what grounds?"

"It's the right thing to do," another sorcerer retorted. Looking closer, I recognized Sage's father as the speaker.

She turned to him, scowling. "There's no legal pathway, Mirrik. Elves would require Hall standing, and I've yet to hear that this girl has a tie to *any* Hall in the Pactlands."

She wasn't wrong. I could claim at least fifteen of the southern Halls, but those weren't doing me a lick of good.

"This is a time to find an exception," he insisted. "My daughter—"

"Oh, yes, *clearly*, what we need here are more human-raised refugees," she snapped. "Aren't your little surprise and the Aniap brat sufficient?"

At that, Jane stood and whirled on her. "The name's *Fortune*, Carinar, and you don't actually need to kiss my grandfather's ass anymore. He can't help you from the penal farm."

Ketling's gavel descended, and with a glower at the representative, Jane took her seat. But the Overseer didn't cede the floor again. "Ms. Fortune," she said, looking down at Jane, then paused. "Or is it Agent Fortune?"

"Trainee, ma'am."

"I see. You're familiar with the youngling's community?"

She nodded. "As familiar as anyone not from East Branch can be. That's its name," she explained. "East Branch. It's a family compound more than a town, and it's back in the woods near Whitford. I grew up in the next town over." She paused, locking eyes with me, then said, "Rumors circulate about the place—they're clannish, they marry their cousins, they run off police and don't go to school. I'd never actually visited until two weeks ago, so I wasn't entirely sure what to expect. It's…well, it's impoverished. No reliable electricity, no running water, certainly no computers. And I do *not* say this to be unkind," she continued, staring at me again, "but the deficits in Maebe's general knowledge are staggering, forget magic. They need help," she said, turning to address the room. "They don't have the resources or the skills to blend into the communities around them, but with guidance and tutoring here, I'm sure they *could* learn. A culture shock, naturally, but at least they wouldn't have to worry about keeping up a cover story in the Pactlands."

The wind itched to burst forth, but I held it in check. Jane had said nothing untrue, no matter how uncomfortable it was for me to hear.

"Ivari and his little buddies established East Branch, then left their children to fend for themselves when times got boring and tough," she said. "I understand that they don't have Halls here to bring them in, but can't there be an exception made? Or would the Forum prefer to leave a group of talented quasi-elven folks alone to scrape by in Georgia?"

She nodded to Ketling and took her seat.

"A proposal," said Teolm over the room's rumblings. "Any claim the East Branch residents might have to Hall ti'Cren would be distant and tenuous, but my grandfather was a ti'Ammaas cousin. With the intermarrying, I suspect that most, if not all, of the East Branchers are my distant kin. Let them come in under my protection for now. Any decisions about reestablishing the lost Halls here can be postponed. For now, I can look after them, ensure their safety."

After a moment of discussion among the representatives, a massive troll, his skin rusty and his hair worn in a black mohawk, stood. "Madam Overseer?" he said in a rumbling bass.

"Representative Foggy Lake is recognized," Ketling replied.

"Thank you." Turning to me, he asked, "How many of your people are children?"

I bit my lip, too conscious of the eyes on me. "Uh...by whose reckoning? Under eighteen or under thirty-five?"

"A fair question. Let's start with the former."

Quickly, I tallied my young cousins. "Well, um...David and I are eighteen, Hannah's seventeen, then there's Zoe, Marshall, Sebastian and Stephanie, Peter, Eleanor, little David, Joseph, Eugene, Tobias, and Winston."

The troll nodded. "And if that were expanded to thirty-five?"

I grimaced. "Going to have to guess on some of these, but...Peter and Monica, Kyle and Laurel, Paul and Amy, Justin..."

"Connor," Jane offered.

"Right, Connor...Heidi...that might be it."

"So, perhaps twenty-three, then." Folding his thick arms over his robe, he said, "Surely we can find tutors for twenty-three."

"Toby and Winston are still babies, if that helps."

He considered that, then looked at Teolm. "If Hall ti'Cren can subsidize them, then I don't see the harm."

"You have my word, Representative," Teolm replied.

"And Hall ti'Dana will assist," said Diriem, sharing a look with Teolm. "Assuming the Forum grants permission."

The vote that followed wasn't unanimous, but the margin was wide enough to leave no doubt.

We were in.

I called before we headed to East Branch the next morning, and so my parents were waiting to hug me as soon as I jumped out of Connor's SUV. Once my mom released me, she gave me a closer look and gasped. "Your ears!"

"Illusion," I said, and held my pendant until they flopped over again. "But convincing, right?"

She touched the little gold necklace, marveling. "How..."

"Magic. And there's so much more—"

"Show us," Dad interrupted, stepping back to give me working room. "What have you been up to?"

At that, Diriem, who'd reluctantly acquired his own stash of Annie's nausea patches, intervened. "You know, there are a *lot* of trees around here, and until Maebe has a few more lessons behind her..."

Dad frowned. "She can blow over *trees*?"

"I wouldn't be surprised if she did." Turning from us to the rest of the gathering community, he said, "We have good news, and we have news that's somewhat concerning."

The elders directed folks to the picnic tables, and once the benches had filled, Grandpa leaned against a tree and tucked his hands into the pockets of his patched overalls. "All right, what do we need to know?"

"First things first," said Diriem, "your record book is safe—Maebe knows where it is, and she approved leaving it with the archivists," he added as I nodded. "A copy was made yesterday as a backup in case of damage, but the actual book is being repaired, cleaned, and protected. The team working on it estimates they'll have it ready for you within a week, and I'll send it back via Jane, if that's acceptable."

The elders traded looks, then reached consensus. "Thank you," said Alan. "Not to be greedy, but any chance of getting a translation for that front part?"

I smiled to myself. Having carefully paged through the book while waiting for the archivist team Monday afternoon, I'd realized that I could read Mary's narrative.

"That's no trouble," Diriem replied. "Now, for the next item on the agenda, I believe Connor's best suited to explain."

This was no surprise to Connor. Jane had called to fill him in the night before, and he'd concurred with Diriem's hunch that the news would go down more easily if it came from him.

"So," he said, raising his voice a degree for the people in the back, "we've all been invited to the Pactlands. Diriem here and a distant cousin of ours will help anyone who wants to relocate get situated. That said," he continued over the sudden mutterings, "I told them that most of us won't want to go, and there's no hard feelings. However, I think we can all agree that the schooling in East Branch is...not as good as it could be."

"Worked out just fine for us," Alan retorted.

Connor gave his uncle a long look. "For the very limited purposes of farming this piece of land, yeah, it's fine. You know what you need to know. But what if something happens to East Branch? What's the backup plan?"

No one rushed to speak.

"There isn't one," said Connor. "If, God forbid, we were to lose this place—and it could happen," he said when the mutterings intensified. "I'm not talking about taxes. Y'all ever heard of eminent domain?"

He was greeted by blank expressions.

"Means the government decides it needs your land for some public project, and it makes you leave. You get paid for your property, but you don't have a choice. Now hang on, that's not likely," he said before people could panic, "but it's something to consider. I'm telling you, swear on my life, y'all aren't equipped to live in Whitford. There's just too much that you don't know. And this isn't Connor the big-city boy talking—I'm pretty sure Maebe will back me up. Right, mitta?"

When people looked my way, I nodded slowly. "It's not just magic where we're ignorant. I see that now. There's...*so* much beyond East Branch, and I've learned enough to know how far behind I am."

"So, here's my suggestion," said Connor. "Send the kids to the Pactlands—not necessarily to stay, but to get educated. If they like it there, they can find a place. If not, they'll come home knowing how to manage their touch, but more importantly, how to survive away from East Branch. Some of them might get jobs in town, help pay to maintain this property. This isn't about dismantling East Branch," he insisted, locking eyes with the elders. "It's about *saving* our home. Making it so that in fifty years, a hundred years, our family's still around in some form. And we *are* a family," he continued with a weak chuckle. "The record book makes that abundantly clear. We're one big, screwed-up family. And we need to do right by each other."

"I want to go," a voice blurted, and I spotted David with his hand raised. "If Maebe's going, I should go, too."

"And me," said Heidi, his older sister.

"What about families?" asked Monica, who stood with her husband, Peter, she holding baby Toby and he with his arm around Eleanor, their young daughter. "Could we go together?"

"Certainly," said Diriem. "Arrangements are being made for anyone who wants an education to receive tutoring at a school in Beukal...our capital," he hastily explained. "It has a dormitory for younger children, but there are some apartments within the dorm for couples. We can make it work." He paused, then said, "I don't need a firm decision today. Maebe will be here for a week or so packing. If anyone wants to accompany her back to Beukal, just tell her, and she can get word to us. We'll plan to bring enough transport next week. And this isn't a one-time offer," he added. "If you change your mind in either direction, we'll take you where you wish to be."

I caught the elders' approving nods as my mom wrapped her arm around me and pulled me close. "I'm proud of you, baby," she whispered. "But if you don't want to go—"

"*Mom.*"

"Just saying..."

After a moment, Grandpa asked, "What's the concerning news?"

Diriem cleared his throat. "Well...while we were working to secure permission for East Branch, we looked to see whether there were other communities like yours out there. All credit here to Maebe, who suffered through a blood trace," he said, and Mom's grip on me tightened. "Thanks to her, we didn't find another East Branch—we found your ancestors. Mary was wrong. They didn't kill themselves to save their children, but rather sneaked away to start new lives."

The crowd fell silent.

"Seventeen of the eighteen live in New York, and from what we can tell, they're very wealthy. The eighteenth was killed because he wanted to let East Branch know what had happened. Their leader was surprised that East Branch still exists and hostile to the idea of supporting you."

I was grateful that he left out the part where I set Ivari's office on fire.

"For that reason, we will be remotely monitoring this place," said Diriem. "We *can't* monitor your ancestors—they have a way of blocking us—but we're going to keep an eye on you for your safety. I've been led to understand that East Branch is quite capable of running off strangers," he said, cutting his eyes to Connor, "but a visit from the original settlers might present challenges beyond your strength. To that end, Maebe's parents have a new phone," he continued, gesturing toward our little knot, "as does Maebe, and before we leave today, we'll see that both are programmed properly."

Jane had given me mine the night before, a slim black phone with a touchscreen and her number already in the contacts list.

"And in case of emergency, if Connor's not around, my dad's willing to pitch in," said Jane. "He's just over in Ragged Gap, and we've explained the situation to him."

"I trust him, no question," said Connor. "Yacovi's good people."

The meeting wrapped up shortly thereafter. As young adults and parents crowded around Diriem with their questions about Beukal, I slipped away from my folks to say goodbye to Jane and Connor.

"It's going to be *weird* not seeing you," I said to Jane, chuckling. "Thanks for putting up with me."

"My pleasure, hon," she replied, and hugged me. "And this isn't the last you'll see of me, not by a long shot. I'm based in Beukal most days, and I'll tell you the same thing I told Sage: you can call me whenever you like. Got it?"

I grinned.

As she updated my parents' phone with my new number, Diriem joined us, a small notepad in hand. "Glad I brought this along," he said, tapping it against his palm. "Ten sign-ups already. Maebe, if you wouldn't mind calling Jane or me with any changes, I'd appreciate it."

I gave him a thumbs-up. "Yes, sir."

"And Connor," he continued, turning to my cousin, "you know the offer is open to you, too, right?"

Connor spread his hands. "Gainfully employed here. That's kind of important to East Branch…"

Lowering his voice, Diriem said, "If it's a question of tax money, I can absorb that. You should learn how to best use your talent."

"Appreciated," he replied, "but I made a commitment to Whitford, you know? Someone's got to come when you call 911."

Diriem grunted, but he didn't argue. "You know how to reach me, should you ever decide otherwise."

"Thanks. And, uh…" Connor rubbed the back of his neck and smiled at Jane. "Would you mind if we keep doing the long-distance thing for now?"

She pulled him close and kissed him. "As long as you need. Although…" Turning to Diriem, Jane asked, "So, with the East Branch folks coming in, does that mean our relationship is approved now?"

He made a face as he considered the question. "There's certainly a path to citizenship now, and it wouldn't hurt if Connor would get a blood test, but as of today?"

"Whatever," she muttered, and rolled her eyes before she and Connor kissed again. "You saw nothing, got it?"

"I never do," Diriem said dryly. "Shall we?"

I followed them to the SUV to see them off, but before Diriem climbed into the back seat, he looked at me strangely. "It's odd, but I thought you'd be a pyromancer."

"Me? *Why?*"

"Because some of those flashes I had of you before we

met carried a suggestion of fire. Ah, well," he said, and shrugged. "Farsight can be imprecise. And don't tell Jane," he murmured, "but there are plenty of pyros. Aeromancers are a rarer breed." With that, he slid into the vehicle and smiled. "See you next week, Maebe."

I stood by the dirt road out of East Branch and watched them drive away in a cloud of dust until I felt a pat on my shoulder and found my parents flanking me. "So," said Dad, "you can make things fly now?"

"Working on it."

"Can you use it to clean up that mess you call a bedroom?" I glared at him, and he grinned and kissed my forehead. "Welcome home, sweetie, even if it's just for a few days. Now, before you run off again, your mom and I are going to need the *full* story. Want to come inside?"

Arms around each other, holding on a little more tightly than usual, my parents and I walked home together.

ACKNOWLEDGEMENTS

Greetings, dear reader! Welcome to the start of a new Pactlands trilogy. Thank you for coming along for the ride, and I hope you enjoyed—Maebe's story is just beginning.

(If, by chance, this is your first Pactlands book and you feel like you've missed something, never fear! You might want to jump back to Hall of Thorns, The Wild Hunt, and Fortune's Child, the three series before this one. Each series can be read alone, but they do work best in sequence.)

As per usual, I send my thanks to the Novel Chicks, who've read more of my work than might be considered healthy. Special thanks go to Adam Domby for his generous feedback.

And yes, here's to you, Mom and Dad.

ABOUT THE AUTHOR

When not writing fiction, Ash Fitzsimmons is an appellate
attorney and an unrepentant car singer.

Find her online:
www.ashfitzsimmons.com